The Girl Who Loves Horses

Pegasus Equestrian Center Series: Book 1

Diana Vincent

This is a work of fiction. Names, characters, places, and incidents are the product of the author's imagination. Any resemblance to real events or persons is purely coincidental.

The Girl Who Loves Horses - Copyright 2012 by Diana Vincent
All rights reserved.

Cover design: Kimberly Killion
www.hotdamndesigns.com

Cover photograph: Katie Kern riding Zoe

Cover photograph by Axl Canyon O'Neal,
Actiontakenbytim@gmail.com

ISBN-13:978-1478389514
ISBN-10:1478389516

DEDICATION

To all the horses who willingly and patiently taught me to ride.

What care I for wings
On the back of a horse I fly
As fast as the wind

CONTENTS

1 PEGASUS EQUESTRIAN CENTER

In the very first stages of training, the horse should be allowed to carry his head in the position which he finds most comfortable – Brigadier General Kurt Albrecht, *Principles of Dressage*

Head high, eyes wide and frightened, nostrils flared and ears flat, a big chestnut gelding galloped toward the line of vertical jumps in a blur of golden red. The young girl on his back clutched the reins tightly, sawing at the bit in his mouth and yelled out, "Whoa, whoa!" His muscles bunched, the veins bulging as he propelled himself forward with thrusts of his hind legs and forelegs reaching up and out. Foam flew back from the corners of his mouth, flecking his glistening neck and shoulders.

"Ease up! Slow him down!" yelled the riding instructor from the middle of the arena.

The rider jerked hard on the reins causing the gelding to thrust his nose straight up in defense. Panicked by the tight hold on his mouth which diminished his ability to use his neck and shoulders, he rushed at the first vertical bar, took off early, clearing it high and wide with inches to spare and landed too close to the next jump. He thrust his body over the second jump, pulling the top rail down with his off hind foot. His abrupt movements and stiff back unbalanced his rider, shifting her forward over his neck and the reins slackened. His head free, the chestnut shook it side to side pulling the reins loose from the rider's hands, and galloped wildly to the perimeter of the arena, veering away from the last jump of the combination.

"Sit back! Pick up the reins!" The instructor moved helplessly toward the frantic horse as she yelled directions to her student.

"Beast!" the rider screamed as she grabbed onto the mane and pommel of the saddle to keep herself on the horse's back. As he neared the exit gate, he slowed his pace and the rider managed to shift back into the middle of the saddle and pick up the reins in a white-knuckled grip.

A small figure watched anxiously at the edge of the arena, following the chestnut with wistful, wide brown eyes. Her heart beat in rhythm with his pounding hooves as she imagined herself moving with him up and over the jumps. But her heart ached for the terror she recognized in his expression and she clenched her fists against her chest to keep her hands from stretching out toward him. *Can't they see how frightened he is?*

The instructor spoke in clipped sentences to the rider. The gelding stood with nostrils flaring in and out in rhythm with his heaving sides and his eyes rolling anxiously. The girl gathered the reins even tighter causing the chestnut to jerk his head upward, and he backed up rapidly, his hind legs bent near the ground. The girl yanked his head toward her knee and dug her heels into his sides to move him away from the rail and into the arena. He jumped into a trot and his rider turned him in a tight circle. At the instructor's command, she spiraled him out, increasing the size of the circle; then yanked at the reins to face him toward the line of jumps.

Horse and rider approached the first vertical at a trot, the gelding with his neck stiff and head high in resistance to the painful hold on the bit in his mouth. Halfway, he broke from trot to canter in spite of the tight hold, and managing his take-off at an easier distance, soared over the first bar, landed with a shake of his head and pulled an inch of reins, giving him enough freedom to thrust up over the second bar and then the third. Clearing the line, he raced toward the perceived safety of the exit gate.

"Let's quit with that," the instructor directed as the rider forcefully brought her mount to a choppy halt. She dismounted and her instructor walked by her side as they led the sweat-drenched, blowing horse toward a large stable.

The small spectator sighed with relief for the frightened animal, finally allowed to stretch his head down as he walked out of the arena. She stepped forward to follow them, hoping one or the other would notice her so she could ask a question.

"I'll have River ride him a few days to see if he can't settle him down and we'll try again next week," the instructor said to her student. "You might want to consider starting him on some medication to keep him calm."

"I might want to consider selling him too," the rider spoke angrily.

"Perhaps, but he certainly does have talent. If we can get him under control he could be the horse to take you to advanced level in a few years. We don't want to give him up until we at least have found you a more suitable mount."

The group neared the stable, an attractive large structure in gleaming white with blue trim and its name, *Pegasus Equestrian Center*, painted prominently above the center doors. Inside, two long cement aisles with rows of box stalls flanked a large indoor riding arena. In the front of the stable were three open bays with crossties for grooming and tacking up horses, a cement-walled wash stall, and a tack room.

As they reached the wide entryway the sound of a shovel banging against a wheelbarrow clanged from inside. The chestnut pulled up and swung his hindquarters to the side, shying at the sound.

"Cut it out," his owner shouted as she jerked down on the bridle reins and slapped at his rump with her riding crop. The horse leaped forward into the dim light of the stable. "You are such a beast!" the girl swore at him again, leading him into an open bay.

"See what I mean? He's too high-strung," the instructor commented over her shoulder as she walked off.

Picking up a halter from a box of grooming equipment, the girl unbuckled the chestnut's bridle and replaced it with the halter, swearing at him as he tossed his head nervously. She snapped the two crossties to the side rings of the halter and tossed the bridle into the grooming box.

"Hi, Crystal," the small observer spoke timidly. She recognized the horse's owner as a classmate from school.

Crystal glanced over her shoulder. "What are you doing here?" she asked curtly.

"Your horse is beautiful!"

Crystal's angry countenance did not change and ignoring the complement and the girl, she walked briskly away, the heels of her tall riding boots clacking sharply on the cement floor.

The small girl looked up at the frightened gelding who started to paw with one foreleg, his posture tense and worried. "Hey, Beautiful," she spoke softly while gazing at him with adoring eyes. He flicked his ears toward her, watching warily as she stepped slowly toward him with her hand outstretched where he could see. Then she gently touched his neck and began to stroke him. "Poor frightened boy," she whispered. The chestnut's hot, damp skin quivered at her touch.

"What are you doing?" an angry voice demanded.

Startled, the girl dropped her hand, stepped back quickly and turned to face the person speaking.

Dark eyes flashing, a skinny teenage boy approached; shaggy black hair framing a brown face with features stone-hard in visible anger.

"H-he's s-scared!" she stuttered, frightened by the boy's irate demeanor and fighting back tears of distress over both her own fear and that of the chestnut.

The boy stared at the small girl, his features shifting to a softer look of curiosity. Over her shoulder the gelding whickered a low sound, drawing the boy's attention. He approached the chestnut, speaking to him softly, "Hey, *amigo*, hey." The horse lowered his head and pricked his ears toward the boy. He arched his neck to bring his muzzle in reach as the boy offered the flat of his hand. He snuffled at the boy's palm, then licked it with his tongue. "A little rough on you again, hey *hermano*?" The boy murmured in soothing tones as he touched the chestnut's hot, wet neck and felt his chest between his forelegs to assess for heat. He moved over to the horse's side and unbuckled the girth, pulled the saddle and wet pad off his back and set it on the dividing wall of the bay, still murmuring reassurances. He bent down slowly and removed the protective boots from the gelding's fetlocks, and ran his hands up and down the lower legs. Grabbing a lead rope from the tack box, he clipped it to the center ring of the halter and undid the crossties. "Let's cool you down." He led the chestnut away.

The girl watched, fascinated as the horse visibly calmed under the care of the boy. Maybe she could have asked him her question, but she had not wanted to interrupt while he soothed the distraught animal, and now they were both gone. Alone, she looked around for anyone that might be able to help her. She walked a little way down the aisle looking dreamily around at the empty box stalls filled with shavings, ready for the horses when brought in for the night. She read the names of some of the horses printed elegantly on brass plaques tacked to the stall doors: *Red Magic, Fala, Neat Trix, Calliope.* In her imagination she pictured herself leading her very own horse into one of these stalls for the night, patting his neck and giving him a carrot as she said goodbye.

Not finding anyone in the stable, she sighed deeply in resignation and returned outside. A building with a door marked *Lounge,* and another door marked *Office* stood off to the side of the stable in front of a parking area. She stepped over to the office door and peeked in through a glass window. Inside, the riding instructor sat at a desk in front of a computer screen.

That must be Teresa Holmes. The girl had looked up everything she could find on the internet about Pegasus Equestrian Center and its part-owner, trainer, and instructor, Teresa Holmes. She knocked on the door.

The instructor called out without turning away from the computer, "It's open."

The girl entered and in a timid voice asked, "Excuse me, Ms. Holmes?"

The instructor looked over at her, frowning with annoyance at the interruption. "Well, what do you want?" she demanded.

"I, um, I saw the ad for a stable hand on weekends."

"What?" She turned toward her now in exasperation. "How old are you?"

"I'll be thirteen in two weeks."

Frowning, the instructor examined the girl; small, really didn't look older than ten, with large brown eyes, a smattering of summer freckles over the bridge of her nose, and wisps of light brown hair escaping from two thick braids. "I'm sorry; you're too young and too little." She turned back to the computer in dismissal.

That is not the right answer! The girl stood still, not yet willing to give up. She gave a small cough. "I'll work for free to prove I can do the job," she offered tremulously. "And if I can, I'd work in exchange for riding lessons."

The instructor turned back toward her and studied her silently for a few moments. "What's your name?"

"Sierra Landsing."

"I assume you're in school?"

"Yes ma-am. I'm in eighth grade."

"Not *ma-am*, not *Ms.*; it's Tess," she corrected, speaking the titles in a sarcastic tone as if the girl had insulted her. "All right; show up here this weekend at seven o'clock and you can help feed and clean stalls. If your work is acceptable we'll talk about arrangements for lessons. If you can't do the work then you'll just have to wait until you're older."

"Thank you, thank you very much." Sierra flushed.

Reaching into a drawer, Tess pulled out a packet of papers stapled together. "Have your parents sign a release." She thrust the papers at Sierra and turned back to her computer.

Sierra left the office smiling and looking around to be sure no one could see, she jumped into the air, circled around with her arms wide, her two pigtails flying around her head, and took off gleefully to where she had left her bicycle.

2 SIERRA

As in life, so with riding, we must fix our eyes on a goal and advance toward it in a straight direction. – Alois Podhajsky, *The Riding Teacher*

"She is such a total nerd," Sierra heard the whispered words amid giggles as she walked back from the whiteboard to her desk. Mr. Perkins, the math teacher, had called her to the front of the class to solve step-by-step one of the algebra problems from the last exam; after announcing that Sierra was the only one who had solved the equation correctly.

The insult prickled at Sierra's feelings and she blushed. That bothered her more than being called a nerd; the fact that she reacted visibly so that the other kids could see her embarrassment. She hated to be singled out, even though she was proud of doing well on the test. But truthfully, Sierra admitted to herself, by definition she probably was a nerd. If a nerd is a person who likes school, likes to read and enjoys studying, then she fit the description. She even liked algebra and thought solving equations fun, sort of like solving a puzzle.

"Way to go," Luke Abrams, the friendly boy sitting in the desk behind her said good-naturedly. Sierra glanced at him and he smiled and gave her a wink.

That caused her color to deepen even more and she stumbled into her desk amid more snickering.

"What a weirdo," someone else jeered.

A girl's voice asked, "Don't you just want to dip the ends of those braids into something...like something sticky?"

"Don't tempt me," another voice answered. The snickering continued.

It was Sierra's second week of eighth grade at her new school, Firwood Middle School, and she still felt very much an outsider. But she didn't think it was just because she was new. Even at her old school in seventh grade, a slow rift had developed between her and her two best friends. By the end of that year, Sue and Emily were phoning each other and doing things together without including Sierra. They were growing up. Both of them already had their periods and Sue had developed woman-sized breasts that she proudly contained in her first bra. (Emily started wearing a bra too, even though her small bumps hardly warranted one.) But at least Emily had bumps. Sierra felt as if her body refused to grow up. She hadn't started having periods, nor did her chest show even a hint of swelling. The last time Sue's mom had taken the three of them to the mall, Sue and Emily only wanted to try on clothes. Sierra wanted to look at the latest model horses or go to the book store. Sierra wanted to talk about horses, a passion the three of them used to share. But Sue and Emily only wanted to talk about boys.

It wasn't that Sierra didn't like boys because she did; she just found it boring to talk about them. She actually liked Luke quite a bit. He was a nice-looking boy with bright blue eyes, an open, friendly face, and always laughing. He had been friendly to her ever since the first day of school; saying hi if they passed in the hallway and making encouraging comments like he did in math class. But everyone liked Luke and she really didn't want him for a boyfriend, just a friend. She didn't feel ready to have a boyfriend. If given a choice, she would much rather have a horse.

Mr. Perkins began explaining new material and Sierra tuned out the snide comments and last few snickers, slipping into the world of numbers and formulas where everything fit.

Algebra was her last class before lunch. When the bell rang Sierra hastily stuffed her notebook into her backpack and shot out of the classroom to head for the cafeteria. She wanted to slip into a table in the back, gulp down her sandwich and juice, and then escape to the library. She wanted to avoid Billy.

In the first two weeks of school Sierra had made only one friend, and not by her choice.

All eighth graders in this school district were required to participate in mandatory ballroom dance lessons as part of first quarter physical education. On the first day of class as the other students paired off with their friends, Sierra found herself in a group of five girls without partners. The instructor, anxious to begin the lesson, randomly paired the leftover girls with the leftover boys. She guided Sierra by the shoulder to stand face to face with Billy Bruber on the dance floor. Somehow Billy interpreted the pairing as Sierra's choice. Ever since, he sought her out and followed her around, sat next to her in the classes they shared, sat at her table uninvited at lunch, and had pretty much destroyed her chances of making friends on her own.

Billy was an obese, bumbling boy with a loud voice and nerve-grating laugh. Besides his unattractive corpulent body, his personal hygiene was not of high standards; in fact, met no standards at all. His shirts usually bore food stains, his teeth had a mossy appearance, and his body odor whenever he perspired (which he usually did while stumbling through ballroom dancing) created an olfactory zone definitely to be avoided. He thought of himself as a comedian but Sierra found his jokes either silly or disgusting. He was not only unattractive but also boring.

Sierra didn't like Billy but she did feel sorry for him and didn't want to hurt his feelings. But she hadn't found a way to discourage his attentions without being rude. In fact, she thought her blandness toward him bordered on rudeness. But Billy, accustomed to overt ridicule and abrupt rejection, interpreted her insipid politeness as friendship.

Fortunately the math classroom was close to the cafeteria and Sierra moved much faster than Billy. She was usually swallowing her last few bites of lunch by the time he arrived to ask the same thing every day, "Is anyone sitting here?" And of course no one was, as Sierra would have to admit.

"Is anyone sitting here?" The question was followed by a grunting laugh, *hngh hngh.*

Without looking up Sierra gathered her empty sandwich bag and juice carton in one hand and shoved away from the table. "Hi, Billy," she greeted with barely a smile. "No one's sitting here and I'm just leaving to go to the library. I want to get ahead with my homework." Food was not allowed in the library, and she knew Billy, clutching a full tray of cafeteria food, would not leave it to follow her. She left triumphantly with just a tinge of shame for slighting pathetic, lonely Billy.

"Hey, Sierra," Billy called to her retreating back. "What's that in your hair?" Followed by his *hngh hngh.*

Sierra ignored him thinking he was playing one of his lame jokes. But when she heard laughter from the next table she wondered. She waited until she reached the solitude of the hallway leading to the library before reaching back to touch her braids.

Oh no! Stuck within the tasseled end of one braid she felt the unmistakable rubbery, sticky texture of chewed gum.

Sierra fled to the nearest girls' bathroom. Inside she passed two girls standing in front of the first two sinks, touching up their make-up while they gossiped loudly. Sierra tried to look invisible as she stepped up to the last sink farthest away. She pulled her braids to the front and studied the mass of sickly-pink, sticky goo clumping together the hairs at the end of one braid. *Bubblegum.* At least it was close to the end of her hair. *Who would do this? When did it even happen?* Probably when that group of boys had surrounded her in the hallway, jostling her as they rushed past to the cafeteria. They had not looked at her, and she just assumed they were oblivious to her presence in their hurry to start lunch. *How could they be so mean?* She didn't even know those boys, but she was pretty sure two of them were in her algebra class. Sierra fought back tears, wishing the two girls would leave before she lost control.

"Oh m'God!" one of the girls exclaimed, sounding aghast. "Is that gum in your hair?"

Sierra nodded, still staring at the end of her braid.

"Yuk," the other girl cried out. "Do you remember Cindy Casselback when she got gum in her hair?"

"I do; there was no way she could get it out. She tried ice cubes and then some kind of solvent that made her hair all frizzy." The girls directed their comments to each other, excluding Sierra from the conversation.

"What can I do?" Sierra asked, feeling helpless.

The first girl looked at her with an expression that plainly inferred, 'how dare you speak to me'. She smirked and answered, "Cut it off. There's nothing else you can do." The two girls laughed. Then ignoring Sierra, they picked up the thread of their previous gossip.

Sierra fled the bathroom. That's what she would do; she would find a pair of scissors and cut off the ends of both braids. It would only shorten her hair by about two inches and she would hardly notice. With her hair unbraided, it fell to the middle of her back so she could afford to lose the inches. Ms.

Braum, the librarian, should have scissors and maybe she would loan them for the brief operation.

Ms. Braum was appropriately sympathetic, and tsk, tsking all the while, snipped off the ends of Sierra's braids, holding them over the trashcan. Then she helped her re-braid the ends.

"Thank you, Ms. Braum," Sierra thanked the librarian with gratitude in her tone.

"You really should report those boys," Ms. Braum stated with a stern expression.

"I don't even know who they are," Sierra answered. "And I really think it would just make things worse to tattle on them, even if I did."

Ms. Braum shook her head over the foolishness of adolescents and returned to her desk leaving Sierra free to find a table and work on her homework for the remaining minutes of the lunch hour.

3 THE COTTAGE

A horse is the projection of people's dreams about themselves – strong, powerful, beautiful – and it has the capability of giving us escape from our mundane existence. – Pam Brown

The yellow school bus pulled to a stop opposite a two-story farmhouse. Sierra hopped down the three steps, flung her backpack on, and jogged along the driveway past the house to an intersecting driveway that led into the yard of a much smaller house; a cottage. Late-blooming flowers – pansies and impatiens that had been planted in the summer and a fine old hydrangea with lingering clusters of blue – ornamented the front yard. A Steller's Jay scolded from a branch of a large maple tree, its leaves just starting to turn from green to orange.

"I'm home," Sierra announced to the jay bird. She went around to the backyard, plucked a ripe apple from one of the apple trees, and entered the house. At the doorway, a sweet, cinnamon smell wafted out as if she needed something to lure her inside. Sierra felt her school troubles drop away. Coming home to the small cottage felt like stepping out of the real world of problems and conflict into her personal separate world of harmony and peace.

"Hi, Mom," Sierra called out, "what are you baking?" She stepped through the utility room into the warm kitchen where her mother sat at the table with a textbook and papers in front of her, doing her own homework. Pam Landsing had started the nursing program at the local university, the reason she and her daughter had moved to the town of Firwood.

"Hi, Kitten," Pam greeted her daughter and reached out her arms for a hug. As Sierra embraced her warmly Pam kissed her on the cheek.

"It smells wonderful in here." Sierra shrugged off her backpack and dropped it on the table.

"I made an apple crisp out of the apples you brought in yesterday. We'll have it for dessert tonight. How was school?"

Sierra plopped into a chair, biting into her apple. A scruffy black cat ghosted into the kitchen from who knew where, and jumped into her lap.

"Hey, Socrates," she greeted him. He kneaded with his paws, tickling her, before he settled into a comfortable position, accenting his contentment with a loud purr. "Mom, does my hair look any different to you?" Sierra asked, bringing the two braids forward.

Pam studied her daughter's hair, wondering the reason for this question. "No," she answered after a few minutes, "it looks the same. What happened?"

Between bites of apple Sierra told her mother about her day. And somehow with Socrates' warm body on her lap, eating a fresh, sweet apple plucked from a tree, and her mom listening with her usual full attention on Sierra's words and commiserating with her over the teasing in class and the cruel prank of gum in her hair; Sierra no longer felt quite as hurt or humiliated.

"I'm so proud of you," Pam said when Sierra told her about her algebra score. "I think the other kids are just jealous of how smart you are."

"Mom," Sierra groaned, "you know kids don't care about being smart." She didn't believe for a minute that was the reason kids picked on her, but she appreciated her mother's sympathy and support. She changed the subject; to the anticipated pleasure of working with horses, much more interesting than her school troubles. "Don't forget, I start my job at the stable tomorrow," Sierra reminded her mother. "I'll be gone before you get home from work." Pam worked graveyard shift Friday and Saturday nights in a nursing home as a nurse's aide. Monday through Friday she attended classes at the university. She never had a day off. But Sierra knew it was her mother's dream to go through nurse's training and then become a registered nurse. She was very proud of her mother.

"That's right," Pam grinned at her daughter. "Sierra, isn't it amazing how things are falling into place for us, as if it was our destiny to move here?"

Sierra understood what she meant, like finding this cottage.

The day after finishing seventh grade, Sierra and her mother packed all their belongings into a U-haul and drove three hundred miles to the college town of Firwood, towing their car behind. Pam had managed to find an apartment to rent through the internet, and as they reached the outskirts of the town, she pulled off the main road onto a country lane to study the map and her directions to the apartment complex.

They had exited off the freeway onto country roads and Sierra's spirits soared as she looked out at stands of trees, rolling hills covered in wildflowers, and pastures with animals grazing. All her life she had lived in a city in an apartment complex. She was used to pavement, supermarkets, gas stations, and strip malls as the scenes one passed going to and from home. She lowered the window and breathed in deep of the country air. That's when she spied the attractive two-story farm house midway down the lane with a *For Rent* sign pegged into the front lawn.

"Mom, look at that sweet house," she interrupted Pam's study of the map.

"Um hmm," Pam answered without looking up.

"It's for rent."

"Honey, we already have an apartment." She added in a mumble to herself, "If I can just find it."

"It would be so cool to live in a house," Sierra dreamed out loud. She knew they couldn't afford a place like that.

Pam looked up and over to where Sierra stared. She also looked with longing at the house, and then smiled conspiratorially. "It would be fun to look inside, wouldn't it? It can't hurt anything to pretend we could afford a place like that…because someday when I'm a nurse working in a hospital, we will live in a house." She added the last in a hopeful tone.

Pam moved the U-haul up the lane and parked across from the house. She pulled out her cell phone and punched in the number printed on the sign. Sierra listened in eager curiosity as Pam asked questions.

"Hello, my name is Pam Landsing…I'm inquiring about the house for rent…I see…What is the monthly rent..? I see…I see…What utilities are included with that? I see…yes, a twelve year old daughter…I work night shift so I worry about her being alone…A school bus..? Yes, we're actually parked here now, across the street…Great, thank you."

She disconnected and turned to Sierra with wide eyes that almost looked frightened. "It's not this house for rent but a smaller one in the back, and we could afford the rent. In fact, it's cheaper than the apartment. Want to take a look?"

"Of course!" Sierra replied, the seed of hope suddenly bursting into full bloom.

A woman stepped out of the front door of the farm house and waved. They got out of the van and crossed the lane. "I'm Mary Robinson," she greeted. Pam introduced herself and her daughter and they all shook hands. Then Mrs. Robinson led them along the driveway that extended beyond the farmhouse, winding around to the back and onto another graveled driveway that angled off to the side.

A small house in desperate need of paint sat in a yard overrun with weeds, piles of broken machinery, and other trash. A sprawling maple tree graced the front yard. In the back were two apple trees, a cherry tree, plum tree, and tangled raspberry and grape vines; all in need of pruning. Off to the side an outbuilding served as a small garage.

"This used to be the caretaker's cottage when this place was a working farm," Mrs. Robinson announced as she unlocked the front door. They entered into a small living room with a large window that framed the maple tree in front. A smell of mold and stale smoke filled their nostrils. The inside walls screamed out for fresh paint and the wall-to-wall carpet was an indistinguishable faded color with many stains. "The last renters were college students; two boys," Mrs. Robinson explained as an excuse for the neglect. She made a sound of disgust and added, "That's a mistake I'll never make again."

There were two tiny bedrooms of equal size and both with dark painted wood paneling, and each with a tiny closet. The bathroom had an old-fashioned claw-foot tub with a shower curtain track that completely surrounded it. The pipe for the shower head projected up from the plumbing at the head of the tub and curved over its interior. The pedestal sink did not look like a modern imitation, but an ancient original model. There were rust stains around the drain and separate faucets for the hot and cold water. Black and white squares of linoleum covered the floor in surprisingly good shape.

The kitchen was bigger than the living room. It had white metal cabinets, a wide and shallow chipped porcelain sink, gas stove, an older model small white refrigerator; and no dishwasher. It had the same black and white linoleum flooring that had been used in the bathroom. Off the kitchen was a good-sized utility room with a deep sink and counter, hook-ups for a washer and dryer, and a wall of sturdy storage shelves. An open box of Mason canning jars sat on one of the lower shelves. Thick layers of dust covered all surfaces and there were trails of mouse droppings here and there.

Mother and daughter looked at each other and both knew without words that they had instantly fallen in love with the small, badly neglected cottage. They took possession of it on the spot. When Arthur Robinson came home, Pam negotiated an agreement where the landlords would pay for paint, rental of a carpet steam-cleaner, and Mr. Robinson would haul away the trash in his pick-up truck. The Robinsons were grateful to have renters willing to do the much needed work, and waived the first month's rent in exchange for their labor; a financial arrangement that suited Pam's tight finances very well. The Robinsons helped Pam and Sierra unload their belongings from the U-haul into the outbuilding where they planned to store things until they had a chance to scrub the interior. Pam contacted the apartment manager and gave him an honest explanation of why she no longer wanted to rent the apartment, and he graciously consented to return the check she had mailed as a deposit.

Over the next month, Pam and Sierra scrubbed the cottage from ceilings to the four corners of each room and into every cupboard and closet nook and cranny. The Robinsons bought the paint they chose; off white for the living room, kitchen, and Pam's bedroom; a pale blue for the bathroom; and Sierra chose a light sage green for her room; a color she thought would produce a complimentary background for her horse posters. Out of curiosity, Sierra pried up a corner of the disgusting carpet and to their surprise, they found hardwood floors underneath. They convinced the Robinsons to tear out the carpeting and instead of renting a steam cleaner they rented a floor polisher. For the final touches, after cleaning, painting and polishing, Sierra helped her mother make curtains for each room from remnant fabrics they selected. The sparkling clean cottage now smelled of fragrant all-purpose cleaner, fresh paint, and floor wax.

With the interior work finished, they tackled the outside. Mr. Robinson hired one of his grown nephews to help with the exterior painting, thinking it was too big a job for one woman and small girl. They chose a rose-tinged light beige for the main color and a deep maroon for the shutters and trim. After the trash had been hauled away, they weeded the yard and pruned the existing trees and shrubs. Pam had always enjoyed the cultivation of house plants and tubs of flowers that she kept on the deck of their old apartment. Having a yard to actually plant flower beds and a vegetable garden thrilled her with the possibilities.

It was while they spent the days working in the yard that the bedraggled black kitten with protruding ribs appeared. All her life Sierra had wanted a pet but Pam never could afford the deposit and extra rent required to have a pet in their apartment. The Robinsons didn't mind at all if they had animals. They had two dogs of their own, a coop with five hens and one rooster, and an old gray cat that always slept curled up in the chair on their front porch. With the expected stipulation of, "as long as you take care of him and clean up after him," Pam consented to let Sierra adopt the stray. She named him Socrates.

Sierra felt safe in the cottage, even when she was alone at night with her mother at work. The Robinsons were homebodies, never going out after dark, and had even offered to let Sierra sleep on their couch while Pam worked. But Sierra pleaded to be allowed to sleep in her own bed – she would be fine; the Robinsons were just a shout away and one of their dogs barked loudly if any living creature ventured onto the property. Pam reluctantly agreed, for the precedent had been set when they still lived in the apartment. There had been two very bad experiences with babysitters: once when Pam came home unexpectedly to find the highly recommended high school girl in Pam's own bed with her boyfriend, and then when she found out the gentle-mannered grandmotherly woman, so sweet to Pam's face, made Sierra stay in her bedroom the minute Pam left the apartment and even once slapped Sierra when she dared to come out. After that, Pam decided she trusted her own daughter, who had just turned twelve, more than strangers, and agreed to let Sierra stay by herself.

After the cottage was fixed up to their liking, Sierra spent the rest of her summer days exploring from her bicycle the area around her new home. Farmland! The neighborhood was a checkerboard of farms: a dairy farm, Christmas tree farm, a farm that specialized in apple products and boasted strawberry and blueberry fields; farms with fields of hay, corn, and pumpkins; and most exciting of all, at least five of the farms also had horses grazing in pastures and three were actual stables with paddocks and riding arenas with jumps set up. It was during one of her bicycle rides after school that she had seen the sign advertising for stable help posted at the entrance gate of Pegasus Equestrian Center.

Living in this cottage, having a pet of her own, gardens for her mom, and now the chance to work around horses and learn to ride, far outweighed the fact that Sierra wasn't making friends at school.

4 RIVER

Saturday, at six-forty-five a.m., the early morning of mid-September greeted anyone willing to leave one's bed with cool crispness and a sharp scent in the air that warned of winter coming. Sierra breathed in deeply, filling her lungs with the freshness of the morning and allowed the crisp feeling to unwind the knots of nervousness in her stomach. She stood outside the locked main door to the stable at Pegasus Equestrian Center, waiting for someone to arrive and tell her what to do.

About ten minutes later, a lone figure emerged from the lane leading into the stable yard, and Sierra recognized the dark-haired boy who had startled her the other day. A large black dog of mixed breed, maybe part shepherd and part lab, trotted at his side. The boy glanced at her without speaking as he walked past the main entrance and out of sight behind the stable.

Should I follow him? He didn't look particularly happy to see her. Sierra decided to wait a little longer to see if someone else might arrive; someone who expected her and would get her started with what she was supposed to do.

Sounds of activity from inside the stable filtered out through the closed door, mixed in with the whinnies of horses. Sierra's spine jumped as the large entrance door rose slowly upwards to the low rumbling of an automatic opener. She spied the boy walking away from the wall where he must have activated the switch to open the doors. Not knowing what else to do, Sierra swallowed down her shyness and stepped inside to catch up to the boy.

"Hi," she greeted, "I'm Sierra Landsing. I was told to be here at seven this morning."

He glanced at her without stopping. "For what?"

"Ms. Holmes…Tess, said I could help feed and clean stalls."

He looked at her more directly now, obviously evaluating the small girl's ability to be of any help. "Have you ever cleaned stalls?" he asked doubtfully.

"No, but I'm a fast learner."

He didn't comment as he continued to walk down the aisle, past horses snorting and nickering and sticking their heads up to the barred grates to look out. Sierra followed, the nervousness in her stomach knotting tighter.

At the back end of the stable an electric cart with its open bed filled with bales of hay had been parked. The boy hopped onto the driver's seat, started the ignition, and drove the cart about a quarter way down one aisle. He jumped out, grabbed an armload of hay, toted it back to the first stall, opened the feed grate and tossed it in to the nickering horse inside. Then he returned to the cart for another armload of hay which he delivered to the next stall.

Sierra's fear seeped away, replaced by frustrated annoyance at such rudeness. In a burst of angry determination she marched up to the boy as he began his third trip to deliver hay and announced, "Tess said I could help feed too."

He tossed the hay into the third stall and without answering, returned to the cart. Sierra persisted in following him, but her heart sank as it occurred to her that Tess had not told anyone to expect her, or perhaps had even forgotten she had consented to give her a chance at the job.

At the cart, he asked without looking up, "Do you know the difference between alfalfa and grass hay?"

Actually she did. She recognized the two types of hay from pictures she had seen in a book she had read on horse care. "This is alfalfa and this is grass hay," she correctly pointed out.

"Read the card on the stall door." He hopped up onto the driver's seat and moved the cart another quarter way down the aisle.

Sierra stepped over to the fourth stall and read the name on the brass plaque, *Fala*. A dainty black mare whinnied and poked her nose at the grate, demanding her breakfast. Below the brass plaque was a card neatly typed with the owner's name and telephone number, the name of a veterinarian and farrier, and a line for its morning and evening feed requirements. *Two grass*, had been printed on the card. Not knowing what the *two* meant, Sierra went back to where the boy had halted the cart, hoping to get a clue by watching what he did.

The boy had jumped out and was again loading his arms with hay. She said, "I'll carry the hay to Fala, but I'm not sure about the amount."

"She gets two grass, like the card says," he answered, sounding annoyed, and walked away with his armload.

Sierra waited, taking deep breaths until he returned. "Didn't Tess tell you that I was coming this weekend?" she asked to his back.

24

He looked over his shoulder and with a half grin that held no humor replied, "No; but she tends to forget to tell me things." He loaded his arms with hay and turned away.

"She told me to be here at seven and if I can do the work she'll give me riding lessons," Sierra explained, trailing behind him. "Is there someone else I should talk to?" She followed him from the stall where he tossed in the hay, and back to the cart.

"I thought you said you'd feed Fala."

"Can you show me what the card means by *two*?" she asked pleadingly.

The boy pulled two sections of hay that easily separated apart from a bale of grass hay, and thrust them into her arms. "Two flakes," he stated, as if she were dense.

"Thank you," Sierra clipped a response, and turned away to carry the hay to Fala. *So, the number on the card refers to how many sections of hay, or flakes.* The mare nickered in anticipation as she opened the grate and tossed in the hay. Sierra watched her greedily thrust her muzzle into the sweet-smelling dried grass and then bring her head up with her mouth full. She looked at the girl with her large, warm eyes, as if saying, thank you, and Sierra felt her irritation draining away. *It's about the horses,* she reminded herself. *I can put up with his rudeness as long as I can be around the horses.*

With determination, Sierra followed the cart down the aisle, reading the cards. The boy stopped the cart after every three stalls and she helped carry hay to the horses in those stalls. He did not offer to let her ride on the passenger seat when he moved the cart.

When every horse in both aisles had been fed hay, the boy drove the cart alongside the door to another room at the back of the stable and jumped out. Sierra dogged after him as he opened the door and entered the room.

"Feed room," he announced and handed her a clipboard that he took down from a hook on the wall. A schematic diagram of the stable with the rows of stalls had been sketched onto a paper, and the name of each horse with his feed requirements had been written in the box that corresponded to his stall. There were ten stalls in each aisle, and currently eighteen horses occupied the stalls.

"Whole oats, crimped oats, cob, sweet feed," he lifted off the lids of a group of bins as he identified the grain inside. He pointed out a long counter loaded with several containers and bags of horse vitamins and supplements, and underneath the counter, stacks of feed buckets with each horse's name printed on one bucket. He picked up the first two buckets and handed one to Sierra. "Just follow the directions on that chart for each horse," he said, and took the first bucket over to the grain bins to scoop in the appropriate feed.

Sierra read the name on the bucket, *Silver*, and found his name on the chart. Copying the routine of the boy, she went first to the grain bins and scooped in the designated grain, then found the supplement to add. They worked in silence, filling all the feed buckets and setting them in the back of the cart. The boy watched from the corner of his eye to make sure Sierra made no mistakes. When all the buckets were filled, the boy climbed back onto the driver's seat of the cart.

"Get in," he directed in a neutral tone.

How generous, Sierra thought with smoldering resentment, but she climbed onto the passenger seat and they repeated the routine of driving and stopping along the two aisles to dump the contents of the feed buckets into the manger of each horse's stall. The boy drove back to the feed room and they stacked the buckets back underneath the counter.

"That's all there is to feeding," he stated and walked away, leaving Sierra alone in the feed room.

Now what? She sighed. She decided to follow after him and continue the painful extraction of information of what chore she should do next. Walking past the stalls of horses munching rhythmically on their feed, her annoyance again diminished as she felt the contented pleasure of the horses fill her own heart with joy. She reminded herself again that she could tolerate a lot just to be around these animals.

Outside, she spied the boy at the end of a lane between rows of white-fenced paddocks. He stooped over the water trough in the last paddock, using a long-handled brush to scrub it out. Then he rinsed the trough, tipped it to dump out the dirty water and then filled it with fresh. He stood and moved on to the next paddock's water trough.

"Can I help?" Sierra offered, venturing up to him.

He scowled up at her from where he hunched over the trough but didn't answer as he started scrubbing.

Sierra waited awkwardly.

He finished scrubbing and rinsing the trough and unbent himself to glare at her. "Look," he said, "girls like you show up here all the time thinking that stable work is easy. I waste my time showing you what to do and after a few days you figure out it's not worth free lessons. Tess was supposed to hire someone who knows how to work."

Sierra flushed with anger. This kid had no idea how hard she could work! She hated being pre-judged. Squaring her jaw she met his cold stare. "I can learn the work and I will not quit," she challenged.

He shook his head doubtfully and sighed. "You can fill the water troughs after I've cleaned them; one quarter full," he stated and moved away to the next paddock.

With a deep sigh of frustration, Sierra turned on the spigot over the trough and filled it to the level he had told her. Going from paddock to paddock after the boy finished cleaning, she filled the other troughs. He again disappeared after he scrubbed out the last paddock's trough, leaving her alone again as she finished filling it with fresh water.

Sierra decided to return to the stable and enjoy the company of the horses. She was here to help clean stalls, so she figured she might as well wait around the stalls until the boy or someone else came to start the cleaning. She heard the electric cart coming down the aisle and saw the boy drive it to the back of the stable and park. Its open space had been filled with fresh hay bales, ready for the next feeding. Steeling herself for more rudeness, Sierra approached as he stepped down from the cart.

"What do you want me to do now?"

"The restrooms need to be cleaned," he answered, walking away from her.

"Where's the restroom?" she asked, trailing him again.

"There's one inside the tack room and the one in the lounge."

Not bothering to try to get more instructions from him, Sierra found the two restrooms. With a little snooping around into cabinets she located cleaning supplies and extra toilet paper and paper towels. *Cleaning bathrooms I can handle and if he thinks he can discourage me with this, well, he's going to be disappointed.* Her mother had raised her to help with housework ever since she was old enough to wield a mop and rag. She wiped down all the surfaces, scrubbed the toilets, swept the floors, emptied the trash cans, and refilled the toilet paper and paper towel holders. The restroom in the lounge even had a shower and Sierra polished the fixtures and wiped down the tiled walls. *I might as well tidy the lounge,* she decided after the bathrooms were clean. She picked up the debris of soda cans, used coffee cups, and food containers; dusted, swept the floor, and emptied the trash. With those chores done she figured it was time to go find 'Mr. Congeniality' for what to do next. Walking back from the lounge to the stable, Sierra noticed the boy's dog lying in the shade of a tree, head on its paws, watching her.

The boy was nowhere in sight. To make use of the time, Sierra strolled down the aisles, getting to know each horse by name and noting the information on the card, trying to familiarize herself with their feed requirements so that tomorrow morning it might be easier to keep up with the boy as they fed. She noted that four of the horses belonged to Pegasus. The other fourteen had names of private owners and she assumed they were boarded horses. She talked softly to each one, noting their personalities. Some completely ignored her, their full attention on their hay. A few would jerk their heads up to eye her with suspicion as she peered through the grate, probably worried that she would take them away from their breakfast. But when she made no move to enter the stall, they returned warily to their feed. The friendlier ones actually left their hay to poke a muzzle at her, just in case she had brought a treat.

She found Crystal's horse, the chestnut gelding, and noted his name, *Red Magic*. She lingered at his stall admiring his impressive beauty. He was one of the wary ones, bringing his head up high to eye her. She spoke softly to him, pleased when he returned to munching his hay and relaxed enough to ignore her presence.

The sound of footsteps warned her that someone approached and she looked over her shoulder to the see the boy, a frown on his face. She backed away in apprehension, reminded of his anger the other day when she had petted this horse. He stepped up to the grate. The chestnut raised his head, nickered a greeting, and took a step toward him.

Sierra watched in awe how the horse responded to the boy. "He trusts you," she commented in a respectful tone.

The boy looked back at her, his frown replaced with a pensive expression. Sierra waited for his retort. To her great surprise he suddenly smiled and said, "He's some horse, don't you think?"

"He's magnificent," she smiled back.

Nodding, he turned away and started down the aisle. Sierra remained frozen, not sure what to do. He looked back over his shoulder and stopped, it seemed waiting for her. "Have you ever worked with horses?"

"No," she replied honestly and stepped up to walk at his side.

"You're the girl hanging around here the other day."

"Yes, I had come about the job."

"What was your name again?" he asked.

"Sierra."

"I'm River."

5 CHORES

Let the love for the feeling of responsibility toward the horse rule all your decisions and actions. – Egon von Neindorff

"We give the horses about two hours to eat their breakfast and then we turn them out for the day," River explained. Sierra followed him to the first stall with the nameplate, *Morrison*. "This is Morris." He grabbed the halter from its hook and opened the stall door. A round-shaped, sturdy bay gelding with a wide white blaze and four white socks watched placidly as they entered his stall. "*Hola amigo*," River greeted the bay softly. "Watch," he said over his shoulder as he deftly hooked the halter onto the horse's head, then removed it and handed it to Sierra. "You try it."

Mimicking his actions, Sierra stood next to Morris's head and awkwardly managed to buckle on the halter. She gave silent thanks to the little bay horse as he stood patiently and even lowered his head. His body radiated warmth and he smelled wonderful.

"Okay," River acknowledged. Then he showed her how to hold the lead rope with her right hand about a foot from where the lead attached to the halter, and the trailing end of the lead looped in her left hand. "Lead him outside."

Sierra stepped out of the stall with the lead in hand and marveled that Morris willingly followed behind. As they neared the main door and the little horse noted the sunlight pouring in, he picked up his pace and came up alongside her.

"Don't let him crowd you," River instructed. He showed her how to tug back gently with the lead so that Morris stayed back. "He should walk right behind you. He should not get ahead of your shoulder or lag too far behind."

"Okay," Sierra agreed.

She led Morris to an open paddock. River opened the gate and told her to walk the horse inside and turn around so they both faced the gate. Sierra unbuckled the halter and watched Morris lower his head and snort as he ambled away.

One by one they brought each horse out of the stable and turned it loose in one of the paddocks or into a large communal pasture. River helped Sierra lead the horses that had good manners; the more nervous and hot-tempered ones he led out himself. Many of the horses after being confined inside all night, tossed their heads, squealed with glee, and took off running and bucking playfully in the paddock, expressing their happiness with the freedom to move; a joy to behold. Sierra grinned in delight and even River smiled as both of them stopped to watch the antics before turning away.

With all the horses turned out, River led Sierra to an equipment bay where he took down two pitchforks. He showed her how to pick out manure from the shavings and shake the pitchfork gently to allow the dry shavings to fall back down through the tines; then dump only the manure into a cart attached to a small tractor. Wet shavings they had to scoop up completely.

As they started mucking out the stalls, the dog that had followed River this morning entered the stable and plopped down in the aisle near where he worked.

"Is that your dog?" Sierra asked as a way of starting conversation.

"I guess," he answered.

"What do you mean you guess?"

"I'm as much hers as she is mine," he answered.

Interesting, Sierra mused. "What's her name?"

"Storm."

"Oh." After a few minutes of silence she asked, "Any particular reason why Storm?"

"She followed me home one stormy night."

"Do you know what kind of dog she is?"

"No." Then he added voluntarily, "She isn't allowed inside the barn when the horses are in."

Although his answers were short, Sierra didn't sense the animosity from River as when she had first arrived. He didn't seem to mind answering her questions about his dog, and even smiled at Storm when she pricked her ears at hearing her name. After that, the two mucked out the stalls together in silence, but it was a companionable silence and Sierra enjoyed the work. *This isn't hard*, she thought, getting into a rhythm of motion with the pitchfork; pick up, swing around, dump.

They had finished the first aisle when another man entered the stables. He smiled as he walked by and Sierra caught a pleasant whiff of something good to eat coming from a basket he carried. The man spoke to River in rapid Spanish and she heard her name mixed in with the Spanish words. Apprehension seeped into her heart. *They must be discussing my work*. After a few minutes of talking, the man approached Sierra.

"Allo," he greeted in accented English. "Mees Tess tell me you work 'eere weekend eef you do okay."

33

Sierra wiped straggling damp hair that had escaped her braids away from her face. "I'll get faster as I get more used to the work," she blurted out defensively.

He laughed pleasantly. "*Muy bien*, good. I am Manuel, I am dee barn maneeger."

"Nice to meet you; I'm Sierra Landsing." She smiled at his pleasant manner.

"Sierra," he nodded with a reassuring grin. He pronounced her name with a Spanish inflection and rolling the *r*s, and she liked the way it sounded. "Reever, 'ee tell me you do okay."

"Really?" She looked over at the boy in disbelief.

"Yeah," River muttered and turned away to toss a pitchfork-full into the cart.

"Thanks," Sierra responded, grinning in relief, and returned to her own mucking with renewed energy.

"You keeds, you take a break now," Manuel ordered. "My Rosa, she make for you to eat." Manuel walked to an observation platform at one end of the indoor arena where several chairs and a small bleacher had been placed, and set the basket down.

"Come on," River directed, leaning his pitchfork against the side of the stall. Sierra followed him to the tack room where they washed their hands and then over to the platform where Manuel unloaded the contents of the basket. Scrambled eggs, cheese, and bits of chorizo sausage had been stuffed inside freshly-made tortillas. A plastic container filled with a chunky salsa and a jug of orange juice accompanied the food. Sierra had eaten a bowl of cereal before leaving home that morning, but her stomach growled at the smell of the enticing food, and she realized she was quite hungry. She sat down on one of the chairs next to River and Storm came over to lie at their feet. The two kids quickly consumed the six tortillas with voracious appetites, breaking off pieces that they tossed to Storm, sharing the feast.

A few boarders began to arrive; either to ride their horses out for a hack on the trails or to work in one of the arenas. Some managed their own horses but a few would call River away, asking him to bring a horse in from the paddock or help with grooming and tacking, and that left Sierra to clean stalls by herself. Her muscles already ached from the unaccustomed work, but she kept up the pace, even with River away.

Finally all eighteen stalls had been mucked out, filled with fresh shavings, and the aisles and other areas inside the stable swept and tidied.

"We're done," River announced as they hung brooms back on the wall in the equipment bay. Sierra looked back down the aisle at the row of fresh, clean stalls, feeling a sense of accomplishment and happy for the horses to have such comfortable stalls to sleep in. She closed her eyes and hugged herself, breathing in deeply the wonderful smells of horse, hay, and even manure.

"What are you doing?" River asked, watching her.

She blushed in embarrassment for she thought he had turned away. "Nothing...I'm just smelling the smells." She was sure River would laugh or scoff at her, but surprisingly he smiled, as if he understood. "Thanks for showing me what to do," she added.

He nodded. "Are you coming back tomorrow?"

"Yes, I told you I won't quit...that is, if I have the job."

"If you want it," he replied.

The silhouette of a figure walked down the aisle toward them. As she came into view Sierra recognized Crystal Douglas dressed in a tailored blue and gold riding pullover that seemed well coordinated with her blue eyes and golden hair, tan breeches, and polished black riding boots.

"River," the girl's voice called out sharply. "Get Magic tacked up. I want the blue pad and matching splint boots."

River's posture stiffened and his jaw tightened. Crystal had spoken her command and walked away. He stood a moment taking in deep breaths before he strode rapidly after her. Just behind her he said, "I'm riding Magic today."

Crystal stopped and turned back toward him. "What did you say?"

"Tess wants me to trail ride him."

"You were supposed to do that yesterday."

"And today."

Sierra watched the interaction, looking at Crystal and then at River, and felt the tangible enmity between them.

"Well, I'm riding him today," Crystal spat out. They stared hard at each other, Crystal with arms folded firmly across her chest and River clenching his fists at his sides.

The tense moment lasted the length of a held breath. Then River shrugged and snapped back, "He's your horse, but you'll have to tack him up yourself." He strode angrily past Crystal and out the stable door.

Sierra let out her breath, watching all with an anxious expression on her face.

"What are you staring at?" Crystal barked angrily at her. Then she too spun around and stomped back outside.

6 THE HORSES

No healthy people, no culture rooted in natural principles, will ever be able to forgo close alliance with the horse and the happiness it gives. – Waldemar Seunig

Sunday morning, Sierra woke with the muscles of her arms, back, and even her legs stiff and aching from the unaccustomed hard work of yesterday. She felt crippled as she hobbled out of bed and dressed in her grubby jeans and sweatshirt. After gulping down a glass of milk with a piece of toast, she stiffly pedaled her bicycle to Pegasus and waited at the stable doors for River to arrive.

He came up the lane with Storm and glanced at her, again without speaking.

Sierra took a deep breath and followed him around to the back of the stable. "Hi, River," she greeted.

He mumbled a response as he punched in numbers on the keypad of a back door, opened it and went inside. She sighed and followed him in, noting where the switches were located as he flipped on lights and the button that opened the main entryway door. Horses stirred in their stalls and whinnied out their greetings. A tabby cat emerged from a shadowy corner to rub against River's legs and meow up at him. Sierra's irritation at his surliness began to ease amid the animal smells and sounds.

River jumped up onto the driver's seat of the electric cart, already loaded with bales of hay, and turned on the ignition. He beckoned to her, "Are you coming?"

Sierra smiled in relief and climbed onto the passenger seat and they began the morning chores.

Monday morning Sierra stared out the school bus window; not seeing the traffic or passing scenery. Rather she imagined the shadow of the bus as a giant black horse who galloped alongside, jumping all the obstacles he met in his way. When the bus slowed and pulled over to its next stop, she calmed her fiery steed, *patience, True Heart.* She imagined him stomping and pawing at this forced halt. Moments later the bus lurched back into the lane and she released True Heart, who burst forward and leaped over the blue Honda to the left of the bus.

A heavy plop into the empty space next to Sierra jounced the seat, and without looking she scooted away closer to the window.

"Hi, Sierra," a voice greeted her, followed by a gargled-sounding laugh.

Great, Billy, Sierra recognized his voice. His mother must not have been able to drive him to school this morning. She glanced at him and politely said, "Hi," with a quick smile before turning back to the window and True Heart.

"Did you finish the English homework?" Billy inquired as he shifted around in the seat, arranging his ample bottom and finding room between his feet for his backpack.

"Yes," Sierra replied without turning away from the window, resisting his attempts to draw her into conversation.

Billy prattled on about a movie he had seen over the weekend, interpreting Sierra's one word responses as interest. His voice invaded into her imagination and she lost True Heart.

Finally the bus pulled into the school loading and unloading zone. Sierra felt trapped as the other kids rushed off the bus exuding laughter and chatter as they pushed their way down the aisle. Billy waited until the last kid had passed before squirming his bulky body into the aisle. He stepped back and with a sweep of his hand, announced, "After you, m'lady," mimicking the accent of a character in his movie.

Sierra could not help a short laugh and rolled her eyes as she stepped past him, because for once he was funny. She began the descent down the steps of the bus moving with slow stiffness, all her muscles aching from the weekend work. At the last step, a heavy weight unexpectedly plummeted against her back. She staggered, lost her balance, and fell to her knees onto the sidewalk. Billy fell heavily on top of her, his backpack knocking the side of her head before sliding away.

Laughter and snide comments encircled Sierra and Billy as kids crowded around, hiding them from the view of the bus driver who seemed unaware of the accident.

"Billy, please get off me," Sierra wheezed, for his weight on her back made it hard to breathe. Billy shifted to roll off and then she was free to pick herself up.

"Are you okay?" Billy asked anxiously, still on the ground where he had rolled onto his side.

Sierra stood, brushing off her clothes and relieved not to find a tear in the knee of her jeans, even though she could feel a painful scrape underneath. "I'm okay," she assured him, keeping her back turned as she adjusted her backpack. It was embarrassing to hear Billy grunt and groan as he pushed himself onto his feet. The first bell had sounded and most of the crowd had dispersed, heading into the building. As much as Sierra wanted to flee, she waited to be sure Billy had regained his feet. She picked up his backpack and handed it to him.

"Justin shocked me," Billy said as he hoisted his backpack over his shoulders.

"What?" Sierra didn't understand. "Who?"

"An electric shock," Billy stated. "He touched the back of my leg with something and it gave me a jolt." As if in proof, Billy rubbed the calf of his left leg.

"He wouldn't…" But Sierra admitted to herself that yes, some of the boys here were mean enough to do something like that…like put bubblegum in a girl's hair. "You should tell someone," she advised.

Billy snorted. "I'm not a tattletale…besides…and don't you say anything either."

A new Chevrolet Suburban pulled up to the curb, doors opened, and Crystal with her best friend Gloria Sanders, stepped out. "Do you smell manure?" Crystal asked in a loud voice as the two girls passed by, and they both giggled derisively. They skipped up the steps to where a boy waited and Sierra recognized Justin Blomquist, Crystal's boyfriend. He greeted the girls with a satisfied grin and began telling them what had happened, cocking his head towards Sierra and Billy. The three went inside laughing loudly.

Billy watched their retreating backs, and then lumbered after Sierra as she started up the steps. "Have you made an enemy of Crystal?"

"Not that I know of."

"That's one person you don't want on your bad side," he warned in an ominous tone.

"I've started working weekends at Pegasus Equestrian Center, where she boards her horse," she told him. "I don't see why that would make me her enemy though."

"Sierra, she doesn't board her horse there. Her father owns that stable; or at least part owner," Billy informed her.

"I still don't see why she would care if I work there," Sierra wondered. She said goodbye as they entered the building and parted for their classes. But she thought back to the last time she had seen Crystal at the stable and the altercation with River. *Could she resent me because I witnessed that?*

Every weekend Sierra spent at the stable. Saturday and Sunday mornings she helped feed, turn out horses, and muck stalls with River. Her muscles developed and she became adept at the work which no longer left her sore. River remained reticent, especially first thing in the morning; but they worked together in companionable silence and Sierra no longer sensed that he resented her presence.

She learned the stable routine. Manuel and his wife Rosa did the chores during the weekdays, and then Manuel busied himself with maintenance of the stable and grounds. Rosa worked at a local Mexican restaurant in the afternoons. Manuel had the weekend mornings off and all day Sunday. Saturday, Manuel brought the horses in for the night and fed them but Sunday night River did the evening chores. Rosa prepared a midmorning basket of food for the two kids every Saturday and Sunday, usually delivered by Manuel, but sometimes Rosa herself. She was a short, plump woman who always wore an affectionate smile, hugged both Sierra and River, and spoke only a few words of English.

River also worked weekdays after school; tacking up and then cooling down the horses used in lessons and helping Manuel bring in and feed the horses in the evening. In between chores, River rode two or three horses that Tess assigned him; either schooling in the arena, hacking out on the trails, or in the open fields behind the stable where a permanent cross country jumping course had been constructed.

After school and after chores on the weekend, Sierra spent her free time at the stable. She visited each horse, petting them and feeding bits of apples or carrots. And then she watched River.

She stayed in the background so as not to get in River's way. She loved watching him handle the horses both on the ground and in the saddle; but especially in the saddle. There was something magical about River on a horse, as if it was the place meant for him in the world. She never saw him wear spurs and he rarely carried a whip. The few times she had seen him use a whip had been as an extension of his hand or leg and only a tap. Yet his mount always looked energized and quick to respond to whatever invisible commands River gave to the animal. The expression in the eye of the horse and the way it would flick its ears back and forth looked exactly as if the horse listened to and understood River.

Tess rode the horses in training in the mornings which freed her up to give lessons in the afternoons, but sometimes she would be finishing up with the last horse when Sierra arrived at the stable after school. Sierra liked watching Tess ride also, but she wondered at the difference in Tess's style from that of River. When Tess rode, Sierra could see how she controlled the horse's every move, with hands and with touches of spur and whip. She demanded of the horse powerful, energetic movements, yet they seemed tense and forced. It was a power that Sierra thought of as a tightly compressed coil which once released, would spring apart with violence and with the potential to hurt something. It was a frightening beauty. When River rode, the horse's energy seemed effortless, fluid, and full of joy. When Tess rode, the horse's energy seemed tightly controlled and explosive.

River knew Sierra hung around watching, and eventually he called her over and let her help him groom, tack, untack, and cool down the horses as they were brought back from their lessons. Speaking few words, he mostly taught by showing her how. She never felt irritation or impatience from him as she struggled with the unfamiliar tasks. Sierra learned to brush coats, pick out feet, and comb manes and tails; how to bridle and saddle a horse; and how to clean the tack before storing it in the tack room.

River also taught her what Sierra liked to think of as horse language, such things as: watch out when a horse's ears are laid back, he's annoyed; be careful around the back end when the tail is clamped tight, he may kick; the combination of ears back, quivering of skin and hunching of back muscles when grooming meant that she had touched a ticklish or sensitive spot. Sierra learned these signals that all horses possess in common, but she also discovered individual characteristics and personality traits in each one. She came to know all the horses not only by their appearances, but also by each one's uniqueness. She learned their names; their registered names (often rather pretentious), and their stable names or nicknames. She loved them all and tried to give equal attention to each horse, but she did have her favorites, one of which was Red Magic, nicknamed Magic.

Magnificently beautiful with a regal presence, Magic had a sweet and timid disposition, easily frightened, but very receptive to kind words and soft handling. River told her he was a four-year-old, very green, and still considered a baby. Sierra thought River loved him best of all the horses and it wasn't difficult to recognize a close bond between the boy and the lovely chestnut.

Crystal Douglas acquired Magic three months ago to replace her older eventing horse Caretaker, nicknamed Butch, a sixteen-year-old dark bay Oldenburg gelding. Crystal had done very well on Butch in combined training events; having won the Pacific Regional Championship at both beginner novice and novice levels in years past. But last season, riding at training level, he came up lame mid-season and she was unable to qualify for the championship event. Campaigned hard all his life and now suffering from arthritis, it was doubtful he would remain sound if moved up to preliminary level and higher. Crystal convinced her father she needed a better mount and Butch was now for sale.

Magic was only green broke, meaning he had very little training under saddle. The plan was for Tess to school him along this year and Crystal was only supposed to ride him during lessons with Tess coaching her. Sierra guessed that the day Crystal came to ride him and got into the argument with River, that she did not have Tess's approval. One of her school friends had come with her that day and Crystal probably wanted to show off. Most of the time, Crystal only came to ride two days a week, the days she had her lessons on Magic. Crystal liked riding in competitions but left the day-to-day training and care of her horses to Tess and River.

Crystal's two best friends, Gloria Sanders and Katrina Lund, also boarded at Pegasus. Gloria owned a well-trained eight-year-old Dutch warmblood, Silver Knight (nicknamed Silver), an impressive gray gelding that stood seventeen hands. She had taken reserve championship last year at beginner novice level, and planned to compete this year at the next level up – novice level. She also took two lessons a week from Tess. Like Crystal, she never groomed or tacked up her own horse, always ordering River to do it for her.

Katrina owned a nine-year-old appaloosa mare, Calliope, and had placed in most of her events last year at beginner novice level, winning one second place, and the rest fourth and fifth places. She also planned to move up to novice level in the upcoming season. Katrina showed up to ride several days a week in addition to her lessons, and unlike Crystal and Gloria, preferred to manage her own horse. Of the three girls, it seemed Katrina was the only one who had a genuine love for her animal.

Five other boarders competed in combined training under Tess's coaching, a high school girl and four adults competing in senior amateur divisions. The other five boarded horses were in training with Tess, and their owners seldom came to the stable. The horses in training remained anywhere from two weeks to six months, and there was a constant stream of horses in training moving in and out.

The remaining four horses were owned by Pegasus and used as school horses for riding lessons. Morrison, a bay quarter horse with a placid disposition and a tendency to laziness, served as a safe beginner's mount. Muffin, a large black and white pony, sixteen years old, had a successful career as a hunter-jumper. He was an excellent first mount for smaller riders to learn to jump and compete in their first show. Fala, a ten-year-old black Arabian mare had a sweet and willing disposition and also was used in competitions. Gunsmoke, a twenty-two-year old retired Hanoverian gelding was occasionally used in lessons for more advanced riders. He had carried Tess through advanced level combined training competitions and secured her reputation as a successful event rider. After eventing, he continued his career in dressage, all the way to grand prix level.

Sierra wondered about River's place at the farm. He seemed to be just hired stable help, taking his orders from both Tess and Manuel. But he pushed the limits of rudeness with many of the boarders and seemed to get away with it. Tess and he barely tolerated each other and the hatred between him and Crystal was tangible. Yet he worked very hard and with no days off.

But what was obvious to Sierra was that River loved the horses, and the horses all loved him. Neat Trix, or Trixie, the temperamental mare when in season, turned her back and threatened to kick anyone who approached her; except for River. Raider, a thoroughbred gelding who often decided he did not want to be caught at the end of the day, never ran away from River. Muffin, who had figured out how to open any latch, untie knots, and even unbuckle a halter, frequently escaped from his paddock to follow River around like a dog, but ran away if anyone else tried to catch him. River treated each horse with gentleness and patience, and surprisingly, Sierra began to sense that he treated her in the same manner as the horses.

7 FIRST RIDE

Riding a horse is not a gentle hobby, to be picked up and laid down like a game of solitaire. It is a grand passion. It seizes a person whole and, once it has done so, he will have to accept that his life will be radically changed. – Ralph Waldo Emerson

One Saturday after they had finished cleaning stalls and had just finished sweeping the aisles, River asked, "When is Tess going to give you a riding lesson?"

"I don't know, she hasn't said anything to me," Sierra answered.

"Are you sure you want to take lessons from her?"

"Of course!" Sierra frowned at him, surprised he would ask that. "Tess Holmes is the best rider and trainer around. I hear Crystal, Gloria, and Katrina at school bragging all the time about all her wins."

"But you've seen her give lessons."

"Yes." Sierra wasn't sure what River was getting at.

"You've seen how the horses look afterwards, and you still want to learn from her?"

"Well, I want to learn from the best," Sierra insisted, but a little nagging feeling crept into the back of her mind. It did disturb her to see how upset and frightened some of the horses appeared after their lessons.

"Have you ever ridden before?"

"Only once; two years ago I got to go on a trail ride for my birthday."

River hung up his broom and paused, thinking. Then making a decision he said, "Come on." He led Sierra to the outside paddock where Morris stood asleep, resting on one hind leg and with his head low and ears flopped to the sides.

"*Amigo*," River called to him. Morris looked up and pricking his ears forward nickered almost soundlessly. He sauntered toward them as River opened the gate and the two kids stepped inside. As Morris reached them River gave him a treat from his pocket, talking to him softly and stroking his neck. Then he told Sierra to put on his halter.

"Follow me," River directed and led the way out of the paddock, but instead of going towards the stable, he headed to the open fields. "You might as well start getting used to the feel of a horse underneath you." River stopped and took the lead rope from Sierra's hand.

"Really?" Sierra's eyes widened in disbelief and a grin split her face.

River showed her where to stand next to the bay's side and then boosted her up onto the middle of Morris's warm, soft back.

"Keep your body loose and feel him underneath you," River instructed and led Morris off at a walk.

The motion was incredible! At first Sierra just enjoyed the soft feel of his back. Then she started to focus on the movement of his muscles; how his hip and shoulder on one side moved forward, then the hip and shoulder on the other side. She felt his rib cage swing back and forth against her legs in rhythm with his walking motion.

"Try closing your eyes," River suggested.

She did and it was amazing how much more aware of Morris's movements she became.

River led on at a leisurely pace around the field, going up and down small hills. The first time going downhill Sierra almost felt like she was going to slip forward over Morris's neck.

"Sit deep and stay centered over his back," River told her. Going uphill, he told her to grab a handful of mane and keep her weight forward over Morris's shoulders.

Too soon River headed back to the stable. "*Andale*," he spoke to Morris who lagged at the end of the lead rope, eyeing a particularly tempting green clump of grass.

"How come you always talk to the horses in Spanish?" Sierra asked; something she had wondered about.

"I don't know…I guess it has softer tones."

"Oh, yeah. I think so too. How come you speak Spanish so well? You don't look Mexican."

"I'm not."

"So..?" She asked again. She was used to pulling information from River bit by bit.

He shrugged. "I've grown up around stables and there are always Cuban and Puerto Rican or Mexican workers. I've spoken Spanish as long as I've spoken English." He turned his attention to Morris, clucking at him to step up his pace and effectively discouraged any more of the questions she wanted to ask. They reached the edge of the field and River told her how to swing her right leg around and then push away and jump down.

"That was so awesome," Sierra exclaimed softly as River handed her the lead rope and they led Morris back to his paddock. "Thanks."

A battered, older model Ford pick-up and equally dilapidated horse trailer sat in the stable yard and in view as they crested the hill from the fields. *Not quite the type of outfit that clients of Pegasus usually show up in*, Sierra thought.

River swore something under his breath and in a solemn tone told Sierra to take Morris back to his paddock. He strode off toward the stable yard and the squareness of his shoulders testified to his distress.

"Something's wrong," Sierra said to Morris as she led him back into his paddock. She slipped off his halter and then hugged him around his neck and whispered, "Thanks." Morris snuffled at her pockets for the treat he knew should be there. Sierra pulled out broken pieces of carrot and fed them to him off the flat of her palm. With a final pat, she reluctantly left the paddock and walked toward the stable yard. She felt a little nervous about River possibly in a confrontation with a client.

A tall, broad-shouldered, dark-haired man stood with arms folded watching as River backed a hooded, blanketed, and booted horse down the ramp of the trailer. Manuel stood on the other side of the ramp to help guide the animal straight back. As soon as the horse felt all four of his feet on level ground he raised his head high and trumpeted out a loud neigh, announcing his presence. Answering whinnies came from the paddocks and horses with ears pricked and heads over the top rails, stared at the newcomer. The horse tugged at his halter, blowing loudly through his nose, and shifting his hind end side-to-side as he looked around.

He's awesome! Sierra watched as River led him around in a tight circle several times to keep his attention.

"I don't even have a stall ready for him," River snapped out angrily at the tall man.

"Ees ready," Manuel informed him. "Mees Tess, she call."

At that moment, a white Lexus pulled into the stable yard; Tess's car.

Manuel spoke to River in Spanish, and shaking his head, River led the new horse away, following Manuel. The fractious animal danced at the end of his lead rope, throwing his head up, and several times River needed to turn him in a tight circle to regain control. They did not take the horse into the stable but down a path that led to a mobile home where Manuel and Rosa resided. There was a small barn and paddock on that part of the property.

Tess had parked her car and stood watching the retreating horse. The tall man strode up behind her and grabbed Tess about the waist and swung her around in glee. He was a handsome man and dressed in tailored clothes that did not match the quality of his truck and trailer.

"Five wins!" he yelled out above Tess's laughter and her cries of, "Cray, put me down!"

He did set her down and the two fell into an embrace and kissed.

"Oh my," Sierra whispered and retreated back into the stable out of sight, not wanting to inadvertently witness a private situation. She heard their voices in animated conversation and then the sounds of the office door as it opened and closed. Only when silence reigned in the stable yard did she dare go back outside. River and Manuel with the new horse had disappeared. She walked down the lane of paddocks and said goodbye to the horses, giving each one a last treat before she headed home.

○—•—○

"What horse was that who came in yesterday?" Sierra asked River the next morning as they mucked stalls.

"The stallion?" he asked back.

"He's a stallion?"

"Yeah, a race horse."

"Tess is training a race horse?"

"No, he belongs to my father." River answered without enthusiasm.

"That was your father?" Sierra asked in surprise.

River didn't answer right away but his next toss from his pitchfork seemed a bit forceful. "Yeah," he finally replied and turned his back to end the conversation.

His father? Having an affair with Tess? Sierra wanted to ask more questions but sensed River didn't want to talk anymore. They finished cleaning in silence. Sierra pushed away the hope that River might lead her out on Morris again. He was not in one of his better moods.

"Let's go get Morris," River stated as they hung up the brooms after the final sweep of the aisles.

"Really?" Sierra asked in surprise.

"If you want," he answered.

"Of course!"

Ballroom dancing could be a lot of fun, Sierra thought, *especially with a decent partner; maybe someone like Luke Abrams.* As Billy awkwardly tried to lead her around the gym floor during PE, she felt like they were doing the *fox trip* rather than the fox trot. For the third time, Billy stumbled and stepped on her foot.

"Sorry, *hngh hngh,*" he apologized adding his obnoxious laugh. "Sorry." The second apology was addressed to Sierra but the first to the couple who had bumped into them. Sierra looked over Billy's shoulder and this time it was Gloria and her partner Greg, who had purposefully jostled against Billy. The two times before had been Crystal dancing with Justin.

"Watch it, blob!" Greg responded rudely to the apology. Gloria snickered and Sierra saw Crystal and Justin with smirks on their faces as they danced nearby.

"Billy, will you quit apologizing? They're the ones bumping into you," she snapped at him, very annoyed. Those close enough to overhear her chastise Billy tittered in amusement; all except Luke. Sierra noticed him watching over his partner's shoulder with a frown on his face.

"Having a little spat with your boyfriend?" Crystal asked in a sugary sweet voice as she and Justin gracefully danced around Sierra and Billy.

Sierra took over the lead from Billy, which wasn't hard to do, and forcefully guided him to the edge of the gymnasium floor, away from the others. She could imagine the fun they were having watching a girl of her small size pushing around Billy's bulk.

Billy remained quiet, except for clearing his throat several times. Then Sierra noticed the embarrassed flush of his down-turned face. *Of course he knows it was their fault,* she realized. *How else could a boy like Billy respond to public humiliation but to try to make a joke of it?* Sierra wasn't sure however, if the target of the bullying had actually been Billy or if Crystal still had a grudge against her. She knew Crystal did not like her; she just didn't understand what she had done to merit Crystal's scorn.

Sierra let her mind drift back to the weekend and the incredible experience of sitting on the broad, soft and warm back of Morris and how awesome to feel his muscles as he walked. With those thoughts she was able to survive PE.

8 LESSONS

Only when you see through the eyes of the horse, can you lead the dance of the mind. — Pete Spates

"When are you going to give Sierra lessons?" River had stepped into the office where Tess worked at the computer.

Tess sighed, her hands hovering over the keyboard and still focused on the screen. "How long has she been working here?"

"Over a month."

"Has she ever ridden before?"

"No." He had continued to take Sierra out in the back field after their chores on weekends, leading her bareback on Morris or another horse with a calm disposition. He didn't think that really qualified as riding so didn't mention it.

Tess sighed again in exasperation. She turned her head toward River, glaring. "You know I don't work with beginners anymore. This is a business, not a babysitting service."

"Are you going to pay her for her work then?"

"She's getting experience with horses for free."

River felt his anger rising. "You're using her," he accused.

Jerking her hands off the keyboard, Tess swiveled in her chair to face River, her face contorted in anger. "Is she complaining?"

"No, she never complains. But you promised her lessons."

"Well, quite frankly, I didn't think she would last. And I have no open lesson spots. She will just have to wait."

"Let me give her lessons then," he offered.

That caused Tess to sit up straighter and stare at River in surprise. "You?" she asked incredulously. "You hate all the girls that ride here."

"Sierra's different," he replied, his own posture stiffening.

Tess studied him. She had known River since he started working for her five years ago at the age of nine, and she realized she still thought of him as a little boy. But the boy standing in front of her was not so little; he was almost as tall as she and in spite of his thinness there was a breadth to his shoulders…and was that a hint of whiskers above his upper lip? *He's what…fourteen now?*…a teenager and certainly of an age to notice girls. *Does he have a crush on Sierra?* She stifled the urge to laugh and the desire to make a needling remark. Of all the attractive, well-off girls that rode at Pegasus, he would be interested in the one that still looked like a little girl and was poor.

"Fine." Tess turned back to the computer. "Get her started." It was really no concern of hers what River's interest might be in Sierra, except as an advantage to her.

River left, barely keeping his anger under control. He muttered a few uncomplimentary remarks to himself, which helped lighten his dark mood as he returned to his chores.

O——O

Tuesday afternoon Sierra stood at the rail of the indoor arena watching Gloria taking a lesson on Silver. Tess sat on the observation platform and called out instructions through a microphone. The big gray cantered around the perimeter of the arena as Tess instructed Gloria to alternately collect him and then lengthen his stride. With his neck arched and his powerful hind legs propelling him, the gray reached forward with his front legs to take longer strides, then shifted back on his hind legs as he shortened his stride for the collected canter. *Beautiful,* Sierra marveled at the gray's apparent ease in making the transitions.

"Sitting trot," Tess called out.

Gloria stiffened and pulled back on the reins, causing Silver to come up with his head, momentarily losing his balance. She jabbed him with her spurs and he jumped back into a canter.

"Keep your hands in front of his withers," Tess yelled, "and just half-halt, don't pull back on him. Now bring him to a trot."

Gloria tried again, and this time Silver anticipated what was expected. He brought his hind end underneath him and came to a trot, keeping his head and neck rounded.

"Better," Tess stated. "Now half-halt again and bring him to a walk, then give him a long rein and stretch him out." Gloria brought Silver to the walk, then let the reins go slack as the big gelding stretched his neck forward and down. She walked him once around the arena, then came to the exit gate and dismounted. Without a word to Sierra, she tossed her the reins and then walked over to the platform to discuss her lesson with Tess.

"Good boy, Silver," Sierra stroked his warm, sweaty neck, then led him over to the crossties and removed his bridle, saddle, and splint boots. She was about to lead him outside to cool him out when Tess came up behind her.

"Sierra," she spoke sharply.

"Yes?" Sierra turned apprehensively, wondering if she had done something wrong.

"River is going to work with you on the basics for awhile; then we'll see if you're ready for lessons."

Excitement welled up to replace the worry that she was in trouble. Sierra smiled.

Then Tess added, "In the future if you have any complaints I would appreciate it if you would come directly to me instead of whining to River."

Sierra's smile converted to mouth agape at the reprimand. *What is she talking about?*

Without waiting for a response Tess walked away, but turned back once abruptly. "You'll need a helmet and boots, those are the rules."

"Did you hear that, Silver?" Sierra looked up into the gentle eyes of the handsome gray. She reached around his neck and gave him a hug, as if somehow he were responsible for the news. She clipped on the lead rope and led him outside to walk up and down the lane. *River must have said something to Tess*, she concluded, *and she thinks I was complaining about not having lessons.*

Outside, Sierra spied River riding back from the trail on Magic. The chestnut looked around happily with his ears flicking side-to-side, very relaxed. It always amazed Sierra; the difference in Magic when River rode him compared to when Crystal rode. River was riding bareback, wearing jeans with holes in the knees, paddock boots, and a black helmet. Sierra stopped at the end of the lane, admiring the beauty of the boy and horse as the sun moved suddenly from behind a cloud, sending a beam of light that caught the coppery red of Magic's coat and gleamed on River's black hair and helmet. It was a vision of two beings harmoniously merged to appear as one. She wanted to look like that on a horse.

"Hi," Sierra greeted as the pair came up to her and River swung off Magic's back. "How did he do today?"

"Great," River answered, stroking the coppery neck affectionately. They walked the horses side by side back toward the stable.

"Tess told me you're going to give me lessons," Sierra announced.

"I'm sorry it's going to be me. I know you want to take lessons from her," he replied apologetically.

"I'm not sorry!" Sierra exclaimed in surprise. "You're a great rider!"

"But you want to learn from the best," he stated sarcastically.

"River, you are the best. Besides, Tess said you would teach me the basics and then she would give me lessons."

"I see," he answered and said no more.

"Momma," Sierra began as they sat down at the table in the kitchen to eat dinner. "I get to start taking lessons."

Pam paused with her fork and looked at her daughter as a smile spread across her face. "Kitten, that's great! And it's about time." Pam had mentioned a few times that she believed Tess was taking unfair advantage of Sierra's willingness to work for free. But Sierra only responded that at least she got to be around the horses.

"I need a riding helmet and boots though," Sierra continued.

"Oh dear, how much will those cost?" Pam asked.

"I looked on-line, and I can get a pair of rubber riding boots for twenty-nine dollars. They're on sale right now through this one tack store. I have that in my savings. But the cheapest helmet costs around forty dollars."

"Well, I'll see if I can manage that at the end of the month. Can you use your bicycle helmet in the meantime?"

"I guess," Sierra replied in resignation. She understood how tight dollars were. "Can I order the boots?"

"It's your money, so go ahead."

Sierra ordered the boots as soon as she and her mom finished cleaning up after dinner, and spent the extra money for one-day shipping. Her boots arrived the next day.

"Saddle up Morris," River said. They had about an hour between cooling out the last lesson horse and before the horses were brought in for the night.

"I'm going to learn to ride and you're going to help me," Sierra chattered soothingly to Morris although nothing seemed to rattle the complacent little gelding and she could have shouted the news at him.

River came down the aisle with a coil of webbed line in his hands. "Let's go." He studied Sierra as she led Morris into the indoor arena, wearing her new black rubber riding boots over her jeans and a bicycle helmet, her brown braids hanging out the back. He hoped none of the girls who boarded here would happen by to see her, because he could imagine the snide comments they would make. It irritated him how often he overheard these girls who could have anything they wanted, owned expensive horses and all the best equipment, make derogatory remarks about Sierra. She sure was plucky though; seemingly oblivious to their unkindness, focusing all her attention on the horses and working hard as if it were a privilege.

"We're going to start out on the lunge line," he said after he had shown Sierra how to adjust her stirrups and mount up at the mounting block.

"Kind of like they start out at the Spanish Riding School?" she asked.

"That's right. How do you know about that?"

"Oh, I've read every book they have in the library about horses, and there's one all about the school and the Lipizzans."

"Okay, *senorita*," he quipped. He clucked to Morris, starting him at a walk on a circle around him.

River is in a good mood today. That helped to ease Sierra's nervousness. It felt different after riding bareback and not as comfortable; the saddle cold and firm rather than soft, warm, silky hair under her seat. It felt awkward to have to bend her leg to fit her foot in the stirrup after having them hanging loose.

"Let the horse teach you to ride," River told her. "If you start from the beginning listening to him, he'll let you know if you're doing things wrong."

Sierra nodded silently, not quite understanding.

River watched for a few minutes and then said, "You're too tense. Let's try getting you to loosen up. Drop your stirrups and swing your legs back and forth. Try rolling your shoulders forwards and then backwards."

Sierra obeyed as River continued to instruct her in a series of loosening exercises: rolling her neck around on her shoulders, holding her arms out to the sides and circling in both directions, bending forward and backwards from the waist, turning at the waist to look over each shoulder, and then turning to touch the top of his tail and then forward to touch between his ears. Finally, he had her reach down on both sides of Morris and try to touch her toes. Then River turned Morris in the other direction and Sierra repeated all the exercises.

Sierra could feel herself becoming more relaxed as the exercises took her mind off the fact she was actually sitting in a saddle trying to ride. She remembered how Morris had felt bareback and as she relaxed, she began to feel the same movements of his body even through the saddle.

"Through your seat and into your body's deep center is how you feel what's happening with your horse and how you communicate back to him. Your legs and hands are just ways to enhance that communication, and they should always be very light. He's talking to you through his back and his shoulders and in the way he holds his head."

Sierra nodded in acknowledgement and then closed her eyes, focusing on Morris's back beneath her and his shoulders and neck movement in front of her. She could feel his muscles moving, but had to admit that it didn't tell her anything. "I guess it's like a new language I need to learn, and I don't understand the 'words' yet," Sierra said, feeling a little chagrined.

"Exactly," River smiled in encouragement. "Nobody understands the first time up, but since you're trying to learn his language you will get it. From what I can see, you're balanced on his back right now and Morris is 'saying' he's comfortable and you're not interfering with him."

"Really?"

River laughed. "Yeah. Want to try a trot?"

"I think so," Sierra answered, feeling both anticipation and fear.

"Put your feet back in the stirrups. You can hold onto that strap on the front of the saddle." River had buckled a strap between two D-rings at the pommel. "I'll signal Morris to trot and I'll control him. Just let his movement push you out of the saddle. You've seen riders post, so you have an idea what to do, okay?"

She nodded, "I'm ready."

River chirruped to Morris and the little bay obediently picked up his pace into an easygoing trot. Sierra jounced awkwardly for the first few strides and clutched at the strap to hold herself on. For a moment she felt like she was going to fall off.

"Don't try so hard; let him do the work," River called out.

Sierra took a deep breath and closed her eyes for a few moments. Within the next two strides she found herself rising out of the saddle and then back down in rhythm with the bouncing movement of the trot. She opened her eyes and stayed in the rhythm. Her grip on the strap loosened. *I'm posting!*

"You're posting!" River echoed her thoughts. "Are you okay?"

Sierra couldn't speak; she was so entranced with the motion. All she could do was nod and grin with pleasure.

River brought Morris back to the walk and let Sierra rest a few rounds, and then had her trot again. Then he reversed the direction so that Sierra practiced the trot going both ways.

"That's enough," he announced, and brought Morris to the center of the circle and to a halt. "I don't want you to get sore." He showed her how to dismount and they led Morris back to the crossties.

"You've got the rhythm of posting already," River praised her.

"I could feel it," Sierra exclaimed. "It was so cool. This has been the best day of my life!"

River shook his head in amusement but he also gave her a very warm smile.

9 THE CANTER

A horse can lend its rider the speed and strength he or she lacks…but the rider who is wise remembers it is no more than a loan. – Pam Brown

The autumn months gave way to winter and the stable routine changed to accommodate the colder conditions. Sierra helped River clip the thick winter coats of the horses so they didn't sweat and become chilled with their work. Winter blankets had to be put on for turn-out, and many frozen mornings they had to chip the ice away from the outside water troughs. It was harder to get out of bed and pedal her bicycle to the stable in the cold darkness; nevertheless, Sierra arrived before seven, every Saturday and Sunday morning. She and River had fallen into a pattern where she turned on the lights, fed Patches, the tabby cat, and was filling grain buckets by the time he arrived.

The lunge lessons continued, at least four days a week and more often if River had the time. Sierra rode alternately the three school horses, Morris, Muffin, and Fala. She progressed from holding on to the saddle strap to keeping both hands on her waist at the trot. The posting trot became easy. She learned to post on the correct diagonal; rising when the horse's outside shoulder moved forward, and back in the saddle when the inside shoulder moved forward. Most of the time she could identify the diagonal by feel instead of looking down at the horse's shoulder. Then River took her stirrups away. She had to go back to holding onto the strap as she learned to post without stirrups, and then the feel of sitting the trot.

"Your control comes from here," River placed his hand over his mid to lower abdomen. "This is your center of balance. If you can learn to control these muscles it will help you stay balanced and in rhythm with your horse's motion."

Sierra nodded, and practiced tightening and releasing her abdominal muscles to keep in the correct position as she learned to sit the bouncing motion of the trot. Within a few weeks she was able to release her grip on the strap and put her hands back on her waist. When she felt secure at the trot, River had her perform all the loosening up exercises she had been doing at a walk, now at the trot.

"I think you're ready for canter," River stated matter-of-factly one afternoon. Sierra was up on Fala, the little black Arabian mare with an agreeable disposition and very smooth gaits.

"Really?" Sierra had been dreaming about riding the canter, wondering when she would be ready. Now, an electric thrill coursed down her spine, a combination of excitement and fear.

"After the trot, it's easy," he assured her. "You can hold onto the strap and put your feet back in the stirrups."

Sierra complied and then sitting up straight and tall, took a deep breath and nodded to River, "I'm ready."

River signaled Fala to canter. The little mare jumped obediently from the trot into an easy, smooth canter gait.

Sierra's abdominal muscles had grown strong with all the sitting trot work, so to her delighted surprise, she felt comfortable and secure when the rhythm changed into a smooth, rocking motion; not at all bouncy and actually easier to sit than the trot. Fala didn't seem the least bit concerned that this was her rider's first time to canter. After the first circle, Sierra felt confident enough to let go of the strap and put her hands on her waist. She felt like she could ride this motion forever!

"Wow, look at rubber boots on a merry-go-round," a jeering voice commented from the side of the arena. River saw from the corner of his eye Crystal, Gloria, and Katrina watching Sierra and snickering together.

"Does she know the difference between a bicycle and a horse?" one of them added, and the three girls burst into raucous laughter. Then Crystal swung her light-colored jacket above her head, as if to put it across her shoulders, just as Fala approached on her circle.

River's stomach lurched as he realized the group stood in a triangle of sunlight pouring in from the other side of the stable. As Fala approached, she was looking into the light and he knew in an instant that the normally quiet mare would shy at the sudden flash of the light jacket; and he also knew with surety that Crystal had planned it. He watched helplessly as Fala raised her head and swung her hips off the circle to face the perceived danger, and her steady gait changing into a choppy trot. Sierra, not expecting the move, lost her balance and slipped to the side. Fala, feeling her rider shift unexpectedly, jumped forward. Sierra could not hold on and continued to slip to the ground, landing on her right hip and shoulder. But at least she remembered to roll with her fall and ended up on her back, looking up at the roof.

"Ouch," Sierra said.

Seconds later River knelt over her, his face taut with anxiety. "Sierra?"

"I'm okay," she assured him. She took a deep breath and pushed herself up to a sitting position. "Really, I am."

"Do you hurt anywhere?" he asked.

Sierra checked in with all her body parts. Other than the sting of where she had landed, she felt okay. "No," she answered and started to stand up. River grabbed hold of her arm and helped her to her feet. Covered in dirt, Sierra took a few steps, rubbing the hip where she had fallen. She looked at River's distressed expression and smiled at him weakly. "I guess I'm a rider now, huh?"

"What do you mean?"

"You know the saying: if you ain't been throwed then you ain't never rode!"

River laughed in relief and helped her brush the dirt from her clothing.

"I should get back on," Sierra stated.

"That's my girl," River smiled encouragement.

Fala had run to the edge of the arena in a panic, frightened by the loss of her rider and the feel of the saddle askew on her back. Now she stood frozen, the lunge line still attached to the bridle and stretched out on the ground. She watched the kids with her ears flicking nervously. River approached her, talking softly in lilting Spanish, "*Aye linda, que pasa?*" He picked up the lunge line, gathering it up. Fala, at the sound of his voice, lowered her head and stepped up to him. River stroked her neck still murmuring to her, and the wide-eyed frightened look in her eye melted away to soft calmness. River readjusted the saddle, tightened the girth, and led her to the mounting block for Sierra to remount. By the time River led Fala back to the center of the arena, the mare acted as if nothing at all had happened.

"Can I trot a few rounds to get my balance and then try the canter again?" Sierra asked as Fala started back out on the circle.

"Good idea," River agreed. "Whenever you're ready."

Sierra touched Fala's sides to signal for trot, and then settled into the saddle taking slow deep breaths to relax and regain her confidence. After three rounds she grabbed onto the strap and nodded to River that she was ready to canter.

"Touch her with your outside leg," he instructed but also helped by giving Fala the command to canter. Again Sierra felt the rocking, smooth gait and pushing down her fear, even dared to close her eyes to really feel the rhythm of this new motion. She opened her eyes and felt confident enough to let go of the strap and put her hands back on her waist.

"Good!" River encouraged. He brought Fala back to a trot and then walk, and reversed the direction so Sierra could canter both ways.

"I don't think it was the canter that caused me to fall but the fact that she shied and I wasn't expecting it," Sierra mused out loud as she and River walked Fala back to the cross ties after the lesson.

"Yeah," River agreed. "You were looking really good before she shied."

"Have you ever fallen off?" she asked curiously.

"Lots of times."

"How long have you been riding?"

"Would you believe even before I was born?"

"How do you mean?"

"My mother was a jockey, and she was riding racehorses while she was pregnant with me."

"Wow, no wonder you ride so well!" The revelation surprised Sierra, but also the fact that River was actually telling her this. "Is your mother still a jockey?"

"She died...she fell off in a race and she was trampled to death."

Sierra stopped in shock to look at him. "River, how horrible! I'm so sorry."

"It's okay. It was a long time ago."

She had a million questions she wanted to ask. *How awesome to have a mother who was a jockey. Did he like that about her? Did he blame the horse that had killed her? Did he ever want to be a jockey? Was it his mother who taught him to ride?* But she knew it must have been horrible for him and she just couldn't think how to phrase any questions.

After a few minutes of silence River said, "I'm named after a racehorse. Did you know that?"

"No." *Of course I didn't know that, I don't know anything about you,* Sierra wanted to say to him.

"Yeah, Raging River, a colt my mother rode to a win. At least she named me River and not Raging." He half-laughed.

"I like your name," she told him sincerely.

He shrugged and made a wry face.

"How would you like to be named after a mountain range?"

"Oh yeah, Sierra," he smirked. "Because you're so big like a mountain."

She laughed. *River is actually teasing me!*

"I like it though," he said.

"Gee, thanks."

"No, really I do."

They were almost to the stable when Sierra blurted out, "My father was killed in a car accident." She hardly ever talked to anyone about the father she had never known; not with her two best friends at her old school, and not even with her mother. She didn't know why she told River just then. "It happened before I was born."

"I guess we have that in common," he said softly. "We've both lost a parent in a bad accident."

Sierra thought about River as she pedaled home. It felt good that he had confided in her. She remembered how he had called her 'my girl', when she wanted to get back up on Fala after her fall, and how she liked that he referred to her that way. *Is this what it feels like to have an older brother?* she wondered, *one who looks out for you and cares about you?*

Sierra was very curious about River. How had he learned so much about horses, and who taught him to ride? Why did he even work at Pegasus since he and Tess didn't seem to get along very well? More than once she had heard Tess speaking harshly to him and River storming away in anger. He didn't care for most of the boarders either. Pegasus Equestrian Center was the most expensive riding facility in the area and catered to the wealthy who could afford expensive, well-bred, talented horses and a place where they could have others do the unpleasant chores of cleaning, grooming, tacking up and cooling out the horses. She knew he despised Crystal and those like her who rode for the glory of winning in competitions, and had no idea of the joy of companionship one developed in taking full care of a horse.

But River likes me! She was sure of that. Well, brother or not, River was her friend and that made her feel good. *Who needs friends at school; I have River and the horses!*

10 WINTER

Equestrian art, perhaps more than any other, is closely related to the wisdom of life…the horse teaches us self-control, constancy, and the ability to understand what goes on in the mind and feelings of another creature, qualities that are important throughout our lives. – Alois Podhajsky

The lunge line lessons continued throughout the ensuing weeks of winter, usually five or six days a week now, as the cold deterred many of the boarders and River had more time to work with Sierra. She now felt secure at all three gaits and on different horses. River had put her up on other mounts besides the school horses so she could feel different ways of moving on horses of different conformations. He even put her up on Magic and Sierra had delighted at the chestnut's natural big and bold way of going. Little by little, River relinquished control, teaching her how to increase and decrease the pace and transitions between gaits, all through her abdominal muscles, weight, and legs.

One day he gave her the reins; showing her how to hold each rein with thumbs on top and the flat of the rein between the last two fingers, letting the excess loop off to the right side of the horse's neck. "These are for talking to your horse, not for control," he said very seriously. He kept her on the lunge line for a few more lessons so she could practice keeping her hands in the correct position and get accustomed to the feel of the horse's mouth through the contact with the reins. Then River ended each lesson by unclipping the lunge line and letting Sierra ride completely on her own.

For Christmas, Pam gave her daughter only two presents; a new black riding helmet in a style that many of the boarders wore, and a pair of second-hand tan riding breeches that she had found on e-bay.

"Momma, these are the best presents I've ever had in my life," Sierra exclaimed on Christmas morning, and hugged her mother in a tight embrace with the strength of all her love, her eyes wet with gratitude.

Sierra received one other Christmas present; on the last day of school before the holiday break. Classes in the afternoon had been cancelled in lieu of a holiday party for the whole school. The gymnasium had been decorated with a Christmas tree and other traditional ornaments, a row of tables with refreshments had been set up, and both ballroom dance and popular music played over the loudspeakers. It was a time when many friends exchanged Christmas presents.

Inevitably, Billy asked her to dance and Sierra consented once. *My Christmas present to him,* she conceded. After the dance she firmly told him she had enough and was just going to watch. She found a corner chair where she stowed her backpack underneath and took out a book to pass the time until the bell rang and they were dismissed.

"Hi, Sierra," Crystal called in sweet tones. Sierra looked up to see Crystal, Gloria, and Katrina approaching. Crystal carried something in a bag. "We have a gift for you; a thank you for your hard work at Pegasus." She pulled from the bag a square package wrapped in bright holiday paper and an elegant ribbon, which she presented ceremoniously.

What's going on? Sierra wondered. *Could this be a peace offering?* Doubtfully, she accepted the gift, a reflexive smile on her face.

"Go ahead, open it," Crystal encouraged.

Embarrassed as the three girls and other kids watched, Sierra nevertheless undid the fancy wrappings and opened the lid of the box. Inside were several red and green tissue paper-wrapped round objects. "What are these?" she asked without thinking.

"Open them," Crystal and Gloria said in unison. Sierra glanced up, filled with suspicion as she noted how they were stifling giggles. Cautiously, she unwrapped one of the spheres in red tissue paper. *Horse manure!* Inside was a rounded clump. She stared at it, frozen in disbelief, and then flushed hot with humiliation. As the three girls as well as the group of onlookers burst into gales of laughter, Sierra jumped from her chair and the box fell from her lap, its contents spilling out onto the floor. The watchers screamed in hilarity as they jumped away from the balls of manure rolling out from their loose tissue paper wrappings.

Sierra looked up to meet the eyes of Crystal, which gleamed back at her with vengeful satisfaction.

Hurt and anger filled Sierra's heart, and she fought back tears, determined not to cry in front of all her classmates. She could think of nothing to say, no clever retort, nor what she should do. But she was certainly not going to laugh and pretend she enjoyed being the brunt of a cruel joke. She wanted desperately to flee, but she didn't think it would be fair to leave the manure on the floor where kids could step in it. And without any doubts, she knew Crystal and her friends would not pick up the mess.

"Jeeze, you guys," someone spoke to the three girls. Luke Abrams pushed his way forward through the crowd of kids. "That is so lame." He didn't look at Sierra; he just picked up the gift box, and then using the edge of a paper plate, shoved the manure and tissue paper back into the box. It took only a few minutes. He completed the job as unobtrusively as possible, and then dumped the box of manure into a nearby waste can.

"You should really let Sierra do that; she's an expert," Crystal informed Luke.

"Yeah, almost as good as River," Gloria chimed in.

Luke ignored the girls and walked away. Sierra shot a quick look at Crystal who stood with a grim expression aimed at Luke's retreating back. Sierra grabbed her backpack and hurried after him.

"Thanks," Sierra offered as she came up alongside Luke. Before he could reply, she turned and fled the gym.

One Sunday afternoon in February, with chores finished, and a cold winter sun shining, River said, "I think you're ready for a trail ride. I need to take Lucy out and you can ride Fala."

Sierra had never ridden anywhere but in the arena, except for the few times when River had led her around bareback. The idea of riding out on the trail sounded fantastic.

They groomed and tacked up the two horses and then led them down the lane to the open field. Once outside, River whistled once, and Storm emerged from wherever she had been resting, her tail wagging happily. She was allowed to follow River on trail rides. River waited while Sierra mounted up on Fala, and then swung easily onto the back of Dancing Queen (Lucy), a light chestnut mare who belonged to one of Tess's high school students.

"Fala's good on the trails and she'll follow Lucy," River said as he started out at the walk across the field. Both horses seemed happy to be outside in the open and looked around with their ears flicking back and forth and stepping out at a lively walk. They reached the start of the trail and continued on in single file. Storm kept a respectful distance behind Fala until the trail led into the woods and then she bounded off to chase squirrels, yet keeping pace with the riders.

This is heaven! Sierra could not imagine anything more wonderful than being on the back of a horse on such a beautiful day. Fala walked out at a brisk pace, needing no urging; the footing soft and comfortable under her hooves. The green needles of the conifers contrasting with the bare limbs of the leafless deciduous trees created interesting patterns in the afternoon sunlight. Sierra loved watching the swinging hind end of Lucy ahead on the trail, her tail swishing rhythmically. The sounds of a few winter birds calling, the squeak of the leather of the saddles, the footfalls of the horses crunching through dead leaves, and their occasional snorts and blowing, all together created a pleasing blend, a natural symphony. She admired the straight back of River and his easy posture in the saddle as if he grew out of it, a part of the horse. Occasionally he would reach down to pet Lucy's neck, and Sierra could hear him humming a tune. The trail curved through the forest with hills of varying steepness, and she was delighted to find she had no problem keeping a secure position going both up and down hills. She remembered how awkward and a little afraid she had felt the first time River had led her downhill on Morris. Every once in awhile, River looked back to check on them, and he smiled as Sierra grinned reassurance that they were fine.

"Do you want to trot a little?" he asked.

"Sure!"

"Okay, but if these girls get too frisky, we'll go right back to a walk. They both seem to feel pretty good. Are you ready?"

"I'm ready," Sierra answered, and shortened her reins in preparation, taking a gentle hold in the same way as on the lunge line.

River started Lucy into an easy trot. Fala stepped eagerly into a trot right behind her. River kept the pace slow, and both horses minded their manners, enjoying the easy pace and each others' company. Sierra felt confident and in control, able to slow Fala with half-halts when she needed to, and secure in letting her pick up the pace as well. They trotted on for several minutes with River glancing over his shoulder from time to time to make sure they were behind him and doing okay. Then he brought the pace back to a walk.

"This is the best day I've ever had in my whole life!" Sierra declared after the trail looped them back to the open field and they had dismounted.

"That's what you said after your first lesson," River teased.

Sierra laughed and made a face back at him as she stroked Fala's silky neck. Two humans, two horses, and one dog returned to the stable; all five in high, contented spirits.

11 CROSS COUNTRY CLINIC

You cannot train a horse with shouts and expect it to obey a whisper.
– Dagobert D. Runes

"What's wrong, River?" Sierra asked hesitantly, swinging her last pitchfork-full from the stall she was cleaning. River had paused in his work and stood leaning on his pitchfork, staring intently at the ground with his thoughts obviously somewhere else. Although they never talked much, this morning he had been quieter and grumpier than usual and she knew he was upset about something.

He looked up, pulling himself back from his reverie, and with a deep sigh resumed forking up wet shavings. He finished the last few forkfuls before he finally answered. "I don't know what I'm doing here." He stood still again, leaning on the pitchfork.

Sierra's stomach knotted in apprehension. *Is he thinking about quitting?* She waited.

"You know the clinic Tess is teaching today?"

Sierra nodded. Today was the first Saturday in March and the beginning of training and conditioning for the upcoming competition season. Crystal, Gloria, Katrina, and two other boarders were all competing in combined training events, a competition consisting of three phases: a dressage test, cross-country jumping, and stadium jumping. Tess also had a group of students who trailered their horses to Pegasus for lessons. Today the clinic with eight students participating would be held in the back field to work on cross-country jumping.

"Crystal is going to ride Magic today."

"Oh." Sierra knew how he felt about Crystal riding the young chestnut.

"She is such an idiot." He moved on to the next stall. Sierra followed and worked in the adjacent stall while he talked. "She did very well on Caretaker because that's exactly what he is. He takes care of her and carries her in spite of her bad riding. He's used to heavy hands. But when he came up lame, instead of getting another well-trained horse, she gets her father to buy her Magic."

Sierra listened intently, glad that River was willing to confide in her.

"I had made up my mind to quit last summer. Then they brought Magic in, and I can't help it; he's such a special horse. She's going to ruin him. Can you imagine how he's going to react if she tries to jump him outside today?"

"Don't you think Tess will be able to help her?" Sierra offered meekly. After all, that was what the clinic was all about; learning to jump an outside course.

In response, River made a noise of disgust.

Sierra felt very confused. She had watched Tess ride and thought she always looked like she knew what she was doing; in total control of her mounts and consistently getting clean jumping rounds and accurate dressage movements. She knew the history of Tess's career, having looked her up on-line. As a teenager, Tess had cleaned up as a junior rider in three-day events; competitions of the three phases of combined training spread out over three days. She consistently won at the regional end-of-season championship events, both as a junior and an adult amateur all the way to advanced level; and twice had qualified to try out for the Olympic team. Now as a professional in her mid-thirties, she continued to maintain a reputation as a formidable competitor at the local level, and had coached a few students to considerable success.

"I think she's a good rider," Sierra stated her opinion.

"Yeah, she has that reputation."

"What do you think?" Sierra asked timidly.

"She rides well enough on a talented horse that likes to be held and told exactly what to do, and since there are some horses like that, she can show and win. She knows what kind of horses she looks good on, so those are the only ones she shows. She isn't able to do anything to improve a horse without natural talent. She can't ride a horse like Magic either. He won't tolerate a tight hold." River spoke with bitterness.

"Oh, well…" Sierra could think of nothing to say, but she thought about what River had told her as they worked in silence. She respected his opinion but still, how could she doubt the opinion of the eventing community? After all, Tess had qualified to try for the Olympics. You had to be good to have that opportunity, didn't you? She felt very confused, ignorant, and unwise. But, she admitted to herself, there was no question in her mind as to who was the better rider between Tess and River. Tess always looked confident and in control. River looked like a part of his horse; they moved as one and the horse moved with free, expressive movements, as if taking jumps was entirely his own idea. She had seen River ride a horse in the arena performing circles, figure eights, lateral movements, and most beautiful of all, canter flying changes. Never once could she detect any signals from River. It looked like all the movements were the horse's idea.

After awhile Sierra asked, "What are you going to do?"

He looked at her, his eyes dark as smoke. "Tess wants me to warm up Magic for Crystal. If I do, he has a better chance of getting through the course in spite of her. But all I can think of is the look in his eyes when I hand the bridle reins over to Crystal. It's as if he's saying, 'how can you do this to me?'"

"Oh, I see what you mean."

The sound of trailers pulling into the stable yard, and horses clomping backwards out of the trailers, signaled the arrival of the outside riders and the onset of the clinic.

Eight riders galloped around the perimeter of the field, warming up their horses and themselves. Sierra stood near a group of parents and friends of the riders, all clustered behind Tess where they could watch and hear her instructions. Tess stood at the edge of the field near the mounting block, studying the riders intently.

"Rein them in and gather back over here," Tess called through a megaphone. The group of riders obediently slowed their horses to a canter, then a trot to ride back to Tess.

Sierra watched Crystal on Magic, anxiously hoping she would not upset him too much in the warm up. Magic tossed his head a few times and shook it side to side, and she could see Crystal fighting with the reins. Magic's usual long stride looked short and choppy as Crystal struggled to keep him a stride's length behind Gloria on Silver.

Tess glanced over at Sierra and ordered, "Where is River? Go get him."

Nervously, Sierra straightened her posture, looked back up the empty hillside, and then started up the slope. She did not know what River had decided. He had retreated into his barrier of silence as they finished the morning chores and then disappeared. It was Sierra who tacked up Magic for Crystal and helped Manuel get the other horses ready.

She was halfway up the slope when she saw River approaching. He wore his riding boots and breeches and carried a helmet. Sierra sighed with relief. "Hi," she greeted as he came alongside her.

'"Hi," he answered distractedly. They kept walking in silence back down the hill and up to the group. The riders were walking their horses in a circle around Tess as she described and gestured to the jumps they were to ride for their first course.

Tess glared at River as he and Sierra approached. "Crystal, River will take Magic around for his first time."

Crystal dismounted with her jaw set in angry lines and a fixed frown. Although Tess had told her the plan, and in her heart she knew she would have a very difficult time trying to jump this course on Magic, she still found it humiliating to be de-horsed in front of the spectators. She jerked hard on the reins causing Magic to toss up his head, as she led him over to Tess.

River avoided Crystal's stabbing look as he took the reins from her, talking softly to Magic as he led him to the mounting block. He adjusted the stirrup length for his longer legs and mounted while Tess repeated to him the jumps she wanted him to take.

"Es facil, hermano," River whispered to the chestnut as he walked him away from the group and urged him into a trot, posting. Magic stretched his head into the soft hands holding the reins, finding his balance on the hilly terrain as River directed him in a large trotting circle. He visibly began to relax under the hands of this familiar and trusted rider, gaining confidence. He snorted and shook his head once; just for the reassurance he could move his head. River squeezed the reins between his fingers as he touched his legs to Magic's sides, and the big horse jumped into a canter.

They approached the first obstacle, railroad ties stacked in a block formation at various heights and with two upright ties set as posts on the ends; a solid jump, two feet in height at its lowest level. Magic pricked his ears forward as River guided him toward the obstacle, his eyes wide, and he snorted again. He had been faced with jumps in the arena but never outside in the fields and it confused him. But River touched his mouth through the reins, not pulling, just letting him know he was there, and *yes*, River's legs told him to keep going forward. Trusting his rider, Magic adjusted his stride at the approach and sailed over the jump.

River smiled and touched his hand to the chestnut's neck. "*Que bien*," he encouraged. They approached the next jump, a large log with its diameter creating equal height and width. River did not sense any hesitation this time as they approached, as if Magic had figured out that jumping occurred outside as well as in an arena. The chestnut instinctively adjusted his stride and again thrust up and sailed over the log in a beautiful arc.

All River's doubts and negative feelings were at least for the moment dissipated in the joy of the free and powerful motion of the horse beneath him. They galloped around the field taking each obstacle of the course without hesitation as the chestnut instinctively shortened or lengthened his stride, a natural jumper. With each thrust of his hindquarters, River allowed the movement to push him forward over the withers, his hands following the arch of Magic's head, keeping contact without obstructing his jump. They covered the course as one, with a mutual purpose and with mutual joyful exuberance.

"Magnificent!" One of the onlookers exclaimed. "That horse is incredible. Where did you get him, Tess?"

He's Crystal's new mount; we found him at the import sale. He is a Trakehner, bred in Germany."

"What a fantastic rider," another observer commented. "Who is he, Tess? I've never seen him at any of the shows."

"That's River Girard; he doesn't compete," Tess answered.

"They certainly make a good pair!"

Sierra watched in rapturous awe. She could feel the rhythmic pulsing of Magic's hooves in the ground below her feet, and she found her body wanting to move forward with each thrust of the powerful hindquarters over the jumps. She was breathless as River and Magic finished the round and galloped the last distance uphill toward the group, the chestnut's dark red mane and tail floating like a banner heralding his arrival.

The onlookers clapped at their arrival, calling out, "wonderful," and "awesome ride!" River jumped off and stroked Magic's neck as the horse nuzzled at him. Reluctantly he led him back to the mounting block where Crystal waited, proudly aware of the admiration directed toward her horse, but resentful that she was not riding.

"Just point him at the jump and stay off his mouth," River hissed at Crystal as he readjusted the stirrups and held Magic's head while she mounted.

"Don't tell me how to ride my own horse," Crystal snarled back at him. She pulled heavily on the reins causing Magic's head to jerk up, and walked him back to the milling group of horses and riders.

"Hi, River," a girl in the group of onlookers called out to him, then giggled and whispered with the girl standing next to her. Sierra recognized two of her classmates that she knew hung around with Crystal's crowd at school. River glanced at them without answering and joined Sierra where she stood at the edge of the group.

"He was perfect," she whispered.

"Yeah, he was, wasn't he?" River agreed with her. She glanced sideways at him, disturbed by the look of anguish on his face as his eyes followed Magic.

Gloria rode next on Silver, who valiantly completed the course without errors, but also without the effortlessness exhibited by Magic. His stride became choppy at times as he tried to approach a jump at the right pace, his rider inexperienced in judging distances. Tess yelled out instructions through the megaphone, coaching Gloria through the course. Two more riders took their turns; the first had two refusals at the ditch, and the second rider's horse ran out at almost every obstacle. Tess had walked to the middle of the field as she coached each rider over individual jumps.

Tess signaled for Crystal next. Crystal gathered her reins in her usual abrupt manner, and started down the hillside at a choppy posting trot and with Magic's head stiff in the air. She kicked him into a canter and began the warm-up circle.

"Move your hands forward but keep your reins short," Tess called. "Don't let him pull the reins from your hands!" Magic shook and tossed his head, frantic with the tight hold. His canter became unbalanced and choppy, his leads disunited. "Keep him moving forward!" Tess directed. Crystal whacked Magic with her riding crop and jerked his head toward the first obstacle. "Don't let him rush!" Tess yelled again.

With his head high, neck stiff, and ears laid back, the frightened horse rushed headlong toward the railroad tie jump, fighting for his head. He jumped high and wide, and after landing, galloped towards the woods beyond the field. Crystal screamed at him and jerked hard at the left side of his mouth to steer him back on course. Magic submitted to the painful pull and turned back to the left, now heading for the log. His speed increased, his only defense against the painful jabbing at his mouth that prevented him from reaching with his head and neck.

Tess continued to yell, "Take control; pull him back to a trot if you have to."

Somehow Crystal completed the course, managing to forcefully jerk Magic to a trot before each jump, then whipping him with her crop as he tried to veer away. He refused once as he came to a cross-rail fence at an awkward angle and could not get his hindquarters underneath enough to thrust. He tried running out to escape the hard hold on his head, but each time, Tess yelled for Crystal to "circle him and get him over!" Finally, they completed all twelve obstacles of the course and returned to the group. There had been no grace, no fluidness, no freedom; and no applause from the onlookers.

"Well, you got him over the course," Gloria greeted her friend, the most positive thing she could think of to say.

"Temperamental, isn't he?" an onlooker commented.

"Look after him, okay, Sierra?" River asked her in a mournful tone. Sierra answered yes to his retreating back as he sprinted up the hill and out of sight.

The rest of the riders completed their rounds, and then Tess worked with individuals over problem obstacles. "You can cool your horses out; then we'll meet in the lounge," she announced as the last rider finally trotted successfully over the jump that her horse had refused several times.

Sierra trailed the group back to the stable and made sure she was available to take Magic from Crystal, who tossed her the reins and walked away chatting with another girl. Manuel arrived to help with the boarders' horses, and took Silver from Gloria. Katrina took care of Calliope herself, but the other two boarders left their horses in the crossties, and Sierra and Manuel untacked, rinsed off, and cooled out the four horses. River did not return to help.

Without knocking, River stepped into the office where Tess worked on training schedules at the computer. "I'm quitting," he announced.

Tess pushed her chair back from the keyboard and turned to face him, frowning. "What for this time?" she asked with irritation undisguised in her tone.

"How come you didn't talk that girl out of buying Magic? You know he's not the right horse for her."

"That is absolutely none of your business," Tess stated coldly. "But for the record, I tried to discourage her and I tried to talk her father into saying no; but he gives her anything she wants."

"I can't stay here and watch her ruin him," he snapped back with equal ire.

"He will hardly be ruined."

They stared icily at each other for a few moments; then River turned abruptly to leave.

"Fine, quit! You're just like your father," Tess lowered her voice to a snarl.

River froze; then looked back at her with an expression as if she had slapped him. "I am nothing like my father," he stated emphatically, clenching his fists at his sides.

"Right, and you don't have a temper either," she retorted sarcastically. She deliberately turned back to the computer and heard him slam the door as he left.

12 CHANGES

Never push more than you can control and never hold more than you can push. – Arthur Kottas

Sunday morning Sierra punched in the keypad combination to let herself in through the back door of the stable. As she flipped on the lights, welcoming whinnies from the horses greeted her, just in case she had forgotten they were hungry. "Don't worry," she called out reassuringly, "breakfast is coming." Patches emerged from the shadows to entwine herself between Sierra's legs, purring loudly. Sierra scooped her up and scratched behind her ears as she stepped into the feed room to grab the bag of cat chow and fill her dish. With a heavy heart, Sierra began filling the grain buckets, holding on to her scanty hope that River would show up in the next few minutes.

A short while later footsteps echoed down the cement aisle and Sierra's heart leaped with relief. But the footsteps were accompanied by cheerful whistling (*that's not River*), followed by Manuel's voice greeting the horses. As he came into view he called out, "Mees Sierra," we work togedeer today, yes?"

"River's not coming?" Sierra asked as she stepped out of the feed room, even though she knew the answer.

Manuel shrugged and smiled sympathetically. "No, today no. 'Ee queet. Come, I show you 'ow to drive dee cart."

Sierra and Manuel fed the horses and completed chores until time to turn the horses out. Always cheerful, whistling or singing, Manuel was easy to work with, but her heart ached for River's unhappiness, and she already missed him. "What will Tess do without River?" she asked Manuel.

"Reever, 'ee queet before. Maybe 'ee come back." Manuel shook his head and with a big sigh added, "Until 'ee do, I no get day off."

"I'm sorry, Manuel, Sierra commiserated. "I can clean stalls by myself so you could have a little more of the day free."

Manuel argued with her at first but Sierra finally convinced him that she didn't mind at all, and he gratefully left her alone cleaning stalls to return to Rosa.

When the stalls were cleaned and filled with fresh shavings, Sierra dejectedly strolled down the lane of paddocks to visit each horse before she went home. If River had stayed, they would be saddling up now to ride out on the trails, the usual activity on weekends. Not for the first time that morning, she fought back hot tears wanting to spill from her eyes. She wondered if she would ever have the chance to ride and take lessons again without River. She mentally added up the time since she had started lessons; five months and she could walk, trot, and canter a horse independently in the arena, perform circles and figure eights, and could trot and even canter a horse with confidence on the trails.

And she had jumped!

In her last few lessons, River had set up a row of six cavalletti; poles set on the ground equal distances apart and spaced so that her horse either trotted or cantered over them without losing his stride. River had already taught her how to shift her weight forward into two-point position, the correct position for jumping, and had her practice that position in the arena and on the trails. "As you round the corner and approach the cavalletti, get up into two-point," he had told her. "You can grab mane if you start to lose your balance because he will move bigger over the poles." After she became accustomed to riding the line of cavalletti, River added a low cross-bar jump two strides from the last pole. When she trotted over the last pole, her horse took two strides and jumped the cross-bar. What a thrill to feel her horse's back arch up underneath her as he seemed to fly over the low jump.

Sierra loved caring for the horses, but riding them was the ultimate joy of her life. She lay in bed each night reliving the day's riding experience; analyzing the feel and what River had told her she had done well and what she needed to improve. Her last thoughts before falling asleep were on horseback as well as her first sleep-hazy images as she awoke in the morning.

Sierra had given each horse a treat and a pat and was on her way to her bicycle when she saw Tess's Lexus pull into the stable yard. Tess usually took weekends off except for clinics or horse shows, so when she stepped out of the car dressed in her riding clothes, Sierra realized Tess must be here to take over riding the horses she would have assigned to River. Tess headed toward the stable, a very unpleasant expression on her face, and half way there looked up to notice Sierra. Her expression deepened into a scowl of annoyance.

What have I done now? Sierra never felt comfortable around Tess, always feeling like Tess regarded her as a pest that distracted River from his work.

"Sierra," Tess beckoned to her.

"Yes?" Sierra came up to her apprehensively. *Is she going to fire me because River is gone?*

To Sierra's great surprise, Tess said, "You've been very dependable helping out. Can I count on you to continue with the weekend chores?"

"Yes," Sierra answered, still unsure of what Tess had in mind.

"River has quit," Tess stated bluntly. "You'll be working with Manuel. I can also use your help afternoons with the lesson horses. I know you were helping River and you know what to do, so if you can commit to these extra duties and I can depend on you, I can give you a regular lesson slot twice a week...Tuesdays and Thursdays at three-thirty."

"Yes, I can do that," Sierra answered in a state of shock. "I would like that...thank you."

After school, Sierra worked alone doing the chores that had been such a pleasure when she and River had worked together. She still enjoyed the company of the horses as she readied them for lessons and cooled them out afterwards. But a great emptiness had seeped into the atmosphere of the stable without River. They had never talked much, but she missed his quiet competence, his ability to calm the nervousness of any horse, and how she trusted him to keep her safe. She wasn't afraid of any of the horses, but some were definitely higher strung and harder to handle than others. Whenever a horse got himself wound up, River had always been right there to help her or at least tell her what to do.

And although they never spoke of it, she knew he loved the animals as much as she did. *How can he stand it to be away from the horses?*

On Tuesday for Sierra's first lesson, Tess ordered, "Saddle up Fala. We'll start with a lesson on the flat so use a dressage saddle."

Her nerves tight, Sierra tacked up the mare, feeling apprehensive in a way she had never felt before a lesson with River, as she imagined the critical scrutiny of Tess. *But this is what I have dreamed of,* she reminded herself. "I'm glad she picked you," she told Fala as she buckled the throatlatch of her bridle and brought the reins over her head to lead her out. Sierra had probably ridden Fala more than any other of the horses and the mare's familiar smooth gaits and willing personality would make the first lesson easier. Sierra led Fala into the arena at exactly three-thirty and waited at the mounting block.

"Aren't you warmed up?" Tess spoke in exasperation as she stepped up onto the observation platform and picked up the microphone.

"No, I wasn't sure if you wanted to watch my warm-up," Sierra replied, already intimidated by this first greeting.

"I expect you to be warmed up and ready to work by the time I arrive, "Tess informed her. "Mount up and let's see what River has taught you." She didn't disguise the annoyance in her tone.

Sierra mounted and moved Fala to the perimeter of the arena at a walk and with the reins long and loose to encourage the mare to stretch her neck; the way she always started her warm-up with River.

"Gather up the reins and establish contact right from the beginning," Tess ordered through the microphone.

Sierra complied and sensed surprise and perhaps confusion from Fala at so soon being asked to lift her head and round her neck to accept contact with the bit. But she submitted willingly, perhaps as comfortable with Sierra as Sierra was with her.

"I don't believe in wasting time plodding around with your horse's nose on the ground. The sooner they learn that once in the arena it's time to work, the easier it is to overcome their resistance," Tess instructed, watching Sierra walk Fala once around and then reverse direction. "Pick up a posting trot and come onto a twenty-meter circle in front of me."

Abdominal muscles pulled in, Sierra touched her legs to Fala's sides and squeezed gently with her fingers on both reins to move the mare into a trot. Fala moved energetically and in a relaxed' manner as Sierra guided her onto a circle in front of Tess.

"She is too strung out; she needs to be rounder," Tess called out. Sierra looked up at her instructor, not sure what she meant. "Shorten your reins and establish contact with the bit."

Sierra felt confused. She thought she did have contact with the bit. She could feel both sides of Fala's mouth through the reins to her fingers, and when she squeezed on one or the other rein, the mare yielded her head obediently to that side. *Don't I already have contact?* Nevertheless, Sierra shortened the reins, trying to keep her hold soft, but she felt a touch of resistance against her hands and a stiffening of Fala's gait.

"Change through the circle," Tess called.

What? Sierra didn't understand what Tess wanted her to do. "I'm sorry, what do you mean?" she asked.

"Oh for pity's sake," Tess groaned. "Didn't River teach you anything? Ride her through the middle of the circle and reverse direction."

Sierra flushed as she complied. She had done this before under River's direction; he just hadn't used that terminology. She trotted Fala around, and unconsciously let the reins slip slightly in her hands back to a point where she felt she had light contact, and Fala moved forward with more energy.

"Rounder!" Tess yelled. "You've let her pull the reins from your hands. Shorten those reins."

Again Sierra took up a bit more rein, not liking the response from Fala, yet determined to learn what Tess wanted her to do. Fala's ears went flat in a sign of distress and her movements felt stiff.

"Sitting trot," Tess ordered.

I can do this. Sierra tightened her belly as she eased her seat deep into the saddle, letting her lower spine move with Fala's motion. Inadvertently, she released her hold on the reins again and Fala stretched her nose slightly forward as she moved into what Sierra felt was a more relaxed trot.

"Sierra, how many times do I have to tell you not to let her pull the reins from your hands? Ride her over here and halt." Sierra complied as Tess jumped down from the platform and came over to Fala's side. "This is what I want you to feel," she instructed. She reached over Fala's withers and gathered up the reins so that Fala arched her neck toward her chest. "Grab hold here," she ordered. Sierra took up the reins where Tess indicated and held on. "Do you feel the contact?"

"Yes," Sierra answered meekly. She certainly did feel the bit in Fala's mouth but it felt like she was hanging onto it.

"Now squeeze the reins with both hands."

Sierra obeyed and Fala tucked her nose in even deeper, her muzzle almost touching her chest.

"She's overbent now," Tess explained, "but that's okay. I want you to feel the amount of tension there needs to be in the reins at all times. You should maintain about ten pounds of pressure equally in both hands. Until you learn this contact you are not going to be able to push her up into the bit for collected work. Do you understand?"

Sierra nodded. But she wondered. River had always said the reins should feel as if she had a baby bird in her hand. She needed to hold firm enough to keep the bird within her hand but not so tight as to hurt the bird.

"Take her back out onto the circle and we'll try some canter."

The rest of the lesson progressed in the same manner with Tess over and over yelling at Sierra to "shorten the reins," or "rounder!" Fala became tense and resistive, and Sierra felt her own muscles tighten, making it hard to stay in balance. Their transitions were choppy and stiff and she had a hard time keeping her feet in the stirrups. Her shoulders ached trying to keep Fala from pulling the reins from her grip. At last Tess called out "enough for today," and finally Sierra was allowed to release the reins and let Fala stretch her neck.

"Any questions?" Tess asked as Sierra led Fala to where her instructor had jumped down from the platform to debrief.

"It's very different from how River taught me," Sierra replied honestly.

"River is a backyard rider," Tess stated. "He doesn't compete, and he's always been too easy on the horses. At least you've developed a secure seat, but I think maybe it was a mistake to allow him to teach you for so long.

Wait a minute! Sierra wanted to protest. She felt more confused than ever. Tess was essentially telling her that River had taught her incorrectly.

"River has never taught anyone before," Tess continued. "I was surprised when he offered to get you started. But I should have realized that without a background in showing or formal instruction that he would establish in you some bad habits."

Sierra nodded as she listened, feeling traitorous to River.

"But I think we can correct them soon enough and no permanent harm. Did he take you out on the trails?"

"Yes, at least twice a week, sometimes more."

Tess nodded thoughtfully. "Don't be discouraged. You've got a good start. In addition to your lessons, I think it will improve your seat and confidence if you ride one or two horses out on the trail every day, and include some trot and canter. Do you think you can do that?"

Sierra certainly hadn't expected to hear that. "Sure!" She answered.

"Good; I'll put a schedule of which horses you should ride each day on the notice board in the tack room and how much trotting and galloping you should do on each horse. I'll have you ride two horses a day except on your lesson days, and then you only ride one. Is that agreeable?"

"Yes. Thank you, I would like that."

Sierra led Fala back to the crossties and started removing her tack. She heard a trailer pull into the stable yard, which certainly wasn't unusual. But then she heard Tess yell angrily, "Where is he?"

"Hey Baby, what a greeting," a man replied, his voice wheedling in tone.

"You are not going to unload that mare," Tess stated emphatically.

"Listen, I'll find him, don't worry," the man soothed. "The mare is in heat now. This can't wait."

"My partner is not going to tolerate your horse here for free."

"Hey," the man's voice also took on an angry note. "River worked here all last summer when I didn't have a horse here. That's got to be worth something."

River's father! Sierra realized who the man was arguing with Tess. Her curiosity overtook her judgment and she moved forward into the shadow of the stable doorway to peer out. The same dilapidated truck and trailer was parked in the yard with the ramp down. Manuel with his eyes wide and a lead rope in his hand stood by the ramp, looking back and forth between Tess and Cray Blackthorn as they argued.

"Either you find River and have him back here by this weekend, or you start paying full board, or take your stallion away," Tess stepped up closer to glare menacingly into Cray's face.

"Okay, okay, I said I'll find him."

"He's fifteen years old! Can't you control him?" Tess demanded.

"About as well as you can," he retorted in a mocking tone.

Tess spun away and Cray signaled to Manuel to go ahead and unload the mare.

Sierra began to get a clue as to why River worked here. Was his father boarding his stallion here in exchange for River's labor? River was only a kid; that couldn't be legal.

Undiscovered talent, Tess mused as she looked over the training schedules for the competition horses. She had no idea Sierra had made so much progress in only a few months. River had taught her well. She congratulated herself on how she had managed to unload the conditioning rides that she would have assigned to River; and have Sierra think it was a favor she was offering her. *Well, the truth is it will be good for the girl to have more saddle time and nothing like riding cross country to gain a secure seat and confidence,* she told herself, assuaging her conscience. *I might actually have her ready to compete this season.*

Tess felt irritation welling up again as she shoved the schedules aside and picked up a stack of bills. River had only been gone five days but in that short time she had to devote extra hours to the conditioning rides; valuable time she needed to do office work. Maybe she could catch up with Sierra taking over those rides. But she still needed River's talent in training the horses who would compete this season. Besides the conditioning rides, she used him to school the green horses in dressage and some jumping. But most importantly, River had a gift with the horses; somehow he knew instinctively how to calm and relax them. If she had River ride the competition horses a few days before an event, they seemed to become more manageable. She depended on his abilities to help maintain the reputation of Pegasus as a successful eventing stable…she needed River more than she cared to admit.

13 LESSONS WITH TESS

Dressage becomes an art only when it's a joy for the horse as well as for us. – Klaus Balkenhol

"When I say shorten the reins I mean pick up those reins and shorten them!" Tess yelled out harshly. "Do not let her pull the reins from your hands. She has to learn what is expected of her. If she tries to pull the reins use your whip to push her forward. Now!"

Sierra shuddered involuntarily at being yelled at...again, and struggled to comply with Tess's demands. She rode Fala in the lesson, and the mare fought constantly against the tight hold on her bit. She either tossed her head or held it high with her neck stiff and hollow, resisting the pressure. Sierra took up two inches on the reins and whispered to the mare, "Please, Fala, relax," and willed herself to relax as well. But every time Tess shouted at her, Sierra could feel her spine and muscles tense up. She simply was not accustomed to being yelled at.

Fala snorted her displeasure and shortened her stride into a choppy trot.

"Use the whip," Tess yelled.

Sierra tapped Fala's flank with the long dressage whip causing the mare to jump forward in alarm and break into a canter.

"Give her a hard jerk on the mouth and bring her back to the trot," Tess demanded. "Breaking the gait is an evasion and she is being very disobedient. She has to learn to maintain the proper frame."

Frustrated, Sierra obeyed and jerked hard on the reins. With teeth gritted, she used all her arm and hand strength to hold tight to the reins and forcefully guide Fala around the serpentine pattern Tess had instructed her to ride at a collected trot. Fala made a sound of unhappiness, and guilt surged through Sierra as she realized she had transposed her anger at Tess into her treatment of Fala.

"All right, let's quit with that," Tess allowed, after Sierra completed the figure. "Finish by letting her stretch on a twenty-meter circle."

Sierra let her breath out slowly as she released her hold on the reins. Fala snorted and tossed her head several times. She thrust her nose warily forward, as if anticipating a sudden jerk on her sensitive mouth. The mare trotted two circles before she tentatively dropped her head and neck forward and down.

"Back to walk," Tess ordered.

Sierra obeyed and let the mare walk once around the circle before she brought her to the center and dismounted.

"You have got to develop a sense that you are the master," Tess insisted in the debriefing after the lesson. "You are not being cruel to expect obedience. Nothing you are doing hurts the horse. In fact, it is dangerous to give into a horse's will for it is only natural they will take the advantage if you give it. Your horse must be obedient and submissive to your aids at all times. Once they learn, then you'll find you do not have to ride with as much force. Do you understand?"

"I think so," Sierra replied.

"You think so," Tess retorted, sounding irritated. "Practice taking charge during your rides this week. I would like to see you more in control by your next lesson."

"I'll try."

Tess turned away in dismissal.

"Come on, Fala," Sierra whispered and led the mare out of the arena and over to the crossties. As she removed the tack she watched Fala, how she stood with tense posture, her head up and eyes wide. Her coat glistened with sweat, not just underneath where the saddle had been, but her neck, chest, and flanks. It was like a slap when Sierra suddenly realized the mare looked just like Magic that first day she had come to the stable and watched Crystal taking a lesson.

"You can relax now, the lesson's over," Sierra spoke in a soft, soothing voice. She offered a piece of carrot on the flat of her palm, but Fala would not lower her head to even sniff at the treat. *A horse too tense to be interested in food is a really upset horse.* Sierra felt guilty and sad that it was her poor riding that had resulted in the mare's condition. She draped a cooler over the mare's back, clipped the lead rope to the halter and led her outside to cool her out by walking up and down the lane.

As the mare began to relax, lowering her head and eyeing clumps of grass, Sierra felt her own tenseness ebb. Absently stroking the mare on her neck, she sank deep into troubled thoughts.

The lessons with Tess often ended very much like the lesson today with both horse and rider fraught with nerves, the horse drenched in sweat, and her own muscles aching. Doubts filled Sierra. None of her lessons with River had ever been so stressful. He made sure both she and her mount stayed relaxed and the goal had been for everyone to enjoy the session. *Is that the difference between backyard riding and professional riding?* Sierra wondered.

She thought about the many books she had read on equitation. All the riding masters agreed that the horse needed to relax in order to perform correctly, and training sessions should be joyful for both horse and rider. Relaxation, in fact, was the second tier of the training pyramid that she often came across in the books. Perhaps that was an ideal seldom achieved in the reality of training to compete.

"My last few lessons certainly have not been a joy for either of us, have they?" Sierra spoke out loud to Fala.

But Tess was very successful in competitions and River didn't compete at all. And Sierra yearned to compete.

Since the beginning of the show season, boarders who had entered in competitions arrived with trailers to haul their horses to the show grounds. They emanated a contagious excitement as they groomed, braided, and then booted up their horses before loading them into the trailer. They returned at the end of the day proudly bearing ribbons if they had placed in their class, and full of stories of the event. How she longed to be a participant in that exciting world.

She felt Fala's chest between her legs to check for heat, as River had taught her. The mare's temperature had cooled from very hot to normal warmth and her coat had transitioned from slickly wet to damp. Sierra decided to let the mare graze, to help atone for the stressful lesson. She led her to a grassy area in the back field and Fala eagerly pulled on the lead rope to grab mouthfuls of grass. When her head came up and Sierra offered her the chunk of carrot, Fala lipped it off of Sierra's palm and snuffled at the girl's pockets for more.

"Have you forgiven me?" Sierra asked, offering the mare another treat. She smiled in relief as the mare munched the treats and grass in contentment, her ears relaxed and eyes half closed.

Horses seem to know when you don't mean to harm them and they will forgive you for almost anything, River had once told her. But it bothered Sierra that she would even need forgiveness from her mount. River certainly never did. This was not the kind of relationship she wanted with horses.

Is that what it takes to compete, to forcefully dominate all your horse's movements? Sierra wondered. It seemed to be the method that Tess was trying to teach her. If she wanted to compete successfully would she have to ride as Tess insisted, in spite of how upset the horse became? *Is that why River doesn't compete, because he is unwilling to stress his mount?*

"River, where are you?" Sierra spoke out loud. How she missed him and needed his coaching and advice. Would he tell her to forget about horse shows? She hoped not, for the image of herself wearing a black coat and polished black leather boots over snowy white breeches, and riding a gleaming horse with braided mane, and completing a dressage test or a jumping round with spectators looking on in awe...well, that was a dream that would be hard to put aside. How envious she had been last weekend when Crystal, Gloria, and Katrina returned from their first show of the season, each having won a ribbon. Crystal had won first place on Butch, Gloria had taken second on Silver, and Katrina placed fourth on Calliope.

River had not returned to work by the weekend his father had promised Tess. But apparently something had been worked out because on two more occasions Cray showed up with a mare in season to breed to his stallion.

In fact, it had been a month since River had quit and disappeared.

Pushing aside her regretful thoughts of River, Sierra led Fala back to the stable to finish grooming and put her away. Then she checked the notice board to see which horse Tess had assigned her to trail ride.

"Oh no," she groaned out loud. *Moose.* Once before Sierra had been assigned the big thoroughbred gelding and had returned from the ride with her legs trembling in fear and relieved that she had survived without injury. WinSome Gold, nicknamed Moose, was a seventeen-hand, rangy, off-the-track, bay thoroughbred, whose owner had brought him to Tess to train as an event horse. He seemed talented enough, but he was strong in the head, moved with great bouncing strides, and shied at everything. It had been all Sierra could do to stay on his back and prevent him from bolting as he shied at every stick on the ground, rustling leaf, and shadow on the trail. He would leap to the side, try to spin around, and once half-reared.

With her heart already palpitating in trepidation, Sierra walked weak-kneed to the paddock to bring in Moose. He watched her warily, not particularly friendly, but at least did not run away as she approached with halter in hand. She gave him a piece of carrot which he gingerly accepted, and then she struggled on with his halter. Unlike Morris or Fala, he never lowered his head to help out.

After tacking him up, Sierra led Moose to the mounting block at the edge of the field. The tall gelding was already looking around wide-eyed and blowing loudly through his nose. *My nervousness isn't going to help him stay calm*, Sierra admonished herself, but her heart remained in her throat. She practically had to leap from the mounting block onto his back, for he would not stand still, and once on his back, Moose immediately jumped forward into a trot. Sierra frantically gathered the reins and pulled on his mouth with all her strength, sitting deep in the saddle so that her weight would help bring him back to a walk. He threw his head up, almost hitting her in the face, but finally settled into a jigging walk.

"Easy, easy," she tried to calm him and herself as she turned him to cross the field and onto the trail. They had covered the first few feet when he snorted loudly, lurched to the side throwing her off balance, and then spun and ran back towards the stable. Sierra managed to keep her seat by grabbing mane, but they were half way across the field before she was able to slow him down to his jigging walk and turn him back to the trail. Her hands were slick with sweat on the reins and her heart pounded in her ears. She had no idea what he had shied at.

Sierra struggled on, trying to get Moose around the trail and finish the ride with all her bones intact. Her shoulders ached and she could feel blisters forming between her fingers where she clutched the reins in a death grip. He never did walk, but jigged nervously or lurched between a trot and trying to break to a gallop. Sweat poured down her back between her shoulder blades and her hands remained clammy. "Please, Moose, please settle," she begged and tried to soothe the frightened, worked-up animal.

Finally, they approached the last bend in the trail and Sierra let out her breath in relief. *Made it.*

But as they rounded the turn, the sunlight dappled in front of them and created strange shadowy patterns on the path. Moose flipped out. He reared straight up and this time he did hit her across her nose causing pain to shoot up into her brain. Her weight slipped to the side and as Moose lunged forward Sierra fell.

"Oof," she rolled on contact with the hard ground and then lay still for a moment, listening to the sound of Moose galloping away. Slowly she pushed up onto her feet, feeling for damage. There was a scrape along her forearm and her nose ached, but otherwise she seemed okay. She hobbled clumsily; her rubber boots were certainly not meant for walking. Moose had most likely headed back to the stable at full speed. She just hoped he wouldn't get a leg caught in a dangling rein and hurt himself. Humiliation filled her, to have to return to the stable de-horsed.

But as Sierra stepped out of the woods from the trail, there was Moose placidly grazing in the field, his reins dangling to one side. "Moose," she called out to let him know she was approaching and not startle him. He looked up once and returned to grazing. Thankfully, he didn't bolt as Sierra walked up to him and picked up the reins. His coat was damp and there were a few leaves clinging to the saddle pad where he must have cut underneath a low branch, but otherwise he seemed okay. "Let's go, idiot," she said, but not unkindly, and with a reassuring pat, led him back to the stable.

Sierra told no one about her fall. She never wanted to ride Moose again, but she wasn't sure what scared her the most; riding Moose, or telling Tess she couldn't handle him.

14 PRODIGAL

If life is meant to be a journey of discovery, then riding is a metaphor for life. Riding well is like living well. – Charles de Kunffy

The following Saturday Sierra arrived at the stable to find the main door already opened and the lights shining out into the dimness of the morning. She could hear horses nickering for their breakfast and shuffling about in their stalls. Sudden dread filled her; *one of the horses must have developed colic during the night!* She hurried in through the main door and a shiver went down her spine as she noticed the open door of Magic's stall. *Is he the horse with colic? Please, not Magic!*

As she came close enough to see inside the stall, to her amazement there stood River with one arm around the chestnut's neck and stroking him with his other hand. Magic had thrust his head against the boy's chest. She could hear River talking to him in a low voice but could not distinguish the words.

"River?" Sierra spoke quietly out of habit around horses, although she wanted to shout a welcome.

River dropped his arms and stepped away from Magic with his head bowed and his shaggy hair hiding his face. He mumbled, "Hi," and stepped past Sierra, pulling the stall door closed. He did not look up and headed toward the back of the barn where the hay cart awaited.

"River, what..? Sierra hurried to catch up with him. He looked at her sideways and she saw a purplish bruise and swelling around his left eye. She stifled a gasp and stated calmly, "You've been hurt."

He didn't answer; only continued walking to the hay cart and stepped up into the driver's seat. He turned on the ignition but waited until Sierra climbed up into the passenger seat before driving down the aisle.

"I'm so glad to see you. I've missed you so much," she told him, trying to keep her emotional reaction from producing a tremor in her voice.

"Hmh," he mumbled, keeping his face averted. Silence reigned; well that was nothing new.

They started the routine of delivering hay and then the grain. Sierra was used to River's lack of inclination to talk. But before, the silence had been easy and comfortable; now there was tenseness and the obvious unspoken questions hanging in the air between them. She stole glances at River; he was even thinner, with hollows in his cheeks and shadows under his eyes. He moved slowly, as if parts of his body hurt. *Just what happened to him?*

With the horses fed, Sierra caught up to him as he headed outside. "Please tell me what happened," she pleaded.

"There's nothing to tell. I ran away, my father found me, and now I'm back."

"Did your father hurt you?" Sierra blurted out the question.

River stopped suddenly but still did not look at her. "Sierra, don't ask me questions. I really don't want to talk about it." Then he did glance at her quickly before he turned away and walked toward the paddocks.

Sierra sighed as she followed to help clean the water troughs, a job she had been doing on her own for the past month. She worried about what had happened to River, but knew he was not going to tell her anything unless he chose. Dark suspicions about his father filled her mind, especially after the conversation she had overheard with Tess.

River did his chores, avoiding Sierra, and she did hers; cleaning the restrooms and lounge and then cleaning tack that had been left yesterday by boarders. Then it was time to turn the horses out. Months ago they had established which horses Sierra always took out and those that River handled, and they wordlessly fell back into the same pattern.

They began the stall mucking chores, a time when River could not avoid Sierra. Storm, as if there had been no gap in the routine, sauntered into the aisle and plopped down where she could watch River work.

They had finished the first aisle of stalls when Sierra could not stand the hostile silence any longer. *Why is he mad at me?* She tried again to get River to talk; to try and re-establish their previous easy relationship. "I'm really glad to see you," she offered.

No answer.

"I've been cleaning the stalls by myself on weekends. Manuel started helping me but I told him I didn't mind."

River heaved a full pitchfork of wet shavings into the cart. He sighed and paused a few moments before wielding it again. Sierra wondered if the work was hard for him; if he was in pain from some hurt or if his muscles ached from lack of use for the past month. She realized that she was keeping pace with him one-to-one, rather than him two to three stalls ahead of her as before.

"Tess is giving me lessons now."

"Good for you." His response sounded spiteful.

That hurt her feelings. All the emotions she had felt about River; looking up to him, missing him, worrying about him, and then to have him return and treat her so callously; well… Her confused emotions roiled into a smoldering heavy rock in her chest. Tears began to form but she gulped them back and let a flare-up of anger keep them at bay. She stopped her pitchfork and cried out, "River! Why are you mad at me? I thought we were friends and I've missed you so much." Suddenly her anger dissipated as quickly as it had flared; the burning rock in her chest melted into an iciness that spread through her ribs and down her spine. The tears came in a flood.

River looked at her, stunned. He let his pitchfork fall and stepped over to the stall where she stood gulping back tears, and took her in his arms, hugging her against his chest. He held her tight while she sobbed..

His arms and chest felt hard and strong and secure. He smelled faintly of horses but also his own personal scent which Sierra breathed deeply into her lungs. He didn't smooth her hair or rub her back; things her mother did to comfort her, yet it was a warm and safe place to be. He whispered against her hair, "*Angelita*," so softly she wasn't sure that he had even said the word. *This is what it feels like to have a big brother!*

At last Sierra's sobs receded to sniffles and he loosened his arms. She looked up into his face. His dark eyes that so often looked out with a cold, hard expression were soft and gentle; like a horse's large, warm, and trusting eyes. "I'm not mad at you," he stated.

She nodded and said weakly, "Good." It occurred to her that it was rather ironic; he was the one who had run away and probably beaten by his father, and yet he was comforting her.

"I'm sorry," he said barely over a whisper. He dropped his arms and turned away to return to the stall where he had been working and retrieved his pitchfork.

They went back to work. Sierra pointed at Storm, who sat up stiffly with a worried look on her canine face. "I think we upset Storm." The tension between them had disappeared, but Sierra kept her back toward River for awhile to hide the embarrassment of her blotchy face and red eyes.

"Tell me how things have been with you," River asked after a short period of silence.

"I'm having a hard time riding the way Tess is teaching me," Sierra confessed. She waited, hoping he would have some comments or advice. "The jumping lessons are going okay; it's the dressage that's hard." He just nodded. "She's letting me ride horses out on the trail every day."

River snorted. "She's not letting you ride the horses," he told her. "She's using you to condition the horses. If you didn't take them out on the trail, then she would have to."

Sierra felt stunned. *He's right!* It wasn't to improve her riding that Tess assigned the horses to ride. Sierra thought about that for a few minutes. Nobody likes to be taken advantage of, but truthfully, she guessed she didn't care. She looked forward to the trail rides much more than her lessons. Going out on different horses and trotting and galloping definitely had improved her security in the saddle and her confidence. Plus, it was just plain fun.

"Oh…I guess you're right." She looked over at him scowling over his pitchfork. "But even so, it's so awesome. It's the best part of my day." *Except for Moose.* Suddenly her terrifying ride and fall flashed into her brain. She had told no one, not even her mother, or that she dreaded having to ride the big, flighty horse again. Now she blurted out to River, "Most of the time anyway. Twice she had me ride Moose. I have a hard time controlling him."

River froze with his pitchfork in hand. "What?" he exclaimed. "Sierra, even I have trouble with that horse on the trail." And then more to himself, "What is she trying to do to her?"

Sierra felt tears building again but sniffed them back. *Enough crying!*

"You should tell her you can't handle him."

She nodded in agreement, afraid to try to speak just yet. It was such a relief that River agreed she shouldn't ride Moose; that it was not just her lack of horsemanship.

He shook his head and went back to wielding the pitchfork. "She's never even ridden Moose on the trail so she has no idea how he acts. He's almost lazy when she rides him inside the arena. But he's off the track; you get him outside and he thinks it's time to race."

Tess has never ridden Moose on the trail? That was news to her. Sierra sighed and smiled, "I'm so glad you're back," she couldn't help but say again. She felt vindicated that even River admitted to a hard time with Moose.

A few stalls later, River brought up the subject of Crystal and Magic. "So Crystal's going to show Magic in beginner novice."

"Yeah," Sierra confirmed. Four riders were going to a horse trial in two weeks; Crystal on Magic, Gloria on Silver, Katrina on Calliope, and Ann McGoverney, the high school girl who owned Lucy. They would compete as a team, representing Pegasus. It would be Magic's first time out at an event.

"What a mistake," River murmured, more to himself.

"Is Tess going to have you start riding him again?" Sierra asked hesitantly.

"He's four years old," River went on, ignoring her question. "He shouldn't even be jumping yet, and he's way too immature to compete."

A whistled tune preceded the arrival of both Manuel and Rosa, bearing a breakfast basket. They greeted River exuberantly amid a flourish of excited Spanish. Rosa hugged him several times, and then as usual, hugged Sierra.

"Deese leetle girl, she work all by alone," Manuel told River as they took a break. Sierra flushed at his praise.

"I'm sorry," River said through a mouthful of tortilla, meeting her eyes. "It was very kind of you to do the stalls by yourself."

Sierra felt embarrassed and turned away to give Storm a chunk of her burrito. The rest of the break, Manuel and Rosa chattered to River, and she finished eating in silence but with renewed happiness to be surrounded by these three people and one dog; like a family.

Sierra and River finished the stalls and then checked the notice board for their riding assignments. Today they were both assigned horses in training with Tess.

The two rode out together onto the trail. The early spring day, although cool and overcast, occasionally broke through with beams of sunlight through the gray clouds. There was a scent of things growing in the air; a hint of warmer weather just around the corner. The horses felt fresh and eager to be out in the open. Sierra rode behind, watching River's back and even without seeing his face she could tell his mood had improved. She could not have been happier herself!

The next Tuesday, Sierra mounted up on Morris for her lesson and began to warm him up. She had hoped Tess would turn her back over to River for lessons, but so far she hadn't said anything; and Sierra remembered that Tess thought River had taught her some bad habits.

Tess arrived and began the lesson, calling out instructions through the microphone. Morris at least never seemed to get upset about anything Tess would ask Sierra to do. He tolerated a short, tight rein without protest, but it did seem as if she needed to push him much more than she ever had when she rode him in a lesson with River. She hadn't even carried a whip then, but now she needed to tap the little bay with it to get any kind of forward movement or upward transition.

After the usual forty-five minutes Tess announced, "We'll end there." Sierra gave Morris a loose rein and walked him over to the platform for the debriefing. "Any questions?" Tess asked.

What Sierra really wanted to ask was if River could take over her lessons, but she held back. *What if River doesn't want to teach me anymore?* "No," she answered.

"Fine," Tess responded. Then she added, "I believe I mentioned to you before that I don't appreciate you going to River when you have a complaint rather than coming to me. If you can't handle Moose, you should have talked to me yourself."

Sierra's eyes widened in surprise. River must have said something to her about Moose. "I didn't complain to River," she started to explain, "I was going to…"

Tess interrupted. "You will not ride him anymore." With that flat statement, she strode away.

It was a relief, but at the same time, Sierra did not like being falsely accused; again.

It is so great to have River back! With the two of them working together, chores were completed in half the time; especially now that Sierra was much more skilled. They rode trails together, and then Sierra watched River working horses in flat work and over jumps. He rode Magic four days a week; getting him ready for the upcoming competition. Magic seemed more settled with River taking care of him. The only upset in the gelding's life now happened on the two days a week when Crystal rode him for her lessons with Tess.

Sierra longed for River to take over her lessons, yet she hesitated to ask him. A small part of her was afraid he might refuse. But mostly it was because she was afraid of how Tess would react. Not because Tess relished giving Sierra lessons herself; but somehow Sierra feared Tess would think she was complaining to River again. And instinctively she knew that Tess would not tolerate anyone preferring River's style over hers. So she continued to take her two lessons a week from Tess. But sometimes she noticed River watching from the shadows.

15 HORSE TRIAL

When I bestride him, I soar, I am a hawk. He trots the air, the earth sings when he touches it. – William Shakespeare.

During River's absence, Tess had taken over training Magic. She tended to leave him till last on her schedule of horses to ride, so many times Sierra arrived at the stable after school in time to watch. Even to Sierra's inexperienced eyes, it was obvious that Tess did not get along with the big chestnut. She fought him constantly; Magic snorting, grinding his teeth, and jerking suddenly with his head. Tess responded with jerks of the reins, hard jabs with her spurs and frequent whacks with her whip.

Once, he reared straight up. Sierra gasped in fear, thinking he would go over backwards, but Tess yelled out at him, and with a combination of her spurs and the whip she pushed Magic forward and then kept him at a hard gallop, lashing him repeatedly with her whip until he was lathered and his sides heaving before she allowed him to slow down. After that, Tess rode him with draw reins on the flat, and over jumps she used a more severe bit and a running martingale.

With River back, Tess reverted to having him take over most of Magic's training sessions. *Interesting,* Sierra observed. She hadn't really noticed the changes in Magic until by contrast, with River again attending to the young horse, those changes disappeared. Magic had been depressed! He had been off his feed, rarely cleaning up his hay. When turned out, he stood in a corner with his head lowered, apparently sleeping all the time. He did not run away from people, but stood with his ears back and looking away when anyone approached with a halter, even to bring him in at night. Sierra visited him frequently to give him attention and treats, which he took half-heartedly when she practically thrust a carrot against his muzzle; whereas the other horses were poking their noses out begging for treats.

Magic perked back to life with River's return. He cleaned up his feed and when turned out, wandered his paddock, searching for something to nibble on; normal behavior for a healthy horse. When River rode Magic, it was as if he were a totally different horse than the one under Tess. Rather than tense, resistive, and frightened; he floated, he flew, he danced. With River on his back it was easy to recognize the inherent talent of the lovely gelding with a rider who could bring out the best of him. *Not bad for a backyard rider!*

Sierra was very curious to know how River had learned to ride. From his mother, the jockey? From his father maybe? And how was it a mere kid could ride Magic so beautifully, whereas Tess, an experienced adult with an impressive professional background, could not? Did it just come naturally to him? Was he one of those horse whisperer type people? She had asked him a few times how he had learned to ride. He just shrugged and said he'd been riding all his life. It was hard to get answers from him.

With the horse trial coming up soon, the training programs for each of the four horses entered had been vamped up. Magic and Silver were assigned to River and Sierra to trail ride for conditioning four days a week, with bouts of trotting and galloping over hilly terrain. Katrina and Ann rode their own horses two to three days a week on trails, with River and Sierra picking up the days when their owners were unable to ride. In addition, the horses were schooled on the flat three days a week and over jumps at least once and sometimes twice a week. Each horse had one day off a week with no work.

Sierra's Thursday lessons were usually over low jumps now, and one week she rode Silver and the next Lucy. Sierra knew that Tess was incorporating exercises to prepare these two horses for the trial into her lessons, but it was good for Sierra also. At least the lessons over jumps were never as stressful as the dressage lessons, so Sierra always looked forward to her Thursday lesson almost as much as she dreaded her Tuesday lesson on the flat.

"Saddle Fala and warm her up in the back field," Tess told Sierra on Thursday.

"This is a surprise," Sierra chatted to Fala as she groomed the mare. She had been jumping small courses in the outdoor arena and starting to feel secure over low heights. This would be her first time jumping in the open field.

Once mounted, Sierra walked Fala down the low slope and then trotted around the perimeter of the field to warm up. The trotting and canter work she rode on the trails had definitely improved her seat and legs, and she felt relaxed and confident as she signaled Fala for an easy hand gallop. Even riding the hilly terrain she felt secure.

"Are you warmed up?" Tess arrived and called out through the megaphone she used in the open.

Sierra circled Fala over to Tess and replied, "Yes, we're ready."

"Let's start right out with an easy course then." Tess pointed out the obstacles she wanted Sierra to take; the railroad ties, the round log, a ditch, a low stone wall, a cross-rail fence, and a log pile.

Fala sensed her rider's excitement as Sierra started her out at a trot to make a big circle before approaching the railroad ties. *This is going to be fun!* The mare volunteered the canter and Sierra let her go, pushing her weight down through her heels and her posture slightly forward over the mare's withers, in two-point. Fala pricked her ears as Sierra guided her to face the jump and she moved forward into a gallop.

"Hold her in," Tess called, "stay in control."

"Easy, girl," Sierra assured the black mare as she shifted her weight slightly back and squeezed the reins, to half halt the rushed pace. Fala flicked her ears back but responded with a shortening of her stride. Then they were within a few feet of the obstacle. Sierra merely shifted forward into two-point and let Fala have her head. They sailed over the railroad ties, and from that point on, Sierra let her go at her own pace and merely steered her towards each obstacle. Sierra was in heaven! Fala needed no urging and seemed as enthusiastic as her rider as they galloped the course, clearing each jump. Sierra exhilarated in the feel of Fala's back arching up underneath as she jumped, and she allowed the movement to push her forward over Fala's neck. Then she settled back lightly in the saddle as the mare landed, moving her hands forward with the motion of Fala's head so as not to jab her in the mouth. Wind whistled in Sierra's ears and an escaped lock of hair partially obscured her vision, but she had Fala's eyes and ears as well as her own to keep them on course. They completed the round and returned to where Tess stood, evaluating her student.

"Well done," Tess said.

Did I hear her correctly? Sierra couldn't recall ever receiving a compliment from Tess.

"How did that feel?"

"Awesome!" Sierra beamed, still a little out of breath.

"How would you like to ride Fala in beginner novice this weekend? One of our team, Ann McGoverney, had to scratch. The entry fee is already paid and they allow substitutions."

Sierra could hardly believe what she had just heard. Her dream to ride in a horse trial could happen this weekend, not sometime in the obscure future! Strangely, sudden terror at the prospect almost overwhelmed her. *Am I ready?* "This Saturday?" Sierra asked feebly.

"I know it's last minute, but if you think you can, I need to know very soon so I can inform the show secretary of the change."

"Um, yes, I want to." Tess frowned at the slight hesitation. "Do you think I'm ready?" Sierra asked quickly.

"You would be entered in maiden beginner novice. There are only seven cross country fences and they will be two-foot-six or less. The entries are either riders or horses who have never competed before. The course will be very similar to what you just rode. I think you are ready."

Sierra finished the lesson in a state of happy distraction as Tess had her school over specific obstacles. Once she even called out, "Sierra, are you listening to me?"

After the lesson Tess handed Sierra a copy of the dressage test she would need to memorize. She asked in a somewhat spiteful tone, "I don't suppose you have a hunt coat?"

Of course Sierra didn't. "No," she replied apprehensively, worried that the lack thereof would prevent her from being allowed to compete.

With a deep sigh Tess continued, "I suppose I can scrounge one up from the hand-me-downs. You're just so small. What about leather boots?"

Again Sierra had to answer no.

"Well, see if you can't sometime in the near future manage to purchase a pair of leather boots and get a hunt coat, both in black." She almost sniffed in disapproval eyeing Sierra's rubber boots. "This is a schooling show so you can get away with those for now, but they're so unprofessional."

"I'll try," Sierra answered. She wanted to add, *you know, I work for lessons, not money,* but bit her lip to hold the words back. It wasn't that she expected to get paid; but Sierra had no idea there would be these expenses involved to compete. She knew what hunt coats and leather boots cost, as well as other show clothes such as tailored riding shirts and breeches, stock ties, gloves, and velvet hunt caps. A catalogue had come with the purchase of her rubber boots, and she spent many an evening pouring dreamily over its contents. Nothing was cheap. Sierra wondered what the entry fees normally cost for the horse trial, and was grateful she was not expected to reimburse Ann.

After the lesson, Sierra with Silver and River with Moose walked their assigned mounts to the mounting block outside. Moose was already starting to prance and look around excitedly. Sierra felt the utmost relief that River was riding the ex-racehorse; not her.

She waited for River to mount first, and marveled at his patience as he over and over waited for Moose to stand politely next to the mounting block before attempting to mount. Moose either swung his hips to the side or stepped forward and River merely brought him back into line and spoke quietly to him. Sierra had given up on getting Moose to stand, even though she knew it reinforced his bad habit. Finally, Moose stood, shifting from one foreleg to the other but at least remained parallel to the block and River mounted. He gathered his reins and stepped Moose away while Sierra mounted Silver.

River looked over at Sierra and smiled one of his rare smiles as they headed toward the trail. "I'm supposed to gallop him today. Wish me luck."

"Are you afraid?" Sierra asked, astonished.

"Of course; he's unschooled and unruly and very strong. I could get killed."

Sierra thought he was kidding, but she noticed a tightness around his mouth that was just a hint of possibly…fear? But there was also a gleam of anticipation in River's eye.

"Let me lead," River said. "He already thinks he's in a race."

"Sure," Sierra agreed.

They walked the horses for a few minutes, and Sierra wondered how River managed to get Moose to actually walk rather than jig. Then River called over his shoulder, "Ready to trot?" She nodded. River and Moose moved off in what looked like a relaxed, forward moving, and controlled trot. Silver readily trotted off after them. Sierra appreciated that Silver was such a cooperative, well-trained fellow, and she had no trouble keeping him two lengths behind Moose so as not to crowd him.

They trotted a while and River brought Moose back to a walk. He turned his head slightly to state, "I'm going to walk a few minutes and then pick up a trot and right into a gallop. Are you okay with that?"

"Fine with me." From her position behind, she could not tell if River was having a hard time with Moose or not.

A few minutes later Moose started to trot and River called out, "Here we go!" Moose exploded into a gallop and took off like a shot. Silver lunged after him, much faster than Sierra had ever galloped before, and the first few moments she froze on his back in a panic. But then she told herself, *This is Silver, not Moose. You've galloped him several times on the trail and he obeys. You can trust him.* She sucked in a deep breath, sat deeper in the saddle and shortened her reins. The obedient gelding immediately responded by slowing his pace. "Good boy," she praised him. *Okay then, I can slow him down and I can stop him if I need to.* Her confidence restored, she loosened her hold and let Silver surge forward again into the fast gallop. It was the fastest she had ever ridden before but feeling in control of her horse, she tuned into her muscles and the feel of her mount, and enjoyed every exhilarating moment.

They sailed around the trail! River glanced over his shoulder only once to make sure Sierra was okay, without slowing the pace. Sierra thrilled at how confident she felt even galloping downhill and around bends in the trail. Silver seemed to be enjoying the pace as much as his rider and easily kept a two-length distance behind Moose.

The trail ran mostly through woods but there was one open area through a field. In this open space a side trail to a large log had been created so that brave riders could deviate from the main trail and take a jump if they wanted. The riders approached that area now, and Sierra was amazed when she saw Moose veer off the main trail toward the jump. *Is that his idea or River's?* She had a split second to decide whether to follow or take the main trail as they usually did. Sierra had never jumped the log before; but it was only about two feet in height and maybe a foot wide; really nothing to challenge either Silver or her. She had jumped higher obstacles last week during her lesson and it was similar to the jumps she had taken today in the field. With her heart speeding up in anticipation, she guided Silver to follow Moose.

Moose and River sailed over the log and galloped on. Sierra moved up into two-point but slowed Silver back to a canter. He collected himself willingly and took the log easily in stride. River glanced back and grinned, and Sierra whooped in glee.

They didn't slow down until they were in sight of the field and then brought the horses to a walk. As they left the trail,

Sierra moved Silver up alongside of Moose, both horses blowing and snorting and content to settle down to a walk.

"That was so awesome!" Sierra beamed at River.

He grinned back, his face reflecting his joy, and Sierra suddenly noticed how handsome he was; with his wild black hair sticking out from his helmet, his brown cheeks flushed with excitement and his dark eyes shining.

"He's starting to listen to me," River sounded very pleased as he reached forward to stroke the giant horse's neck.

"I have never ridden so fast in my life!" Sierra exclaimed, her face still split in a wide grin.

"Were you afraid?" River's features shifted to a look of concern.

"A little at first until I knew I could slow Silver if I needed to. Then I just let him go." She laughed. "Did you see us take the log?"

"Yeah! Did you see us? This guy really enjoys jumping!"

"Was it your idea to go so fast?" Sierra asked.

"No way! But he seemed so comfortable and balanced in his stride so I just let him go. I think my stomach muscles are going to be sore tomorrow."

Sierra looked at him in amazement. River burst out into the most natural laugh she had ever heard from him. This was River's element and he looked truly happy.

16 SHOW DAY

*A horse takes on the mood of the trainer. Therefore, it is important
to make an effort to be as calm as possible.* – Richard Hinrichs

Saturday arrived, blowing and drizzling with spring rain;
but the weather could not dampen Sierra's spirits. Her first
thought on awakening that morning had been, *don't cancel the
show.* Then she remembered that horse trials, like soccer games,
are rarely canceled due to weather. Now she pedaled happily to
the stable with her clothes for the show folded into plastic bags
and stowed in her backpack, all protected by a rain poncho.

As Sierra coasted into the stable yard she saw the six-horse
van already hooked up with the ramps down, hay nets slung
inside, waiting for the horses. Manuel stepped out of the trailer
where he had been hanging the last hay net and called out a
greeting, "Good morning, Sierra. I feed dee 'orses already. You
bring Fala to crossties and I show you to put on shipping
boots."

"Okay, thanks, Manuel."

Sierra soon had Fala groomed and was applying the last two shipping boots after Manuel had showed her how, when River arrived and brought Magic to the crossties.

"Hi, River," Sierra greeted cheerily. He didn't answer. *One of his better mood days,* she thought sarcastically; but then she remembered how upset he was about Magic starting his show career today, so she forgave him. She could hear him whispering softly to the chestnut as he brushed his gleaming red coat. Finished with Fala, Sierra then brought Calliope to the crossties and started getting her ready.

When all four horses were groomed, blanketed, and booted, and their tails wrapped; River loaded each one into the trailer. Manuel secured the ramps and stepped up into the driver's seat of the truck and Sierra headed to the passenger side. Tess and the other team members would meet them at the show grounds. River would remain at the stable to do the chores by himself today.

Sierra had her hand on the cab door handle when River came up behind her. "Sierra," he said, "you're riding too much with your hands. Lighten your hands and ride more with your seat and your stomach muscles." With those words of advice, he spun away and headed inside the stable.

"Thanks," Sierra called after him, but he did not show any indication of whether he heard or not. A yearning flashed through Sierra's heart. His words, so familiar when he had been teaching her, reminded her of how much she missed lessons with him; how much fun they had been.

There was a tangible aura at the show grounds created by the excitement of competitors and their support people with their horses, all milling about amid show officials and crew; everyone with focused expressions on their faces. Horses whinnied, snorted, and whirled around excitedly at the ends of their lead ropes as they were unloaded from trailers and led into their assigned stalls. The paths leading from trailer parking areas to the rows of stalls and to the warm-up areas had already been churned into mud.

Manuel and Sierra had the horses unloaded, shipping gear removed, and settled in their stalls by the time Tess and the others arrived. Tess carried four manila envelopes from which she handed out to each of her students an official number to attach to the horse's saddle pad and a number vest for the rider to wear during the cross country phase.

"I sure wish Ann could have ridden today," Crystal commented to Gloria, intentionally within Sierra's hearing.

"Yeah, well at least the team score is made up of the three top scores," Gloria answered. Sierra understood the implication; that her score would certainly not count in the team placings at the end of the day.

So much for team spirit. Sierra kept the thought to herself, but couldn't help wondering again why Crystal and the others disliked her so much. *What have I ever done to any of them?* She probably would never know.

Sierra diverted her thoughts from her teammates and turned all her attention to Fala, who stood nervously at her stall door with her head out, looking around and whinnying at the strange horses, ignoring her hay. Sierra had about fifty minutes before her dressage test. She hoped both she and her mount could calm down and relax by then.

"Sierra, try this on." Tess came up behind her with a black jacket on a hanger. Sierra slipped it on; it was probably two sizes too big. The tops of the shoulders hung about two inches below her own shoulders, the sleeve hems ended at her knuckles, and the lower hem hung at the top of her thighs. "We can tape up the hem and you can roll the cuffs inside the sleeves and it should do." Tess scowled, as if it was Sierra's fault the jacket didn't fit. Tess produced a roll of duct tape and started securing the folded up hem.

Finally Sierra was dressed in her second-hand breeches, rubber boots, borrowed jacket and borrowed stock tie, and her helmet. *If clothes have any bearing on my score, then I'm doomed,* she thought dismally, comparing her own appearance to that of her teammates in their tailored and well-fitting outfits. The taping of the jacket hem had taken longer than anticipated, and now she felt rushed as she entered the warm-up ring on Fala; only twenty minutes before her dressage test. Fala jigged and flung her head around looking at the strange sights and flattening her ears as other riders on horses passed them. Sierra's grip on the reins tightened as she tried to halt the jigging and at least produce a normal walk. Fala had been shown many times; she was a veteran competitor. *Why is she so nervous?*

Look at what's wrong with the horse and you'll know what's wrong with the rider, words River had said months ago flowed into Sierra's consciousness. *Look at how tense and rigid Fala is carrying herself. Why is she taking these short, choppy steps that are in rhythm with my racing pulse?* Sierra took a deep breath and rolled her shoulders back and forward a few times, trying to release her tension.

Tess stood at the rail of the warm-up ring coaching Crystal, who was scheduled to ride her dressage test right after Sierra. Since this was Magic's first show, he had also been entered into maiden beginner novice. Sierra expected Tess to focus on Crystal and Magic, so her spine jumped in surprise when she heard Tess hiss at her, "Sierra, quit wasting time. Take hold of her, get her round, and move her into a working trot. You only have a few minutes."

That's certainly going to help me relax, Sierra thought sarcastically and annoyed at the last minute coaching from Tess. For once, she ignored her instructor who had already turned her attention back to Crystal. Sierra thought of River's last minute advice. She loosened her hold on Fala's reins, took in slow deep breaths as she drew in her abdominal muscles and sat deep in the saddle. Fala responded; she slowed from her jigging gait and stretched her neck forward. Sierra did not change anything, but merely squeezed the reins at the same time she touched her calves to Fala's sides, and to her delight, Fala snorted, releasing tension, and moved into a relaxed, energetic trot. *We can do this!*

"Number twenty-three, you're on deck," the gate keeper called out to Sierra as she trotted by. *Okay, okay, deep breaths, stay relaxed. Ride Fala just like this,* Sierra coached herself. She would have liked more time to really establish that they had released all tension and were warmed up and limber; she hadn't even had a chance to canter. But at the same time, she had ridden Fala so many times and knew her well. Once she had the mare's attention like this, she should be able to perform the movements of the test. This was actually the first time she had felt connected with Fala on the flat since her last lesson with River. *Thank you, River, for that last minute advice.* She sank her weight deeper into the saddle, squeezed the reins with her fingers, and Fala transitioned from trot to walk. *Yes!* They left the warm-up ring and rode to where the dressage arena had been set up. The rider before them saluted the judge, the signal she had completed her ride. Sierra and Fala could now enter the ring.

"Have a good ride," the rider leaving the arena said to Sierra with an encouraging smile as they passed each other.

"Thanks," Sierra responded in surprise. *Now that's sportsmanship.*

Sierra rode her memorized test with everything around her in a haze, her attention totally focused on Fala and how good the mare felt under her seat. All nervousness and tension had vanished the moment she had trotted down the center line, and in her mind she imagined River's eyes watching and coaching her.

A, enter working trot; C, track right; ME, change rein on half diagonal; EK straight ahead; A, circle left twenty meters, working trot... Only when Sierra halted and gave the final salute to the judge did she become aware again of her surroundings, and to her surprise, heard applause! She gave Fala her head and a praising pat on the neck, and rode out of the ring passing Crystal who was just entering.

"Have a good ride," Sierra encouraged.

Crystal's face was fixed in a grimace, with all her attention on Magic who looked as tense as Sierra had ever seen him, already in a lather.

"Fala, you were wonderful," Sierra flung her arms around the little mare's neck after she dismounted.

"Nice ride," an adult bystander watching the tests commented.

"Thank you," Sierra looked up in surprise but still grinning with pleasure.

"You're one of Tess Holmes's students, aren't you?" the woman asked.

"Yes, I am."

"It certainly shows." The woman turned to another adult standing next to her. "Pegasus always does very well at these trials."

"I can see why," the other agreed.

Sierra swelled with pride. *So people recognize me as one of Tess's students! I represent Pegasus Equestrian Center that always does well.* In the warm glory of such praise she forgot that she had been following River's advice, and her nagging doubts about Tess's teaching style were erased. Sierra determined she would pay much closer attention to Tess and try harder in future lessons. *I guess she really does know what she's talking about.*

"Hey, Sierra," a familiar voice called her name. She turned to find Luke Abrams and Justin Blomquist walking up to her. They must have come with Mr. Douglas; Sierra saw him standing next to Tess, watching Crystal ride her test. "You guys looked really great out there!" Luke greeted her with a wide, friendly smile, and reached out to stroke Fala's neck.

"Thanks. What are you two doing here?" *That was a stupid question,* Sierra realized. Justin, who totally ignored her, had his eyes fixed on Crystal.

"We just came to watch you guys, but I didn't know you'd be here. Is this your horse?"

"No, she belongs to Pegasus. I just get to compete on her today."

"Wow; she's beautiful. What's her name?"

"Fala; she's an Arabian."

"Come on, Luke." Justin slapped the sleeve of Luke's jacket as he strode off. Crystal had just saluted the judge and was leaving the arena. Sierra had been watching the test from the corner of her eye. She knew Magic well enough to recognize the stiffness in his neck and the tense look in his eye. Nevertheless, he had moved with his natural big gaits and Crystal had performed all the movements with precision. It very well could be the winning test.

"See ya around," Luke said in his usual friendly manner as he took off after Justin.

"Girls, put your horses up and meet me at the cross country grounds and we'll walk your course," Tess called out as Crystal dismounted not far from where Sierra stood with Fala.

Feeling almost euphoric, Sierra obediently led Fala back to her stall; happy with Fala's performance and pleased that Luke had recognized her and taken the trouble to say hi. "Fala did great!" she told Manuel as he poked his head over the side of Silver's stall to ask how she did. Gloria and Katrina had finished their dressage tests about twenty minutes ago and were not in sight, and Sierra assumed they had left their horses for Manuel to care for. She hung up her borrowed jacket, removed Fala's tack, gave her a thorough brushing and then made sure she had fresh water and hay after leaving her in her stall.

Crystal just then showed up leading Magic, laughing and talking animatedly with Justin and Luke and two other girls from school who had joined them. She thrust the reins at Sierra and ordered, "Take care of him. I need to go walk the course."

Reflexively, Sierra took the reins, stunned as Crystal and the others walked away. *Hey, I need to walk the course too!*

Luke hesitated and turned back. "Sierra, do you need help?"

Manuel stepped out of Silver's stall and gently took the reins from Sierra. "You go...I take care of 'eem," he stated calmly.

"I can help," Sierra offered although she was afraid Tess would not wait for her to walk the course with the others.

Manuel shook his head and pointed after the group with an insistent finger, "You go."

Thanks," Sierra smiled at him in gratitude and hurried to where Luke had actually stopped, waiting for her. Then he walked with her, straggling behind the group of his friends, commenting on everything around them enthusiastically.

They found Tess with Gloria and Katrina; and then all the riders followed Tess around the course as she explained the best strategies for both the beginner novice and novice level jumps. She pointed out the best approaches to each obstacle, where they would need to slow their mounts and be sure they had control, and where they could speed up to make up time. Sierra and Crystal had only seven jumps in the maiden course. Gloria and Katrina would be faced with eighteen. It was still drizzling off and on and blowing and Tess warned, "It's slippery in places so really pay attention to the footing and slow down in the muddy areas, even if you have to come down to a trot. Any questions?"

When no one had anything further to ask, Tess continued to outline the plan for the rest of the day. "Gloria and Katrina, you have about twenty minutes before you need to warm up for cross country. I suggest you eat a light snack and drink some liquid, and then go get mounted. As soon as you complete your course, take your horse back to the stalls to cool him out. You'll have about an hour and a half to let them rest before you need to warm up for stadium, and that's when I'll walk your stadium course with you.

"Crystal and Sierra, you two are doing stadium jumping next and we have enough time to walk that course now. Then you two should also get something light to eat and drink. You should be in the warm-up ring twenty minutes before your ride time. You'll have a little longer break between stadium and cross country so pay attention to the time and make sure you allow at least thirty minutes to warm up."

They arrived at the big outdoor arena where the stadium jumping courses were held. Tess led Sierra and Crystal first to a large notice board where the course for each division had been posted and told them to study and memorize the maiden course. Then she led them into the arena and around their course, pointing out where the footing looked a little deep or slick and how to make their turns to approach the next jump. Even though they would not have any combination jumps to ride in their course, Tess showed them how to pace off the distances between the jumps in a combination in order to estimate the number of strides between the elements. "You only have six jumps in the maiden class, half the usual course, and there are no time penalties. You don't need to try to cut corners or approach at an angle, so just bring your horse straight on to face each jump and rate his speed. Crystal, if Magic gets himself too worked up, you can even bring him back to a trot." They walked the course twice, and then it was time to return to the stalls, eat a quick bite, and get their horses ready.

I know the course and none of the obstacles are any more difficult, in fact most are easier than what we have jumped at home, Sierra assured herself as she entered the arena after her number had been called. Nervous with all the eyes of the onlookers focused on her, she tried to replace them in her mind with images of the arena at Pegasus and only River's eyes watching. "We're good," she whispered to Fala as she urged her into a trot and then quickly into a canter for her starting circle. Fala flicked her ears, indicating she was in tune to her rider, snorted a release of tension and transitioned smoothly from walk to trot to canter.

As Sierra focused on the first jump, all other thoughts vanished. Fala sailed over the low vertical, and with ears alert, straight on and over a low brick wall, then a turn and over a narrow double oxer. "Slow and easy, Girl," Sierra whispered as she sat deep to slow Fala's increasing pace. The willing mare flicked back her ears, but obediently slowed down, and took the remaining three jumps - a lattice-worked vertical, a small coop, and the final single bar, painted in colorful stripes - all in stride and without errors. Sierra rode Fala out of the arena hearing applause and a few cheers. She spied Luke at the exit gate, beaming up at her and giving her a triumphant fist in the air.

Tess nodded at Sierra and simply stated, "Well done," before she turned her attention back to Crystal who had just entered the arena on Magic.

Sierra dismounted and turned to watch Crystal's ride. Magic, with head high and already in a nervous lather, half-reared as Crystal jerked hard with the rein to turn him onto a circle. "Let go of his head," Sierra breathed out as even she could see how Magic fought for release from Crystal's tight hold. They finished with a clear round although Magic rushed between fences with Crystal sawing at his bit, trying to slow him before each obstacle. Sierra guessed that only his natural talent allowed him to clear each jump and probably the fact they were all very low heights. They left the ring to polite applause.

Outside the arena, Crystal jumped down from the saddle, angrily pulled the reins over Magic's head and jerked forcefully down on his mouth.

"Crystal, don't..." Sierra cried out in alarm at the cruel and needless punishment.

Crystal rounded on Sierra, her eyes narrowed and her mouth a tight snarl. "Don't you ever tell me what to do," she hissed. "Take him back to his stall." She thrust the reins at Sierra, who took them without protest, used to taking orders from Crystal. Then Crystal noticed Justin and Luke watching with wide, curious eyes. "Go see if the dressage scores are posted," she snapped out at them.

"Sure," Justin replied, shrugging off her tone and the two boys set off.

Sierra started leading Fala and Magic back to their stalls, wondering how she was going to manage to get both horses taken care of at the same time.

"You ride dees leetle mare reel good." Manuel said as he emerged from a group of onlookers, and again he rescued her by taking Magic's reins. "I tell Reever, you soon ride better den 'eem, ha, ha!" He chuckled to himself.

"Thanks," Sierra relinquished Magic's reins, feeling more pleased by Manuel's praise than all the compliments she had received from strangers.

Sierra and Manuel had untacked and brushed down the two horses and turned them back into their stalls with an armload of hay to snack on by the time Tess arrived with

Crystal at her side, followed by Gloria and Katrina leading their horses. Both girls were beaming and talking excitedly. They had both finished their cross country course without jumping faults or time penalties.

"Hey guys," Luke called out waving a handful of papers as he and Justin returned from checking out the scores. He handed the papers, the dressage test score sheets, to Tess, who looked each one over before handing them out to each of the riders.

"Crystal, you're in first place," Justin announced. Crystal's entire demeanor brightened on hearing the news. It occurred to Sierra just then to wonder why it was so important to Crystal, somebody who seemed to have everything she wanted, to always win. And then it also occurred to her that it would be very unpleasant if she were to ever come out ahead of Crystal.

Justin and Luke reported on the team's standings so far. In maiden beginner novice, Crystal was in first place, and to Sierra's astonishment, she was in third! In novice, Gloria was currently in first place and Katrina was in fourth. The Pegasus team so far had the highest scores.

For cross country, Tess had told Sierra to wear a long-sleeved red tee shirt or sweat shirt, which fortunately she already owned. Then each of the riders wore a mandatory protective vest, provided by Pegasus in the stable colors of navy blue with scarlet trim. Tess also gave them a satin cover in the same colors, which stretched on over their helmets. The horses wore red splint boots and red saddle pads with PEC embroidered in navy blue. Sierra thought the colors looked great with Fala's gleaming black coat, and with her own complimentary outfit, she felt they must present a grand site as Fala pranced from the warm-up area to the starting box for cross country. Many onlookers smiled at them as they passed by and called out encouragements; "Good luck," or "you look great, have a good ride."

Sierra guided Fala into the starting box in a blissful state. They had warmed up well. Sierra had concentrated on getting Fala to move out at a ground-covering, relaxed working trot to loosen her muscles, and then had hand-galloped her around the perimeter of the warm-up area, taking a low cross-rail jump just once to clue Fala that jumping was coming up. Fala seemed filled with energy, boosted by the excitement of the strange surroundings and other horses, yet she had listened and responded promptly to Sierra's half-halts. Sierra's own adrenalin kept her senses alert and a little on edge; and she felt her muscles were nicely in tune with Fala's movements.

They flew over the course; Fala never once hesitated, not even when asked to gallop through a water crossing (which Tess had not anticipated would be in the maiden course, so they hadn't practiced at home). In spite of the mud flying up and spattering Fala's legs and belly as well as Sierra's legs, and the periods of rain slicking Fala's coat and Sierra's clothing, and partially obscuring her vision, they moved forward without losing their rhythm. It was the most exhilarating and delightful experience Sierra had ever had in her life! They flew between the finish poles without jumping faults or time penalties, and again to applause and cheering.

"Fala, I love you," Sierra exclaimed as she jumped down and hugged her.

Tess walked up with a cooler in her arms and actually had a smile on her face. "Nice ride," she said and helped Sierra loosen Fala's girth and throw the cooler over the mare's back. Then Tess moved back to watch anxiously at the last jump of the course, waiting for Crystal to appear on Magic.

Sierra led Fala at a leisurely pace back towards the stalls but stopped at a point where she could see two of the obstacles on the course, hoping to catch sight of Magic. A lovely paint horse came into view on course with its rider calling to him, "Whoa," as he tried to slow him for the approach to a vertical rail fence at the bottom of a downhill slope. The rider managed to bring the paint back to a trot, and at the slower pace negotiated the downhill without slipping. Sierra remembered that jump and was grateful for the many times of riding up and down hills at a canter and gallop on the trails, so had not been intimidated by the slope and had allowed Fala to stay in a gallop. She also remembered the muddy spot in a direct line to the jump that she had been able to avoid and watched the current rider also steer his horse around the mud, then pick up the canter again and take the jump. *Where is Magic?* Sierra wondered, worried, for they had been the next on course after her and Fala. Perhaps Magic had refused or run out and the next rider had passed them up.

Then Magic crested the hill and began the descent, his brilliant red coat gleaming with the slickness of rain and sweat. Crystal with her hands just inches from his bit struggled to slow his frantic gallop. *Out of control*, Sierra noted and gasped as Magic slipped, one hock bent nearly touching the ground; but he righted himself and flinging his head in desperation, fled on down the hill in a straight line for the jump.

"Look out for the mud!" Sierra yelled.

Crystal's face was fixed in a rigid expression of terror, her eyes on the jump ahead. She did not notice the mud and as Magic tried to veer around, she jerked him back on a straight line and slapped him with her crop. He flung his head up, reared and plunged forward. His front legs came down into the slick mud and he lost traction. Sierra watched in horror as the panicked horse, his legs slipping underneath, struggled to regain a footing, and then his back leg twisted and they went down.

Crystal screamed! She managed to fling her body out of the saddle and away from the thrashing horse. Magic landed on his side, his legs flailing. Somehow he got his forelegs planted and struggled to push himself up but didn't seem able to get his hind legs into a position to lift his weight.

A flurry of activity ensued. Several people rushed over to Crystal and others were running, talking into two-way radios. The next rider had been halted at the crest of the hill. An announcement over the loudspeaker called for the paramedic team and the on-sight veterinarian to come to cross country obstacle five of the maiden course.

"I'm okay, dammit!" Crystal screamed out at the people trying to prevent her from moving until the medics arrived.

Just then Tess came running up followed closely by Walt Douglas, Justin, and Luke. "I'm her father, let us through," Mr. Douglas shouted out and the crowd obediently moved back to let him move up to Crystal's side.

"Daddy," Crystal sobbed hysterically.

Two four-wheelers arrived and two paramedics jumped off the first and rushed over to the crowd around Crystal. Another two men got off the second and joined the people who were standing around Magic, still flailing and struggling to get to his feet. Sierra longed to go over to Magic, but with Fala in her care, all she could do was stand by, a helpless onlooker.

After a short exam by the paramedics, Crystal was helped to her feet and walked with her father's arm around her shoulders. The entire left side of her body was covered in mud. Long tracks of tears streaked her muddy face, ashen in color. On the other side of her, Tess's face was equally drained of color. The crowd parted as they walked over to Crystal's struggling horse.

Two people, one on each side and holding onto Magic's bridle, were trying to pull him forward while several people behind tried to push against his hind end as he struggled to stand. With a mighty groan he at last heaved out of the mud and stood trembling, supporting his weight on three legs. The left hind leg he held bent at an awkward angle at the hock.

"What's going on?" Katrina and Gloria came jogging up behind Sierra, both their faces with anxious expressions.

"Magic went down. I think Crystal's okay, but it looks bad for Magic," Sierra explained briefly. Not having a horse to hold, the two girls hurried to join the crowd, now gawking at the tragic scene.

The veterinarian, who had arrived on the four-wheeler, was examining Magic's leg. He stood, shaking his head and spoke to Tess. "He'll need x-rays, but it's obvious there's a fracture."

"Can you do something so we can get him home?" Tess asked.

"I'll splint the leg and give him pain medication," the vet replied, shaking his head morosely.

The Pegasus truck and horse van pulled up on the nearby road and Manuel jumped out to open the ramp. The vet had finished his first-aid work, and Tess led the limping horse to where she and Manuel and other willing helpers managed to load him into the trailer. The crowd dispersed, the rider who had waited at the top of the hill was signaled to resume the course (her time had been halted during the emergency), and there was nothing for the rest of them to do but load up the other horses and return to the stable. Tess and Katrina actually helped Sierra and Manuel put on the shipping gear and load the other three horses. Then Tess drove off with Gloria and Katrina. Mr. Douglas had already left with Crystal and the two boys. Manuel and Sierra followed behind with the horse van.

17 CANNON BONE

If we are to raise ourselves up to higher levels of equestrian expression, we need to become constructively self-critical and develop a refined degree of self-control. An essential part of this lies in striving to put aside our ego. The earthly ego ever threatens to warp our ability to assess ourselves and our performance objectively. Only when our desire to learn is constantly tempered by modesty and a genuine interest in the horse's well-being, will we be on the path which leads to the blossoming of true horsemanship. – Erik Herbermann

Manuel pulled into the stable yard and halted the rig. A van belonging to Dr. Patterson, Pegasus's vet, already sat parked near the stable entrance. At the sound of their arrival, the others stepped out of the lounge where they had been waiting.

Manuel and Sierra had not talked much during the ride home. Once, Manuel sighed deeply and murmured, *"Pobre Reever."* His words echoed Sierra's own thoughts, *How is River going to react?*

River must have heard the trailer for he came out from inside the stable. His hair shadowed his face as he walked to the back of the van, to Sierra's relief. She did not want to see his expression. River lowered the ramp and stepped inside to stand at Magic's head. Tess came over to help Sierra and Manuel unload the other three horses first. Then River carefully backed the injured chestnut out. Whatever pain medication or tranquilizer the vet had given Magic certainly had taken effect, because he moved very slowly, swaying, and with his head low. He still did not put any weight on his splinted left hind leg.

"Take your time, take your time," Dr. Patterson coached needlessly from the side of the ramp. When Magic was finally unloaded, River led him slowly to the wash stall where Dr. Patterson had set up his x-ray equipment. The others followed to watch, except Manuel and Sierra who went inside the stable to put up the other horses. Sierra still hadn't mustered the courage to look at River.

Dr. Patterson had completed his exam and taken the x-rays by the time Sierra and Manuel finished with the other horses and joined the group. The vet stood in front of his computer at the back of his van, studying the x-ray images with everyone looking over his shoulder. Sierra steeled her nerves to glance over at River. He had remained with Magic, and had his back to her holding Magic's lead. The chestnut stood with his drugged head pressed against River's chest while River stroked his neck.

Dr. Patterson coughed a few times as he moused back and forth between the x-ray images. Then he motioned to Tess, pointing at one of the images. "See here…and here. It's very clear. There is a fracture of the cannon bone."

"What does that mean?" Mr. Douglas asked in a business-like tone.

"We could attempt to repair it. This sort of surgery has been done. I am quite certain he would survive, but there is no way of knowing what level of soundness he will ever achieve. There's a chance he could heal to where he could be used as a pleasure horse. It's doubtful he could remain sound enough to compete, especially at jumping. But it is possible."

Coldness seeped down Sierra's spine and into her arms and legs. She could barely breathe. Her legs felt weighted as she followed the group to stand around Magic.

River looked up at Dr. Patterson, his color pale and mouth tight, and Sierra's heart dropped at the hope she saw in his eyes. The vet shook his head and put a comforting hand on River's shoulder.

"What is your recommendation?" Mr. Douglas asked.

"It depends on what your daughter's attachment is to the horse and how much you are willing to invest. It would of course be different if he were a stallion or a mare."

"He is insured," Mr. Douglas stated.

"I'm sure this injury will qualify for reimbursement of medical expenses. But I should let you know that most insurance companies I have dealt with would consider this injury as justifiable to put the horse down. They would most likely reimburse his insured value."

"Put him down," Crystal snapped out.

Mr. Douglas ignored her and continued discussing with Dr. Patterson. "You're of the opinion he'll not be fit to compete? I paid forty thousand dollars for this animal!"

"Of course there are no absolutes. There is always a chance, but unlikely. I really can't give you any statistics. I would say it's probably a fifty-fifty chance he could recover enough to stay sound for light work."

"Just put him down," Crystal spit out the words.

"Crystal, I only insured him for twenty-five thousand. I would take a big loss."

"We've already lost with this beast," Crystal answered. "He could have killed me!" Her face remained ashen and her lips began to quiver as she sniffed back tears."

River turned. He looked first at Tess who stood with a look of shock frozen on her face, still drained of color. Sierra had never seen her look so distressed. Then River looked at Mr.

Douglas. In the most respectful tone Sierra had ever heard from River, he asked, "Please sir, give him a chance."

Mr. Douglas sighed deeply, puffing out his cheeks, and running a hand over his balding head. "Twenty-five thousand is better than nothing," he said to no one in particular. He could not meet River's eyes. "What kind of time frame are we looking at before we would know how useful he will be?" Mr. Douglas asked the vet.

"An injury like this will take many months, even a year or more. Even with surgery it will require a lengthy recovery."

Mr. Douglas sighed again.

"Daddy, I won't have a horse to ride. Let's just put him down and be done with it."

"You have Caretaker," he answered his daughter.

"Pa-lease," Crystal drew out the word sarcastically, rolling her eyes. "Besides, he's for sale."

"But you could ride him while we shop for another mount, and give this one a chance."

Everyone looked at Crystal, waiting her decision.

"Put him down," she answered with finality.

River snapped his head around to look at her. A flash of rage passed over his face, but he shut his eyes and took a deep breath to regain control. In almost a whisper, he met her icy expression and pleaded, "Please, Crystal."

Crystal's eyes widened in surprise. "And what have you ever done for me but treat me like dirt?" she asked vehemently.

River did not look away. "I'm sorry. In the future I will treat you with the respect you deserve." (Sierra wasn't quite sure how he meant that.)

"Just what does that mean?" Crystal retorted.

"I will greet you with courtesy. I will jump to whatever it is you need me to do. I will be your slave." Sierra heard the desperation in his tone. Tess watched, with a look of horror.

Crystal smiled a slow, malevolent smile. "Hmm," she considered. "Well..." Then she looked away and to her father. "I don't think so. Put him down."

Mr. Douglas shrugged and said to Dr. Patterson, sounding slightly embarrassed. "I guess that's her decision."

"Tess," River turned to her. "Please, don't let her do this. He deserves a chance."

His words seemed to stir Tess up. She actually looked remorseful. "Crystal, in all fairness..."

"Put. Him. Down." Crystal shouted the words and then flung herself into her father's arms. "Daddy, he almost killed me!" she sobbed against his chest. Mr. Douglas made a tsking sound, rubbing her back, and then nodded toward Dr. Patterson.

18 EMPTY STALL

The horses will ever remain our true and ultimate judges; let us always listen to them. – Erik Herbermann

"River, perhaps it would be best if you went away," Dr. Patterson said gently. They had slowly led Magic from the wash stall to a grassy patch at the edge of the stable yard. It would make it easier for the renderers to remove the body. Tess stood next to the veterinarian, her posture still and tense and her face fixed in an expression of horrified shock.

River shook his head, avoiding eye contact with the others and keeping his body close to Magic's head, allowing the chestnut to press against him as he kept a hand on his neck, stroking gently. In a choked voice he pleaded one more time. "Can't we wait a few days?"

"No, son," Dr. Patterson put a hand on River's shoulder. "This is the best decision. I know you don't want him to suffer."

River could not accept this as the best decision. If Magic were to have surgery right away he imagined there would be some pain afterwards, but they could give him pain medicine and he would eventually heal. In River's mind, there was a very good chance he could even heal sound. No one had considered what Magic might prefer.

The vet stepped up to the gelding's neck, palpating for a vein, a prepared syringe in one hand.

"Will he...?" River didn't know what he wanted to ask. He could not watch the needle going in.

"He will just go to sleep...and there will be no more pain."

River looked deep into Magic's large dark eye, searching for blame or forgiveness or some understanding. All he saw was trust. He felt so utterly helpless. He wanted to fight for Magic's right to live but he didn't know how. He could yell, kick, and scream, but eventually they would just drag him away. He had already begged and pleaded. *What can I do...please, what can I do?* "I'm so sorry," he whispered hoarsely, a deep sense of shameful betrayal filling his soul.

Magic emitted a low-sounding moan. His eyes remained open as suddenly his back legs buckled and he dropped onto his hip and then to his side. He made one last attempt to raise his head. Then the opened eyes glazed and he lay still.

River dropped to his own knees staring into the vacant eye with his hands on the red neck. Ice coursed through his veins and he felt frozen.

Dr. Patterson placed a hand on his shoulder. "Come, River, it's over."

River shook his head and then fell onto Magic's neck, his fingers intertwined into the beautiful red mane, and he breathed in deeply of his smell; so that he would not forget...never forget.

The vet and Tess stood by helplessly watching the boy silently sob into the velvety coat of the dead horse. Not until the men drove up in the rendering truck and came over to place their chains, did River finally allow Dr. Patterson and Tess to lift him up by his arms. Wordlessly, he fled.

Tess started to leave, then turned back on a sudden whim and taking a pocket knife from her purse, cut off a thick lock of mane.

Ironically, the Pegasus team had scored the most points at the trial, enhancing Tess's reputation as the best instructor in the area. Gloria finished in first place in junior novice and Katrina moved up into third. To Sierra's amazement, she came in first in maiden beginner novice since Crystal had been eliminated and the previous second-place rider had a refusal cross country. With two firsts and a third, they were the winning junior team.

But the day that Sierra should have been able to cherish as a dream come true was a day she could only remember as a tragedy.

River was at the stable when Sierra arrived the next morning, already delivering hay down the first aisle.

"Hi," she greeted him timidly as she joined him at the cart.

He did not respond or even look at her. He looked terrible; his clothes disheveled as if he had slept in them, bits of shavings in his hair, and his eyes puffy with deep shadows beneath.

"You're here early."

"I never left," he answered, grimly.

Sierra struggled for something to say as he walked away from her with an armload of hay. Her mind mulled over all sorts of the usual but so ineffective expressions. *I'm sorry, I feel your pain, such a tragic loss.* Nothing seemed right to actually speak out loud. She pulled two flakes of alfalfa from the bale and carried them to the next stall.

When River hopped onto the cart and Sierra took the seat beside him she tried again, "River…"

Not looking at her, River drove the cart forward. "I'm okay," he said icily. "It's only a horse, not the end of the world."

"No, not just a horse," Sierra replied.

River stopped the cart three stalls down and jumped out, effectively telling her in his non-verbal way, end of discussion. Sierra felt tears forming; even though she felt like she had cried herself dry last night in her mother's arms. *I loved that horse too. Maybe I would like to talk about him.*

They had reached the end of the aisle, and there was Magic's empty stall; his name plaque still displayed on the door and his halter hanging on the hook. River tossed his armload of hay to Muffin in the stall next door. He started to turn back to the cart, but suddenly shifted and instead stepped over in front of the empty stall to peer into the vacant interior. "Just a horse." His voice choked on the last word and he bolted toward the stable entrance and out of sight.

Now the tears flowed freely down Sierra's cheeks. Horses were nickering impatiently, oblivious to the tragedy in front of them, and only concerned with the delay in their breakfast. Sierra finished delivering the hay alone, through misty eyes, glad that Manuel had taught her how to drive the cart. The horses could wait a bit for their grain, and she went outside to find River, wiping her tear-streaked face.

He was sitting under the tree where Storm rested, his arms around his dog and face buried in her fur. Sierra sat down on the other side of Storm who looked up at her with her beautiful canine eyes that seemed full of understanding.

River let go of Storm and sat up, his expression frozen. They sat silently for several minutes. Storm thrust her nose at

Sierra's hand and she petted the silky fur on her neck and scratched behind her ears.

"You stayed here all night?" Sierra asked to break the silence. *Lame; why can't I think of something comforting to say?*

"Yes." Silence reigned for several more long minutes.

"You want to know why I don't compete?" River asked suddenly, fixing his gaze somewhere in the distance.

"Yes," she answered, surprised by the question.

"Because I'd be good…really good. I know it."

"So..?"

"I wouldn't be just a stupid stable boy. People would look up to me. I could probably ride all kinds of rich people's horses."

"And that would be bad..?"

"I could be very successful and I would get used to that; and I would turn into someone like Tess. I would forget about what's inside a horse and look at them only as dollar signs."

"What are you talking about?" Sierra felt baffled.

"I think Tess used to like riding; maybe when she was a kid."

"You don't think she likes riding now?"

"Does she look happy when she's riding?"

"Well, it's hard to tell…" But Sierra visualized River's expression riding. There was no question he was happy on a horse's back. She compared it to the look of grim determination when Tess rode, and had to admit that she didn't look happy.

"I think it's what happens when people turn something they like into the way they make their living. I don't want it to happen to me."

Sierra thought about that for a few minutes. She wanted to argue with him; she was sure it didn't have to be that way but really didn't know how to defend her opinion. "What are you going to do?" she asked.

"I don't know."

"River, please don't run away again," Sierra pleaded as it occurred to her he might consider it a solution.

He shook his head. "No, running away is too much work. You spend all your time trying to get food and stay warm." He glanced at her briefly. "When I ran away before my father didn't find me. I let him find me because I got too hungry."

"Oh," she responded ineffectually. "Well...good then."

They sat a while longer in silence. River picked up a stick and started making patterns in the dirt at his feet.

"I miss Magic too." Sierra let it slip out.

"Yeah, I know." He looked sideways at her and met her eyes for a few moments before looking back down at his feet. "It's Tess's fault. She pushed him too hard." He started tossing pebbles at the patterns he had drawn. "Did you see what happened? He panicked, didn't he?"

"I think so," Sierra replied. "He hit a slick spot."

"Some horses are mature enough to start competing at four. Magic was just too timid. Everything made him nervous. One year could have made a big difference in his confidence."

"River, you can't blame Tess..."

He interrupted with cold, hard anger in his voice. "I can and I do."

"If anybody's to blame, it's Crystal."

He snorted derisively. "Crystal is a total idiot, but she'll do what Tess tells her. And I do blame her too." He added under his breath, "I hate them both."

Sierra heard pain as well as anger in his tone, and her heart ached for him.

"I'm not going to run away again, but as soon as I turn sixteen I can legally quit school and then I'll leave. I know people at the track and I can get a job as a groom or exercise boy. It won't be any better than here but it will be away from Tess and my father."

"You can't quit school!"

He snorted a short laugh.

"River, you can't." Sierra looked at him bewildered. When he didn't say anything in response she asked, "Don't you want anything more out of life than that? Don't you want to go to college?" Then she felt foolish, sounding like an adult.

"College," he said in a distasteful tone. "I'm flunking out of high school so that's a likely possibility."

"Flunking! Why?" Sierra didn't know anyone who had ever failed a grade. Sure, some kids did better than others but everybody passed.

"Because I'm stupid," he answered and he said it in a way that she realized he meant it literally, not that he was making stupid decisions.

"You are not stupid."

"You don't know."

"I've met some stupid people before and you are not one of them," she told him. "I do know."

An expression flickered over his face as if he wanted to believe her.

"I'm going to be a veterinarian." Sierra didn't understand why she told him her dream just then. She certainly didn't want him to think she was trying to sound better than him.

"Good for you," he said sarcastically.

"You'd be a good vet." Sierra knew it to be true. She had watched River helping Dr. Patterson when he came to examine a horse, give vaccinations, or float teeth. Dr. Patterson always complimented River and had actually told him he had a gift with the animals and should think about becoming a vet some day.

"Sierra, just shut up." With that unkind retort he jumped up and strode back to the stable.

Sierra sighed and stroked Storm's fur. The dog sat up rigidly, following River with her anxious eyes. If ever a dog could show concern, it was definitely in Storm's attitude.

"Storm, what are we going to do with him?"

Storm licked Sierra's face in answer and Sierra hugged her before getting up and returning to chores.

19 EIGHTH GRADE ENDS

In riding a horse, we borrow freedom. – Helen Thompson

After Christmas break, Billy finally gave up chasing Sierra around. She guessed that with no more ballroom dancing he lost his excuse of having her as his partner. His absence freed up space around her so that she had a chance of making friends on her own.

One day after biology class where they had been discussing all the possible careers that involved the study of biology, a classmate caught up to Sierra in the hallway.

"You're Sierra, right?"

"Yes."

"Hi, I'm Allison. So you want to be a veterinarian. I want to be a doctor." The girl chatted amicably about her ambition to follow in her parents' footsteps, both physicians. Then at lunch the next day, she sat down at Sierra's table, and from then on they ate together and then went to the library to work on homework, often helping each other.

"You know, if we go to the same university, we could study together and be lab partners. Pre-med and pre-vet are almost all the same courses."

Sierra thought that was pretty advanced planning since they were both still only in eighth grade, but she laughed and agreed that was a great idea.

Tall, willowy, with a combination of Caucasian, African, and Japanese heritage, Allison Ferguise was an exceptionally beautiful girl. She had inherited the best features of all three races; flawless creamy brown skin, lovely almond-shaped brown eyes, and curly, soft black hair. Sierra guessed someday those around her would recognize her unique beauty, but she was just a little too exotic in looks for most of the boys at Firwood Middle School with their narrow, Hollywood tastes. But what Sierra liked best about Allison was her intelligence and insights, and she loved the long in-depth discussions they had about everything in the world around them.

Allison liked horses but not with the same passion as Sierra. "I'm afraid of horses," she confessed. She loved anything to do with art and appreciated horses for their natural beauty. And being a good listener, she liked hearing Sierra talk about her own emotional experiences riding and working at the stable.

Allison had a talent for analyzing everyone around her with astute insight, and Sierra loved to hear her explain the politics of their small middle school world. One time Sierra asked her about Crystal. "How come a girl who is so self-centered and rude even to her friends is the most popular girl at school? She's pretty, but she's not as beautiful as you are, or even as pretty as Katrina."

"Simple," Allison explained. "She's rich and has a rich attitude. She expects people to look up to her and envy her. Let's face it, money is power. Crystal wears the most expensive clothes, owns the latest model phone and has all the latest gadgets. Her mother drives her to school in an expensive car and you know she'll get a new car of her own as soon as she turns sixteen. Even the teachers give her more slack than other kids because her father has been financially supportive of the school's sports' programs. Kids hang around her hoping to cash in on her assets. They don't realize that of course; they think they are truly friends.

"But your family is well-off and you're beautiful. How come you don't hang out with all the popular kids?"

"For one thing, I'm too different. But mostly because I don't want to."

Sierra thought about that and accepted her statement as the truth. Allison didn't hang around with the elite of the school but it wasn't because she was a reject like Sierra. "Why do you think Crystal dislikes me so much?"

"Now that's a mystery I haven't figured out. There's something you have that she wants, but who knows what it is?"

"It's certainly not my job at her father's stable."

"Yes, but she started noticing you after you started working there. What's at the stable that you have and she doesn't?"

"Nothing," Sierra answered. "I didn't even know how to ride when I first showed up so it's not like she could be jealous of my superior riding skills."

"Hmm," Allison mused.

"The only thing I can possibly imagine is that I work with River, and she can't stand him."

"Ah yes, the stable boy," Allison said pointedly. Sierra had talked a lot about River; how exceptionally well he rode, how he started teaching her to ride before he ran away, and even that she suspected his father abused him and was using him for child labor. Allison found River quite intriguing.

"I think your River is definitely the key. Maybe she is jealous of your friendship with him."

"I doubt that, she hates him."

"Just remember that hate and love are often separated by a very thin line," Allison said philosophically.

"Whatever," Sierra laughed.

"Think about it. Who hated who first?"

"I wonder." An idea suddenly occurred to Sierra. "Maybe it's River she's jealous of."

Allison and Sierra had been friends since January. But since the weekend of the horse trial, a few other changes also occurred at school.

The biggest change was Luke.

Luke had always been friendly to Sierra, but now he actually sought her out. The Monday after the horse trial, he came up to her locker to congratulate her on her win and then walked with her to class. They had two consecutive classes together; history and then algebra, and a few times he also walked with her from one class to the other. He didn't seem at all self-conscious to be seen with a nerdy girl like Sierra. Once he sat down with Allison and Sierra at lunch for a few minutes, to ask a question about a homework assignment.

"Why, I do believe you have a beau," Allison said in a fake southern accent after Luke left their table.

Sierra laughed, "He just wanted to ask a question about the homework and we happened to be sitting here."

"Right," Allison answered and smiled knowingly as Sierra blushed.

Sure, Luke has bright blue eyes that always seem to be smiling, and sandy blond hair in a brush cut that tempts me to stroke my hand over the top of his head, and yes, he's incredibly cute. Sierra laughed to herself. *Here I am thinking about a boy; a subject I used to think really boring. Luke is just a friend!*

Katrina also acted different towards Sierra. She didn't go out of her way, but if she happened to pass Sierra in the hall, especially if she was not with Crystal or Gloria, she would smile and say 'hi'.

"That Fala sure is a sweet mare," she even congratulated Sierra after the horse trial. "You two are a pretty good team, at least at beginner novice level."

But not everything had changed. Crystal and Gloria were as snobbish as ever and continued to plague Sierra with small cruelties; such as filling the inside of her locker handle with peanut butter, or dropping a half-sucked lifesaver on her open notebook when one of them walked by her desk, saying, "Oops, so sorry." They never lost an opportunity to comment about her wardrobe such as, "Why, Sierra, what a lovely pink tee-shirt that looks so much like the blue one you wore yesterday. It goes so well with that pair of jeans that goes so well with the blue tee-shirt. Oh my, why it's the same pair of jeans you wore yesterday!" Sierra never understood what was so incredibly funny about that, but they and their friends laughed hysterically.

What Sierra found very interesting however, was that for days after Magic had been euthanized, Crystal mourned around school playing the tragedy of the loss of her 'beloved horse' to the utmost; bursting into tears, crying on someone's shoulder, and receiving sympathetic attention from everyone, including the teachers.

A few changes also occurred at the stable. Caretaker was sold and his new owner hauled him away to her own barn. Three weeks after the loss of Magic, Crystal's new horse arrived on a Saturday morning while Sierra and River were cleaning stalls.

When Manuel arrived with breakfast, a little earlier than usual, he announced, "Mees Tess she call. Mees Crystal's new 'orse ees coming today. Maybe soon."

Not long after, a truck and trailer pulled into the stable yard. Sierra and River set aside their pitchforks and went outside to meet the new arrival.

"River, come give us a hand," Tess called from the stable yard. She stood at the back of the trailer undoing the fasteners for the ramp. "Oh good," she said as River stepped up and finished lowering the ramp; then disappeared inside the trailer. A few minutes later he backed out a black and white paint horse.

Of course he was beautiful. Sierra could not imagine Crystal settling for anything less than magnificence. With his shipping sheet and boots pulled off, his contrasting black and white patches gleamed in the sun. His legs were white up past the knees, he had a white rump, a large white patch on each side of his neck, and a narrow white blaze on a black head. Both his mane and tail glistened a raven-black color.

River led him around the stable yard, letting him blow and snort at the new smells. Horses whinnied from the paddocks, greeting the newcomer.

"Why'd she get another baby?" River demanded.

"He's six years old; hardly a baby," Tess answered.

"Too young for Crystal."

"River, I would appreciate it for once if you would keep your opinions to yourself," Tess snapped back at him. "He's been shown for two seasons and has done very well. He's obedient and certainly not green. I believe he is perfect for Crystal."

River mumbled a few derogatory remarks under his breath.

"What's his name?" Sierra asked.

Tess glanced at her, as if just now aware that Sierra was even there. "Galaxy." She turned her attention back to River.

"Walk him around for a bit and then find him an empty paddock. We'll put him in Mag…" She caught herself and then said, "Put him in Butch's old stall." She turned away and walked into the office.

Sierra joined River leading Galaxy down the lane of paddocks. "What do you think of him?" she asked.

River shrugged. "He seems nice enough. He's already settling down."

"I think he's beautiful!"

"Sierra, you think all horses are beautiful." The corners of River's mouth turned up slightly. It was the first expression even close to a smile she had seen on his face since the loss of Magic. It surprised her how it warmed her heart.

May arrived with only a few weeks before eighth grade graduation and summer vacation.

In the cafeteria, Sierra had just started eating her sandwich, waiting for Allison, when her friend arrived, obviously excited about something.

"Has Luke said anything to you?" Allison plopped her backpack onto the table and sat across from Sierra, leaning over.

Sierra shook her head, her mouth too full to speak.

"I think he's going to ask you to the eighth grade ball," Allison whispered conspiratorially.

The eighth grade ball was the only evening event that the school sponsored; right after the graduation ceremony. It was currently the hottest topic at school. Although not required, no one ever went without a date, and it seemed the only gossip lately concerned who was going with whom and what everyone was going to wear.

Sierra almost choked. "What?" She gasped when she finally managed to swallow down the food in her mouth.

"He asked me in the hallway this morning if you were going."

"Allison, that hardly means he's going to ask me."

"Oh yeah?"

Sierra felt a little angry with Allison for teasing her. "Luke is a very nice boy who is decent enough to be friendly with me, even though I'm sort of an outcast at this school. I think he probably feels sorry for me."

"Little Sierra," Allison sighed. "You really don't know how attractive you are, do you?"

"Allison!" Sierra answered, annoyed.

"Luke is the only boy bright enough to notice. But if you were to take your hair out of those little girl braids and wear even just a little make-up, all the boys would notice your big brown doe-eyes and your very pretty face."

Sierra stared at her friend, dumfounded. Was Allison making fun of her?

Allison laughed at her expression. "You should see the look on your face." But then she said in a serious tone, "I'm just telling you the truth."

"Allison, please," Sierra said in exasperation.

"Whatever," Allison sighed. "I'm going, you know."

"What?" No, Sierra did not know and this was quite a surprise. Allison was more mature than Sierra and she noticed boys in a very different way. But she had never expressed interest in any of the boys at school.

"Yeah, Chris Wong asked me last night."

"Oh my God," was all Sierra could think to say, responding with a typical teenage girl phrase. Chris was a slight-built boy, probably two inches shorter than Allison, and wore black-rimmed glasses that he was always adjusting on his nose.

But he was one of the smartest kids in school. "You've never said anything about liking him."

"Actually, he took me completely by surprise. But I like him well enough. He's got an admirable brain."

Sierra laughed. Of course Allison would only date intellectual types.

"Anyway," Allison continued. "If Luke asks you, maybe we can all go together."

Sierra wished Allison had never said anything, because after that, she could feel herself blush whenever she saw Luke, and then she avoided him. She didn't want him to ask her to the ball. The idea of going with a boy – well, it would be a date, and that terrified her. *I'm not ready to start dating.*

But Luke never did say anything to Sierra about the dance; not even to ask if she was going.

Graduation came and Pam took her daughter out to a popular Italian restaurant to celebrate after the ceremony; while most of the other graduates went to the eighth grade banquet with their dates, and then to the ball.

"I'm so proud of you," Pam said again for about the hundredth time.

"Thanks, Mom, I know." Sierra felt overly stuffed after eating every bite of her linguini with Alfredo sauce, tons of fresh bread, and a Caesar salad.

"Um, I'll be right back." Pam dabbed her mouth with her napkin and left the table." A few minutes later she returned with two large packages which she presented to Sierra. "Your graduation present."

"Mom, thanks!" Sierra's eye lit up with anticipation. "Should I open them here?"

"Yes, why not?" Pam encouraged, beaming.

Sierra tore off the wrapping paper of the largest package and her heart jumped as she recognized on the box the name of a company that made riding apparel. She lifted the lid and beheld a beautiful pair of black leather boots. "Ohh," Sierra cried out. "They are so beautiful!" She jumped up and hugged her mother in the tightest hug she could muster. She knew the boots were an expense they really couldn't afford.

"You've earned them," Pam squeezed back. "I got them at the tack store downtown, so if they don't fit we can exchange them. Now, open the other one."

Grinning, Sierra returned to her seat and opened the second gift. Inside was a tailored black hunt coat. She looked up at her mom, her eyes already glistening with tears of joy.

"I found a pattern and made it. I hope it's what you want."

"It's perfect!"

20 SUMMER

In everyday life man uses his hands a great deal, but in fact they are not very useful for controlling the horse. On horseback the rider must overcome his natural desire to use the hands for everything. – Michael J. Stevens, *A Classical Riding Notebook.*

The first afternoon after graduation, Tess approached Sierra while she was tacking up Tequila, her assigned ride that day.

"Sierra, I have an offer for you."

"Yes?" Sierra turned in surprise.

"If you can commit to helping with morning chores everyday during your summer vacation, rather than just weekends, and help River get horses ready for training rides in the mornings and lessons in the afternoons, Pegasus can sponsor you for two events this season. Plus we can pay the required membership fees for the USCTA and USEA. How does that sound to you?"

"Great!" Sierra replied. "I would love to do that."

"Good, I would like you on the Pegasus team. You need one qualifying ride to participate in the Pacific Regional

Championship this fall. If you can qualify in one of your events, we can also sponsor you in the championship." With her usual abruptness, Tess walked away.

"Yes!" Sierra exclaimed out loud. She finished putting on the bridle and led Tequila outside.

"Sierra, are you going on the trail?" River called to her from the outdoor arena where he was schooling Crystal's new horse.

"Yeah," she answered.

"I'll come with you." He dismounted and led Galaxy out of the arena and came up to where Sierra waited for him.

"How's he going for you?" she asked as they walked the horses to the field's mounting block.

"He's very lazy," River replied. "I think he was started too young, over-trained, and pushed too hard, and now he's bored with arena work. If Tess would listen to me they would take him out of the arena and just trail ride him for a few months; see if that wouldn't spark him up a bit. He's not a bad horse, but he has no enthusiasm."

Sierra loved to hear River talk about the horses; always amused at how verbal he could be when it was his favorite subject. They mounted up and started toward the trail.

"Did Tess tell you that Pegasus is going to sponsor me in two events?" she asked.

"Yeah, I'm glad." He sounded sincere and even smiled at her.

"Did you say something to Tess?"

"No, you've earned this on your own; winning your very first time out!" He grinned again.

"Thanks; Fala was wonderful." Sierra had longed to tell River all about that day; how his advice had helped her in the dressage test, and how sweet Fala had behaved for her. But Magic's tragedy prevented her from wanting to bring up any reminders of that day.

Since the day they had sat together with Storm, they had not talked about Magic. Their routine had resumed the usual pattern of working and riding together as if nothing had happened. But Sierra knew River mourned for Magic and smoldered with hatred for Tess and Crystal. She had no idea how she could help him.

It was a perfect day for trail riding with the sun shining but enough breeze to keep things cool. Sierra rode ahead on Tequila who had far more energy than Galaxy. They walked and trotted and walked again.

"I'm supposed to gallop the last stretch," Sierra called over her shoulder to River.

"Good," he answered, "go ahead whenever you're ready."

Tequila could be heavy in the hands at times, so Sierra shortened the reins and took a tighter hold as she signaled him to canter. He seemed eager and started out at a steady pace, but he wanted to speed up every few strides. Soon Sierra felt as if she was in a tugging match with him to keep him at the pace she wanted. He didn't scare her like Moose, but she still felt frustrated at her inability to maintain control. They rounded the last bend and she pulled him hard, actually causing him to throw his head up as he came back to a walk. They stepped off the trail onto the field and River came up alongside her.

"You're riding too much with your hands," he stated casually.

It was the last thing Sierra wanted to hear after fighting with Tequila and feeling as if her shoulders might be pulled from their sockets. "He's willful," she snapped back in frustration. She had been doing everything Tess was trying to teach her to take control; shorter reins and quick hard jerks in succession. But with Tequila on the trail, it all seemed to no avail.

River looked at her with eyes suddenly opened wide. Sierra had never snapped at him before or questioned his advice. Then he shrugged and said, "You're starting to ride like Tess."

That felt like a kick in the stomach because from River, it was not a compliment. Sierra brought Tequila to a complete halt, more abruptly than she wanted. River halted next to her. "Just what am I doing wrong?" She asked with irritation still thick in her tone.

River said softly, "You don't need reins to stop your horse."

"Yeah, right," she retorted back.

River narrowed his eyes and started to say something, then seemed to change his mind. "Watch." He dropped his own reins so that they lay loose across Galaxy's withers and moved him forward a few steps and halted. He turned Galaxy to the right a few steps and halted, then back towards her and halted again. He never touched the reins.

Sierra's frustration turned to shame and despair. *How does he do that?* "Galaxy is a much better trained horse," she said defensively.

In answer, River dismounted. "Get off," he ordered.

For a moment Sierra considered kicking Tequila into a trot and fleeing. But she swallowed down her feelings of resentment and humiliation and jumped off.

River handed her Galaxy's reins, and then agilely swung himself up onto Tequila's back. He dropped the reins around the horse's withers again, and moved Tequila forward a few steps, halted, turned him a few steps, halted, and then back towards Sierra and halted again; exactly as he had on Galaxy. He swung out of the saddle and handed Sierra the reins, taking back those of Galaxy.

"River," she began humbly as they walked the horses back to the stable. "I don't think I will ever ride as well as you."

"Yes you will. You used to be able to stop a horse without reins. Don't you remember how you were changing gaits and halting on the lunge line before you ever started using reins?"

Sierra did remember, although the wonderful harmony of those lessons had receded from her present reality to a lost, but cherished past. "I always thought you were the one in control," she said.

"No, most of the time I wasn't doing anything."

They walked in silence but Sierra's mind was bombarded with thoughts; comparing how riding used to feel under River's coaching and how it felt now with Tess.

"River, there's no way I could have slowed Tequila on the trail without using the reins. He had his own ideas about how fast he wanted to go."

"I'm not saying go galloping out on the trail without reins. I just wanted to remind you how little you need reins for control. The reins are a way of asking your horse to listen to you. Reins help you collect a horse. And galloping on the trail, yeah, I certainly use reins but I slow first by sitting deep and using my stomach muscles."

Sierra nodded and then blurted out, "Why won't you give me lessons anymore?"

"I thought you wanted to take lessons from Tess."

"Yes, before I knew anything. I loved my lessons from you and I almost hate my lessons with Tess," she confessed.

"I don't think Tess wants me to teach you again," he replied thoughtfully.

"What am I going to do?"

"I can't tell you what to do," was his most unsatisfactory answer.

Two weeks later, Sierra rode Fala in her second horse trial, at junior beginner novice at a rated show. Crystal rode Galaxy and along with Gloria and Katrina, competed at junior novice level. Ann McGoverney competed at the next highest level, junior training.

It was a much more pleasant experience than Sierra's first event; no rain and no tragic accidents. She started out tense and nervous, but once in the warm-up ring and focusing on Fala, she was able to tune out the background and calm her nerves and muscles. She and Fala were in fourth place after their dressage test, and then finished with clean rounds in cross country and stadium. The second and third place riders after dressage each had one refusal cross country and time penalties. At the end of the trial, Sierra finished in second place, and had earned her qualifying ride to compete in the regional championship.

Crystal had been in second place after dressage and went clean cross country, but with time penalties, and Galaxy took a rail down in stadium jumping which knocked her into third place. Gloria finished in fourth and Katrina in sixth place.

"Why were we only second in dressage?" Crystal demanded of Tess. "We didn't make any mistakes."

"No, it was a good test," Tess replied. "But he's lazy. He needs to move with more energy. The horse that scored higher moved with more impulsion than Galaxy and the judge liked that. We'll work on perking him up. I have a method I'm going to try to get him to pick up his feet when he jumps too."

"Something better perk him up," Crystal threatened.

Sierra remembered what River had said about giving the horse a few months of just trail riding. But she doubted if that was in Tess's plans. Crystal wanted to compete with him now, and she wanted to win. Sierra felt uncomfortable about Galaxy's future.

21 RAPPING

All rapping (poling) is forbidden in Eventing Competitions, and shall be penalized by disqualification. EV111: Abuse of Horses, United States Equestrian Federation Rules for Eventing, 2010

At the end of each lesson with Tess, Sierra tried to muster the courage and explain she would like to quit and take lessons from River again. But Tess always seemed impatient and sometimes disgusted with her, and Sierra never felt like it was the right moment.

After the trail ride when River demonstrated riding without reins, Sierra decided to read again some books written by masters of classical dressage, and she checked out several from the local library. In every book, the authors stressed the importance of relaxation of the horse as necessary for correct performance. Several authors talked about the use of the body, referring to the abdominal or core muscles as the center of a rider's control. Everything she read confirmed that River rode in a classical style. *He is not a backyard rider, he is a classical rider!*

At her next lesson on the flat, Sierra asked, "I've been reading some books on dressage. They talk about how to use your abdominal muscles and weight and I wondered if you were going to teach that to me."

Tess answered in her usual tone of exasperation. "I may not use those terms but every time I tell you to sit deep I'm telling you to use your weight. Classical dressage is the basis of what I'm teaching but you need to realize in competition today that there has to be some deviations from what is considered pure classical. Using your weight becomes more important when you collect for the upper levels. You've heard of the training pyramid, haven't you?"

"Yes," Sierra answered. "It starts with rhythm, then relaxation, connection, impulsion, straightness, and then collection."

Tess gave her a look of disgust that she had actually memorized the pyramid. "Right; and you have to get your horse round and on the bit in order to keep in rhythm. When they accept the bit then they will relax."

That was not actually how Sierra understood what she had been reading, but she didn't ask any more questions.

A week later for her Thursday jumping lesson, Tess told Sierra to saddle Galaxy. Sierra had ridden Galaxy on the trails a few times and felt very comfortable on him. In fact, she agreed with both Tess and River's assessment; he was very lazy.

Sierra had warmed up in the outdoor arena, trotting and cantering big circles and figure eights and was ready when Tess arrived. She looked forward to what it must feel like to jump on the big horse.

"We're going to try to get him to pick up his feet today," Tess announced. "He takes too many rails down when he jumps...lazy." She directed Sierra down a line of cavalletti poles at a trot, which forced Galaxy to use more impulsion, even though he still knocked against the rails a few times. Then Tess set up a line of six low jumps with only a stride in between. The first time through, the heights were all set the same at two feet, and Galaxy easily cleared them all. Then Tess began raising the last bar two inches at a time. One of Tess's adult students joined her where she stood near the last jump of the line.

Galaxy cleared the line with the last bar at two feet, then two feet, two, and two feet, four. At two feet, six, he pulled the rail down as he dragged his hind legs over.

"Again," Tess called out. The adult student and Tess each stood on one side of the jump standard at the end of the line.

Sierra cantered around the arena and up in two-point, steered Galaxy back to the line of jumps. He slowed at the approach as if to say, "What, again? I'm bored."

"Use the crop," Tess instructed.

Sierra slapped his hindquarters with the jumping bat and Galaxy reluctantly picked up the pace and started down the line of jumps. Sierra sensed he was going to pull the rail again as he lazily launched himself to jump the last of the line. He had no energy. Suddenly Sierra heard a loud crack and from the corner of her eye, saw that Tess and her student each held opposite ends of a long bamboo pole. They had lifted the pole to smack against Galaxy's hind legs as he jumped.

Galaxy's head came up in shocked surprise and he leapt forward, snorting and rushed off in a full gallop.

"Take advantage; push him on and bring him around again," Tess ordered.

Sierra was stunned. *What just happened? They hit him with that pole! Were those nails in it?* She rode almost passively, letting Galaxy gallop around the perimeter of the arena, trying to make sense of what Tess had done.

"Bring him through again," Tess yelled, noticing her hesitation.

Sierra steered Galaxy back toward the line. He approached it now with his ears pricked forward and blowing. He seemed confused and frightened, but he started down the line, clearing the jumps. Over the last obstacle, Tess and the student brought the pole up again, hitting his hind legs.

"Again," Tess ordered.

Feeling numb with shock, Sierra let Galaxy gallop around and again took him down the line. He jumped every jump high and wide with a foot to spare.

"Great! Do you feel that?" Tess was grinning. "He'll remember to pick up his feet now."

"Very effective," the adult student exclaimed.

The lesson over, Sierra led Galaxy back to the crossties. Her entire body felt shaky and her nerves raw. Galaxy, usually the most placid horse, held his head high with his eyes rolling, still in a state of terror. Sierra removed his tack and inspected his belly and legs and her stomach flipped when she found two trickles of blood congealed on the inside of one hind leg. *This is abuse and I was part of it.* A wave of nausea roiled her stomach and she felt dizzy. She leaned against Galaxy's shoulder, stroking his neck and telling him over and over, "I'm sorry."

Sierra led him to the wash stall, relieved that he at least didn't show any signs of lameness. She rinsed off the sweat and carefully washed his leg. The wound was barely a scratch; nevertheless, it had drawn blood! She used a sweat scraper to remove excess water from his coat and then walked him up and down the lane to dry. When she finally turned him out into his paddock, he seemed his old self and readily accepted the carrot pieces she offered him. He had forgiven her.

"Never again," she promised him with a final pat, and then walked slowly back to the stable to put his tack away. She stood in the middle of the tack room and looked around at the rows of saddles on racks, the bridles on hooks, and breathed in the rich smell of leather and saddle soap.

She needed to talk to Tess, but she was afraid to confront her. To disagree with Tess she feared would end her place at Pegasus. But Sierra was determined not to be a part of what had happened in her lesson today; never again. She began cleaning Galaxy's bridle while she formulated words to say to Tess in her mind.

Sierra heard the clop of horse hooves into the crossties, and then out again, and knew River had returned from his trail ride, untacked, and had led his horse back out. Not long after, the tack room door opened and River came in carrying a saddle and bridle.

"Hi," he greeted. He set the saddle on the cleaning stand and hung the bridle on the cleaning hook suspended from the ceiling. When Sierra didn't answer he looked over his shoulder where she had stepped away from hanging up a bridle, and now stood still as stone, hugging herself. "Sierra?"

She couldn't answer. She shook her head and then tears began to flow and she burst into sobs. "Ri...iv...er, I can't..."

River's eyes flew open wide and then narrowed. In three long strides he reached Sierra and took her into his arms. She buried her face against his chest, and they sat on the cold, cement floor where he held her in his lap as she sobbed uncontrollably.

Eventually she was able to gulp out what had happened.

"Oh," he sighed in understanding. "Rapping."

"What's that?"

"Using a pole to hit the horse as he jumps. It teaches him to jump big and tuck his legs. Sometimes it's called poling."

"It's horrible and cruel. It freaked Galaxy out and she made him bleed."

"Yeah, I think she uses a pole with nails in it. And she didn't tell you what she was going to do?"

"No, it freaked me out as much as Galaxy. But she had me go around and she hit him again. And…and…I did it. I let her hit him again." More sobs followed.

"No, you didn't. Sierra, you are in no way responsible for what she did."

She could feel River's muscles tighten. She looked up into his frowning face and his eyes were smoldering with anger.

"I'm going to lose this job. I'm going to tell her I can't take lessons from her and she'll probably fire me." Sierra choked back more sobs. *Enough crying!* "I don't want to leave the horses."

"Yeah, she's spiteful enough to let you go. But she'll regret it. You work harder than any girl she's hired before."

"What can I do?" Sierra wailed, though she didn't think River would have any more of a solution than she did.

"I'll go with you to talk to Tess."

Oh yes! Sierra's first reaction was of relief, but moments later she knew it wouldn't help. "No, she always accuses me of complaining to you."

"What?" He seemed surprised and she told him about the two times Tess had accused her of complaining to River rather than going to her first.

He shook his head in disgust. "You're too sweet for this place. Maybe you can work at another stable."

"I don't know of any other place, especially one close enough that I can ride my bicycle to. Besides, I would miss you."

His face softened and he smiled. "Thanks." He pushed a damp stray lock of hair off her wet cheek. "I would miss you too."

He could be so sweet! That wrenched at her heart even more when she thought about not seeing him, or working and riding alongside him every day.

"Maybe she won't fire you. She's smart enough to know what a good deal you are for her. In fact, maybe you should tell her you don't want lessons and ask for pay." He laughed sardonically.

"Do you get paid?" Sierra actually didn't know.

"She pays me half wages because my father keeps a horse or two here during the winter and breeding season. I mostly work here because my father makes me."

"River, that has got to be against some kind of child labor law."

"Who knows? It doesn't matter. He leaves me alone as long as I'm working." He shifted his body and Sierra moved off his lap so they could both stand up.

"Thanks, River…for being my friend."

He nodded, frowning.

Sierra went into the restroom and washed her face and smoothed back her braids. Her face was blotchy and her nose red from crying, but she was okay with Tess realizing how upset she was. Taking a few deep breaths she left the restroom. "Here I go," Sierra announced.

"Good luck," he encouraged from where he stood cleaning tack. She was halfway out the door when he asked, "Sierra, will you come back and let me know what happens?"

"Of course," she smiled back and then walked with determined steps to the office where she had seen Tess go after the lesson. All Sierra had to do was recall the image of a very frightened horse and the blood on his leg to stoke her courage as she approached the door. Anger was very effective armor against timidity.

Sierra knocked on the door and stepped inside without waiting for an answer. "Ms. Holmes," she addressed Tess who looked up from her computer, annoyed. She knew Tess hated to be addressed that way. Without waiting for a response, Sierra rushed on. "What you did in my lesson today, the rapping, and without telling me what you were going to do...well, it was horrible. I don't want to take lessons from you anymore."

Tess turned away from her computer to stare at her in disbelief. "What?"

"I don't want to take lessons from you anymore." Then Sierra added with less assurance. "But I would still like to work here."

Tess pushed back from her desk and folded her arms across her chest. Her face puckered into a disdainful expression. "Well, you ungrateful little..," she huffed. "You don't know anything. Rapping is an accepted method to teach a lazy horse. Look it up. You might find it in the same book as the training pyramid," she added sarcastically.

Sierra's anger boiled into rage. "No," she spoke with assurance. "It is in none of the books that talk about the training pyramid." It was just one more thing that bothered her about Tess; that she disapproved of her reading books on horsemanship. Tess should encourage her students to read books.

"Horses need to learn discipline, just like children. Didn't your mother ever spank you when you were being an insubordinate little girl?"

"My mother has never hit me," Sierra answered truthfully.

Tess's eyes narrowed and she spat out the words. "Get off my property! There is no place for you at Pegasus."

Sierra fled.

River waited for her, watching from the main door of the stable. "What happened?" he asked.

"Fired."

River squared his shoulders and started walking toward the office. Sierra grabbed his arm. "No, it's okay." He shrugged her off and kept on walking. Sierra ran after him and grabbed his arm again. "No, River, please. You'll only make things worse."

He paused, taking deep breaths to get his temper under control. "Yeah, probably true," he mumbled and looked at her with an anguished expression. "What are you going to do?"

"Give up riding. I guess I really don't have a choice."

He walked with her to her bicycle. "I may have an idea," he said. "I have to talk to somebody and then I'll let you know."

"Really?" Sierra replied with a glimmer of hope. "I won't be here. How will you tell me?"

"I know where you live," he answered to Sierra's surprise.

"How do you..?"

"A friend of mine lives near you. I've seen you going to your house. It's that little one behind the Robinson place, right?"

"Yes." She swallowed, and then impulsively, hugged him tightly. Then she got on her bicycle and rode home.

A short, compact rider with a tan weathered face and tight black curls smattered with a touch of gray, reached forward to lightly touch the arched neck of his gray gelding as the horse stretched willingly into contact with his bit. "Good, good," his rider whispered, satisfied that his mount was relaxed and warmed up, ready to attempt more advanced movements. With a gentle squeeze of both reins, a drawing in of his center muscles and touching the sides of his mount with the calves of his legs, he asked the gray to step up underneath himself so that the power from his hind end elevated his movements. The gray responded and with powerful steps from his hind legs, moved forward as if floating, into passage. "Ahhh, so good, my little Fiel," the rider sighed with pleasure after maintaining the animated passage for the length of the flat sandlot. "Now, perhaps…" he increased the aids to shorten the gray's stride to piaffe. The gray's ears flicked back and forth and his tail swished in rhythm as he trotted in place. "Ahh," the rider breathed joyfully. Again he touched the gray's neck as he lightened his seat and legs and allowed the gray to stretch his neck forward and shift into an easier working trot.

It was then the rider noted the figure watching from the shadows of the maple trees that shaded the exercise area. *Who is that and why is he sneaking around?* he wondered, annoyed. The gray rounded the corner approaching the maples and the man brought him to a square halt, opposite the skulking figure. "You are trespassing!" he called out; a slight Portuguese accent infiltrated his speech.

River stepped out of the shadows. "Hi, João."

The man squinted, and then breathed out a long sigh. "River?" He blinked hard, and brushed a hand across his eyes. "Too long, it has been too long," he exclaimed as he dismounted. River stepped forward and with head bowed, allowed the man to pull him into a warm embrace. Then he held River by the shoulders and looked intently into his face.

River met his eyes and flushed before ducking his head with a shamefaced expression. "I'm sorry," he mumbled.

"I know, I know you are. How is it you don't know I understand? Why do you stay away?"

"João, I just…" River could not think of an answer. The two walked side by side, João leading the gray gelding to a small stable next to a two-story house shaded within another grove of maple trees.

"Your father came looking for you a few months ago. Did you run away again?"

"Yes," River answered without further explanation.

"Why didn't you come to me?"

"I did," River replied. "But you weren't home and I couldn't wait. I just wanted to say goodbye. Anyway, I wasn't gone for very long."

"How you hurt me when you won't let me help you. River, I promised your mother…"

"I know, I know. It's not your fault I'm such a loser. I'm sure she doesn't blame you."

João made a sound of exasperation. "I can help you with your school work. Why are you so stubborn?"

"No one can help me. Why can't you accept the fact I'm just too dumb?"

João stopped in his tracks and grabbed River by the shoulders again. River ducked his head. "Look at me," João ordered. "Look at me." He grabbed River's chin and made him look up. "You are not dumb. No," he insisted as River tried to look away. "You are not dumb."

"Okay," River agreed and only then did João let go of his face. They resumed walking.

"I have this friend…at the stable where I work," River began.

22 JOÃO MATEUS

Anything forced and misunderstood can never be beautiful. And to quote the words of Simon: If a dancer was forced to dance by whip and spikes, he would be no more beautiful than a horse trained under similar conditions. – Xenophon

A week passed. The cottage that Sierra loved so much became unbearably confining. Her mother had classes through the summer, so Sierra moped around alone, her thoughts inevitably drifting to what might be happening at the stable, and as time dragged on, every time she noticed the clock she couldn't help but despair, thinking, *River and I would be turning the horses out*, or, *I'd be saddling up to trail ride*, or *River and I would be cleaning tack about now*. She had chores at home that took almost no time for she had become very efficient at them in order to spend all day at the stable. She planned and cooked meals, having them ready for Pam when she got home from school. Other than that, Sierra had nothing to do. Allison lived in another part of town that was too far to get to on a bicycle, but they talked on the phone for hours. Allison proved a true friend. She listened to Sierra's story; sympathized and assured her she had made the right decision to confront Tess. Day after day she listened to Sierra whine and complain, but she had no ideas as to what Sierra could do.

In the evenings, Pam hugged and soothed her daughter and told her how proud she was that she had made the right choice. After several days however, as Sierra's mood did not improve, Pam began to chastise her for her persistent moodiness. But it was impossible for Sierra to foster a cheerful attitude when her thoughts constantly drifted to the horses and River, and how much she missed them.

One evening, sitting with her mother over bowls of ice cream with her mind as usual back at the stable, she asked, "Mom, if you knew of someone that might be abused by their father, what would you do?"

"Who, Honey?" Pam looked up with her spoon hovering, her face showing concern.

"Someone I know from school."

"Do you mean sexually abused?"

"No, no, nothing like that."

Pam spooned in a mouthful of ice cream while she thought. "It's tough. The correct answer is probably you should tell me who, and I should call Child Protective Services. That's what they teach us in nursing school."

"What would happen?" Sierra asked.

"They would investigate and make a decision as to whether it was safe for the child to remain at home or if the child should be placed in foster care. It all sounds very ideal, but unfortunately, a child may be taken out of a bad situation and placed into another equally bad situation. Removing someone from their family, even when abused, doesn't always make things better. And just the fact that a report has been made resulting in an investigation can stir up trouble."

"So, I should do nothing?"

"Maybe you should tell me what your suspicions are."

"No..," Sierra said after a few moments of thinking. "I'm not really sure and I don't have any kind of proof."

"Perhaps you could talk to the person and see if that person might appreciate outside help. That might be a good place to start."

Sierra nodded, "Yeah…"

"Are you sure you don't want to tell me more about it?"

"Not yet, but thanks, Mom."

Another week passed and Sierra sank into miserable ennui. She considered going back to Pegasus and humbly apologizing to Tess, to see if she could at least get her stall cleaning job back. Or if not, just be allowed to visit the horses and River. But depression and boredom are not good bases for courage, so she did nothing.

One evening Sierra stood at the kitchen sink cleaning vegetables from their garden to make a salad to go along with her first attempt at making lasagna. Pam was relaxing on the couch with her feet up, still dressed in her scrubs from school. She had opened her textbook to study but had fallen asleep.

Poor Mom. Whenever Sierra thought about how hard her mother studied and worked with never a day off, her own troubles paled. Even during her school breaks Pam picked up extra shifts at the nursing home to supplement her income. Sierra was glad she could help out by at least taking over dinner preparations so her mother could come home and rest. And Sierra was actually enjoying learning to cook.

Someone knocked softly at the front door. *Strange*, Sierra thought. Their cottage being set back from the road prevented salespeople and evangelists from calling. No one ever came to the door except their landlords. And Mrs. Robinson always knocked loudly in a pattern and called out to announce her presence.

"Mom, I'll get it," Sierra called out, not wanting her mother to have to get up until dinner was ready. But Pam had already awakened and answered the door. With a carrot in hand, Sierra peeked around from the kitchen into the living room, curious to see who was there.

River stood in the doorway. "Um, is Sierra here?"

"Yes, she's here," Pam greeted with a warm smile.

"River!" Sierra cried out happily. "Mom, this is my friend from the stable."

"I'm so glad to meet you, River. I've heard so much about you. Won't you come in?"

"Um," he looked down at his feet, struggling with his social skills.

"Come into the kitchen, I'm fixing dinner," Sierra invited.

"I just came by to tell you about my friend." River seemed nervous and self-conscious in front of Pam.

"Cool! Hey, want to stay for dinner? Mom, can he stay for dinner?"

"Of course." Pam stood with the door wide open and gestured for River to step inside.

"No, I...um,"

"Why don't you stay," Pam encouraged. "If it's all right with your parents."

"Yeah, if you're brave enough," Sierra added. "I made lasagna for the first time. I wouldn't mind a guinea pig besides us."

"Um, well..." He thought for a moment. "Okay."

"Come with me." Sierra had come over to the doorway beside her mother, and she now gave a little tug at River's wrist to get him going. She led the way into the kitchen, and he followed, glancing around. "Dinner's almost ready; I'm just finishing the salad." Sierra pulled out a chair from the kitchen table as she walked back to the sink with the carrot. River took the hint and sat down.

"Your mom's a nurse?" he asked.

"Not yet. Well, she's a nurse's aide right now, but she's going to college to be a nurse."

He nodded thoughtfully. "I like nurses."

The oven's buzzer sounded. "Lasagna's done," Sierra announced as she grabbed pot holders and carefully removed the casserole.

"It smells good."

"It does, doesn't it?" Sierra agreed and then asked over her shoulder, "how come you like nurses?"

Soft purring filled the silence and Sierra glanced back again to note Socrates had transferred himself from the seat of one of the other chairs into River's lap. River seemed intent on stroking the cat's soft fur, but finally explained, "When my mother was killed they took her to the hospital and me too. Nobody knew what to do with me. Then this one nurse took me to the cafeteria and made me eat some food. She sat with me and talked to me a little. I don't know what she did to make it happen but she took me home with her. She and her roommate were both nurses. Between the two of them, they arranged their shifts so someone would be there to look after me. I lived with them for two months before the social worker people located my father."

"How old were you when that happened?" Sierra asked.

"Eight."

"You miss your mom, don't you."

"Sometimes." He coughed. "What I came to tell you is I talked to my friend with a horse. He wants to meet you and see if you'd like to ride."

"Really?" Sierra carried the salad bowl to the table, her face lit up at his news.

River looked at her and smiled. "Really."

"Ohhh!" Sierra cried out in glee. "River, thank you, thank you."

"You're happy about something." Pam stood in the doorway, smiling. She had changed from scrubs into jeans and tee-shirt. Sierra told her the news.

"That sounds encouraging."

Sierra set an extra plate and brought the lasagna to the table and they all sat down. In motherly fashion, Pam began the interrogation. "Who is this man and where does he live?"

Throughout dinner, River answered Pam's questions.

João Mateus, originally from Portugal, was a retired jockey, an old friend of River's mother. He also knew River's father, having ridden a few race horses that his father had trained. When he was ready to retire from racing, he found some affordable acreage for lease in this area and moved in, bringing his one horse. River thought he now did some kind of accounting work from his home.

"I can take you there tonight if you want to meet him," River offered.

"Please, Mom."

"I think that is a good idea. I would like to meet him. More lasagna, River?" He had already eaten two platefuls.

"Um, okay. It's really good," he complimented Sierra.

"Thanks."

They finished dinner and River helped Sierra clear the table and put the dishes in the sink to soak. "I'll wash them later," she said, anxious to meet his friend, or in truth, anxious to meet his horse.

Outside, they found Storm sitting under the maple tree, her tail thumping as they emerged from the house. Pam graciously consented to let her ride in the car with them, and Storm jumped into the back seat next to River, who gave Pam directions to a place not far down the road from the cottage; easy bicycling distance.

They pulled into a gravel driveway that paralleled a mesh-fenced pasture and led up to the house and small barn. Several large trees shaded the yard and pasture, and what looked like a riding arena that was just visible behind the barn. Pam parked the car and as they were getting out, a man and Border Collie emerged from the barn.

Storm bounded forward and she and the Border Collie touched noses, their tails wagging. Then they romped off together, obviously not strangers to each other.

The man approached, his face crinkling into a welcoming grin; his twinkling eyes surprisingly blue. "River has told me about this young lady," he welcomed Pam and Sierra graciously.

"This is Sierra," River stated, the best he could manage for introductions.

"I am João Mateus," he introduced himself and offered his hand to Pam. "Please, you call me João."

"Nice to meet you; I'm Pam Landsing and this is my daughter Sierra." Pam accepted the proffered hand with a smile.

João turned to Sierra and offered his hand. Sierra accepted, her small hand clasped within a warm, firm grip. "It is a pleasure. So, you are the young equestrienne that River has told me about."

Sierra liked him already. She liked his warm face and direct manners. She smiled back and replied, "Yes sir, or at least I want to be an equestrienne."

"Ah, a respectful young person; you should learn from her." João clapped River on the shoulder and laughed at River's scowl. "Well then, shall we go meet Fiel?"

"Yes, please," Sierra answered enthusiastically.

"I have just brought him in for the night and he is having his supper, but we will introduce you." He led them into the little barn.

The smell of horse and hay and the sound of horse teeth munching, welcomed them into the barn's interior. In a roomy box stall, a dappled gray horse with a dark gray mane and tail stood contentedly over a mound of hay. He looked up and whickered softly as they approached. He had a large head with a Roman nose and soft, kind, intelligent brown eyes with long white eyelashes. The sights, smells, and sounds all washed over Sierra, filling her soul; the equal of food offered to a starving man.

"This is my little Fiel," João introduced the horse with obvious pride. Fiel stuck his head over the boards of his stall and João affectionately rubbed his nose.

Sierra stepped up to peer into the lovely equine face. "Hello, Fiel," she greeted in a soft voice, and reached her hand slowly forward to stroke his neck. Fiel stood a few moments but when he realized no one was going to offer him a treat, he stepped back to his hay.

"What kind of horse is he?" Sierra asked.

"He is Lusitano. His dam was imported from Portugal but he was bred here in America. He's twelve now."

"He's beautiful."

João laughed. Well, maybe not so beautiful standing in his stall, but when he is in motion, ahh..." He made a gesture to indicate something fine.

"Sierra thinks all horses are beautiful," River smirked and she made a face at him.

"Well, Miss Sierra, I tend to agree with you." João laughed. "Why don't we sit down and discuss what you wish to learn. Shall we leave Fiel to enjoy his supper, and we will go up to the house for a little refreshment?" They traipsed behind him up to a front porch the length of the house, where a table and chairs waited.

"River, you help me serve the ladies." João pulled out chairs for Pam and Sierra and then he and River went inside to return a few minutes later. River carried a pitcher of ice tea and João had a tray with glasses and a decanter of a dark red liquid.

"Perhaps Pam, you would like to sip on genuine Portuguese aged port?" João held up the decanter. "Or if you prefer, iced tea?"

"Port would be lovely," Pam accepted to Sierra's surprise. Her mother hardly ever drank alcohol. João poured a small glass for Pam and himself, and River and Sierra had glasses of iced tea. Then João asked Sierra about her riding experiences. He seemed especially interested when she tried to explain her confusion at some of the methods she had learned from Tess; how she found them to be very different from how River had tried to teach her and from her understanding of the books she had read. Sometimes his brow creased into a deep frown, especially when she repeated the incident of the rapping used on Galaxy.

At the end of her account, João said, "I feed at six in the morning and then I leave him alone to enjoy his breakfast. About eight, I tidy up in the barn and then we ride. After that he goes in the pasture to be lazy the rest of the day until I bring him in at night. You may come tomorrow, perhaps between eight and eight-thirty, and we will see how you ride. Does that sound acceptable to you?"

"Yes, it sounds wonderful!" Sierra exclaimed. "Is it okay, Mom?"

"João, I think you are very generous. Can Sierra help you out with chores?" Pam offered.

"Thank you. River has told me what a hard working young lady she is. I will accept some help with the chores, but I prefer to clean the stall and care for my own horse. It helps me stay in shape as well as informs me how things are with Fiel."

"I'll do anything you want me to," Sierra offered ambitiously. "But how does cleaning the stall tell you about Fiel?"

"A good question," João settled back in his chair, a man who liked to talk. He reached for a pack of cigarettes and a lighter on a small stand behind him and lit one as he talked. "Please excuse my bad habit," he apologized, especially to Pam. "Such a bad addiction." He shook his head, admonishing himself.

"Now I will explain. When I clean his stall morning after morning, I know how many piles of manure he has produced during the night. I note the consistency. This is important because a horse's digestive system is quite primitive on the evolutionary scale. If there are only a few piles, well, I worry. Maybe he is developing a blockage in the intestine, and I watch him very closely. I can give him something to help if I suspect he might be getting colic.

"Then when I bring him from the stall to the cross ties, I see how he walks first thing in the morning. Does he have stiffness in his joints; soreness anywhere? When I brush him, I notice scratches, bumps, swellings, anything unusual. Since I groom him every day, I know what has always been there and what is new. Plus, I know what kind of mood he is in as he stands in the crossties. Is he lazy today or irritable? Perhaps I worked him too hard yesterday. Is he alert and fresh-acting? Thus I will plan the riding session."

"Wow," Sierra listened, fascinated.

"That's incredible," Pam commented. "I see why you think the chores are important."

"A true horseman is involved in all facets of his animal's life. There is more to horsemanship than riding."

Sierra nodded in agreement.

"This is one reason I am pleased to work with you, Miss Sierra. River has told me how you worked at the stable for many weeks to clean stalls, groom horses; all these kinds of chores and you were not even given lessons to compensate. I think you have the heart and spirit of a true horsewoman."

Sierra flushed at his praise and actually felt tears forming which she fortunately was able to hold back.

They talked awhile longer with João now asking Pam questions about her schooling as they sipped on port and tea. River, as usual, didn't say much of anything, but he seemed relaxed in the company. Storm and Charlie, the Border Collie, had finished cavorting and they had joined the group on the porch to lie panting at their feet.

"João, I want to thank you again for your generosity toward Sierra. She hasn't been in the best of spirits since losing her job at the stable," Pam said as she set down her empty glass. "Well, I have school in the morning and more homework to do, so regretfully we must say goodnight."

João walked them to the car, shook hands again with Pam and Sierra, and they returned home. Sierra turned to River in the back seat to exclaim, "River, he is wonderful. Thanks so much."

"S'okay," he answered, looking out the window.

23 NEW LESSONS

It is my firm conviction that that is the most effective and practical method of riding which is based on the sensitive persuasion of the horse, i.e. on the attainment of its mental cooperation, and which, without the use of force, balances the animal during the performance of its physical activities.
– Lieutenant Colonel A. L. d'Endrödy

Several minutes before eight in the morning Sierra pedaled into the driveway of the small farm and parked her bicycle at the side of the barn. The morning sunlight gleamed off bits of metal here and there in the yard and dappled the ground beneath the trees. Happiness flowed throughout her; it felt so good to be back in a world that centered around a horse. Even so, she harbored a bit of nervousness as to what to expect today with João Mateus.

The door of the house opened and João, puffing on the end of a cigarette and carrying a coffee mug, stepped out. An exuberant Charlie preceded him, bounding up to Sierra with his tail wagging and greeted her with a lick on the hand.

"Miss Sierra," João greeted cheerfully. "It is so very fine to see you."

"Good morning, Mr. Mateus," she answered back. Her own smile outshone his in brightness.

"Let us go see if Fiel is finished with his breakfast. And please, call me João."

"Okay...João. And you don't need to address me as miss either."

"A good bargain," he chuckled in agreement.

And so the day began. Sierra followed João around as he explained and demonstrated how he liked the chores done. Together they cleaned the stall, scrubbed water buckets, and tidied the inside of the barn. Then João led Fiel into the crossties.

"He is in a good mood today; I think eager for work. This is good," João commented as they worked together grooming and saddling Fiel, who stood patiently but alert. "So, I will ride first. You will watch. One can learn much by observation."

Sierra agreed to everything. She already felt as if she had learned an entire book's worth as João explained the parts of the horse as they groomed; especially which muscles and joints were important for executing the different gaits and movements.

João led Fiel to the sandy area behind the barn. A full-sized dressage arena of twenty-by-sixty meters had been set up with a border of low rails. White-painted plywood boxes with black dressage letters had been placed within the rails at the specified distances of an official dressage ring: A at the center of the entry to the short side, then K, V, E, S, H, along one long side; C at the center of the top of the arena; then M, R, B, P, and F, along the other long side. Shade trees grew along one edge of the area providing shade, and a hedgerow at right angles provided another border. Flowers bloomed in planter boxes at each of the four corners of the dressage ring.

What an attractive place to ride. Sierra found it very pleasing to behold.

João mounted and walked Fiel on a long rein a few times in both directions of the ring. Fiel stretched his nose almost to the ground, snorting frequently, and his ears flopped lazily to the sides. Then João gathered the reins and Sierra observed an incredible transformation. Fiel's head came up into a regal arch; his muscles bunched and rippled as he stepped up into a collected walk; the expression in his eye was one of serious concentration; and he pricked his ears forward or flicked them back and forth, listening to his rider. João sat as if an appendage growing gracefully out of his horse's back, his body moving harmoniously with Fiel. Sierra never detected any movement in his hands or legs; always held steady and still. Invisible to her, João signaled Fiel to move forward into an energetic working trot. The relaxed, almost lazy-appearing horse that had entered the ring was transformed into a powerful, gracefully elegant, and magnificent being. She watched in awe.

"This is good," João spoke. "We start with good energy. Now we will collect." Invisibly, João communicated to Fiel and the forward moving trot changed to powerful, upward thrusting movements from his back and hocks. The lovely gray moved around the ring in circles and figure eights, transitioning from a collected trot to medium trot. Sierra sucked in her breath in appreciation as he crossed the diagonal at extended trot, his hocks pushing up underneath his body as he reached forward with outstretched front legs. Then he performed a shoulder-in down one side of the ring, and haunches-in along the other. Turning the corner, he moved across the diagonal in half-pass, his legs crossing underneath his body as he moved in a lateral direction. Then all the movements were repeated in the opposite direction.

From invisible aids, Fiel transitioned to a collected canter, executing flying lead changes as his rider guided him through a serpentine pattern. Then he transitioned from collected to medium and back to collected canter in both directions around the perimeter of the ring.

The session ended with Fiel, obedient to his rider's invisible aids, transitioning down to a collected trot, then into passage (a very collected and elevated trot where he appeared to float above the ground), and finishing with a few steps of piaffe (a collected and elevated trot in place). The trot work was repeated in the opposite direction. The beautiful animal's expression radiated joy and pride, his breath came in rhythm with his gaits, and his tail waved as if a victorious banner. João brought him down to a square halt, and with words of praise and pats on the neck, gave him the reins, allowing Fiel to stretch his nose forward and down as he walked off from the halt.

"Very nice, good energy; a happy horse today." João beamed with pride and pleasure as he walked Fiel over to the mounting block and dismounted. "Now, you will try."

Sierra approached, shaking inside in nervous intimidation. *How can I possibly ride such a talented, well-trained horse?* João helped her mount and adjust the stirrup length.

"Begin at the walk, loose rein; everybody relaxed," he said in a soothing tone, aware of Sierra's nervousness. "I will observe your position."

It felt so good to be back in a saddle. Sierra didn't sense any tenseness or the likelihood of a spook as she sat astride Fiel's broad back; his calmness helping to quell her inner trembling. She pressed her legs to his side and he immediately stepped up into a trot; not what she expected!

"No, no," João spoke calmly as he jogged alongside and gently touched the inside bridle rein to bring Fiel back to a walk. "You see, too much leg just now." He spoke just as patiently and calmly to Sierra as he had to Fiel. "Almost for walk you need only touch the reins to say 'listen' and then touch with the leg. No pressure; just a whisper of a touch. Let us try again." João stopped and Fiel obediently halted. "Try again…softly."

Sierra squeezed the reins between her fingers and noted the flicker of Fiel's ears. Her legs hung down next to the saddle girth and she moved them just to touch Fiel's sides. He stepped forward into the walk.

"Good, good," João praised. "You see, use very little. One goal is always to use as little aid as possible." He continued to coach Sierra as she halted Fiel, then moved him forward into a few steps of walk, then halt, and repeated over and over; all the time walking at their side and correcting just a fraction of her leg position or placing his hands over hers to caution, "Too much with the hands; quiet the hands."

"Now, a little trot."

Her inner trembling returned at the thought of an increase in gait, but she pulled in her stomach muscles, squeezed the reins and touched with her legs. She felt she had done well when Fiel obediently stepped up into a trot, but after only a few steps, João said, "Uh oh, back to walk." And then Sierra was back on a lunge line with the reins and stirrups taken away. "You are riding too much with the hands. I see you have a good seat and you know how to use your legs, but we need to develop control from here." He indicated his abdominal muscles. *Just what River had been telling her.*

In spite of the regression of returning to the lunge line, Sierra felt it was an excellent lesson. Her spirits soared at her good fortune to have found such a wonderful teacher. *Just like River!*

They walked Fiel back to the barn and removed his tack, and then to a graveled area outside where they rinsed off his sweat with a hose (no fancy wash stall here). Fiel tolerated all with patient good manners. Sierra fed him pieces of carrots and then they turned him out into the pasture to relax for the rest of his day.

"Shall we have a cup of tea?" João invited.

"That would be great," she readily agreed. *So very European.*

Sierra followed João into his tiny but cozy kitchen where he prepared tea as if it were an important ritual; setting a kettle of water on a burner, rinsing a ceramic teapot with hot water, suspending loose tea in a tea ball into the pot, and then pouring in water after it had just come to a boil. He set the pot, two cups and saucers, and a plate of tempting pastries on a tray, and they carried it to the table on the front porch. The morning had heated up, and Sierra was sweaty and grimy after riding, but it was pleasant in the shade of the porch where a breeze wafted through from time to time. Charlie emerged from his important canine activities to join them at their feet. João gave him a dog treat from a box on the stand and then pulled out and lit up a cigarette, apologizing again for his bad habit.

"Fiel is wonderful! Thank you again for letting me ride and teaching me. You don't know how much it means to me." Sierra felt happiness infuse throughout her being as she sipped her cup of tea. It also made her feel very mature.

João chuckled, "Ah, but perhaps I do know." His eyes crinkled as he laughed.

"You ride so beautifully, like River!"

At that he burst into a loud guffaw. "Oh my," he gasped amid his laughter. "Let us say River rides like me."

Sierra blushed, realizing what she had just said. "Oh, yeah; I didn't mean it like that sounded. Did you teach River to ride?"

"Now that one, he almost taught himself to ride." João took a last puff off his cigarette and stubbed it out. "If there is such a thing as a natural born rider, then it is that one; like his mother." He took a sip of tea, smiling at a memory.

"How do you know River?" Sierra asked, full of curiosity and realizing she might find many of her answers about River from João.

"I know that one since a baby. Renee, his mother, she and I were good friends even though we often rode as rivals in a race. But his mother understood the heart of a horse, like me. Sadly, not all at the track do." He pushed the plate of pastries toward Sierra. "Here, please. Young people, they must refuel after a morning of riding."

Sierra selected a scone with a sweet lemony and biscuit flavor. She loved the combination of a bite of scone and then a sip of tea.

"River...I remember him all around the stables; barely walking and we could not keep him off the thoroughbreds. He would climb up the sides of the stalls and somehow crawl onto their backs. Those horses, they all put up with him. I still don't know why they stood still for it." He laughed softly. "Renee lost him once when he was maybe five years old. I remember her with frantic tears running around, 'have you seen River?' (He mimicked a female voice.) And where do you think we found him?"

Sierra shook her head, fascinated.

"Sound asleep curled up next to Wind Lass's belly where she lay down in her stall. She had won the cup just that day." Another swallow of tea and he continued. "Renee sometimes put him up in front of her on a colt after the morning workout. Some people criticized her for that; too dangerous. But who could blame her when you could see such absolute joy on the little boy's face?"

Sierra had seen that look on River's face so she knew what he was talking about.

"A few winters we worked at the same farm off-season. His mother started him in a saddle, but I taught him some too."

"Tess Holmes calls him a backyard rider," Sierra told him.

"Hmmph," João responded. "Well, I have seen that woman ride. I have been to some of the events. I do not like to criticize but she rides her mounts with heavy hands and much force. I have only seen her on lovely, well-bred warmbloods, and yes, even with her style of riding, they perform well. But I am not happy to see the look in the eyes of her horses. They are not horses happy in their work."

Sierra almost wanted to burst into tears. All the lessons she had taken from Tess; not only was her horse stressed but herself as well. She should have followed her instincts long ago. "River probably told you I was taking lessons from her."

"Yes, Sierra," he spoke to her with such kindness and understanding. "As a student it is important to respect your teacher and I believe you tried. But for you to confront her after the rapping incident, something you knew in your heart was a wrong thing to do, well, that takes much courage."

"Thank you," Sierra replied, barely above a whisper, and fighting back tears. She sighed deeply and then diverted the conversation. "What do you mean by the 'heart of a horse'?"

"I think you know what I mean, don't you?" He gave her his crinkly-eyed smile.

"Maybe."

"I have lived my life working around horses and I am still humbled by what fine creatures they are. I believe God created horses to be an example for mankind."

Sierra nodded. "I like that," she agreed with him. "I do know what you mean." She thought for a few minutes as she finished the last bite of scone. "I think Tess sees horses as something to conquer and control."

"A good observation," João said. "Sierra, it's not subservience that makes a well-trained horse; it's willingness. And by their very nature, most horses are willing to do what we ask. Our responsibility is to learn how to ask them. That is the purpose of your weight in the saddle, your legs on his sides, and the soft touch of your hand to the bit in his mouth. That is how you communicate what it is you are asking. And if it is not beyond his physical capability and if it does not cause him pain or frighten him, he willingly will do all you ask if he understands what it is you are asking."

Sierra nodded in agreement with his wisdom.

Sierra left the farm in a dream state. She missed all the horses at Pegasus and working with River, but she felt compensated to have found a teacher that she respected; who would teach her in the same manner as River, and in accordance with the philosophy of the riding masters she read about. She thought long and deeply over João's words and determined that she would strive to never become a dominating master of her horse, but his respectful leader and partner.

"Horses are herd animals and by nature, are most content and secure when they have a leader they trust to keep them safe. That is the role of a true horseman," João had explained.

Pam and Sierra were sitting down to dinner with Sierra chattering almost non-stop about her day, when they heard a soft knock at the door.

Pam raised her eyebrows. "Are you expecting River?" she asked.

"No; I'll get it." Sierra went to the front door.

"Hi," River greeted, standing on the doorstep.

"River, I wasn't expecting you," Sierra broke into a grin. "We're just sitting down to dinner and there's plenty of food. Come join us."

"Um, no, sorry, I don't want to bother you. I just wanted to see how things went with João."

"I can't wait to tell you all about it," Sierra's voice and smile gleamed with her eagerness to share her experience.

"Hello, River," Pam called from the kitchen doorway. "Come in and have dinner. I've set a plate for you."

River rubbed his hand over his mouth and relented, "Um, okay."

Two to three times a week, River dropped in for dinner; supposedly to hear about Sierra's lesson on Fiel. He could not help but feel welcomed by Sierra's obvious delight in seeing him and her enthusiasm as she told him all about her time with João and Fiel. Then she plagued him with questions about the horses at Pegasus and always asked him to say hi to Manuel and Rosa.

"Mom, are you okay with River coming over so often?" Sierra asked after the first few evenings.

"Of course, Kitten. He seems like a very nice boy."

"He sure does eat a lot. I can't plan on leftovers."

Laughing, Pam assured her, "The day I can't afford to feed a hungry teenage boy is the day I am truly destitute. I like to see him getting plenty to eat. I lived with a growing boy in the house, remember? (Sierra had an Uncle John, her mother's brother.) I know how much they need to eat." Then in a more serious tone, "He's the friend you were asking about, that might be abused, isn't he?"

"How can you tell?" Sierra asked, surprised.

"It's nothing in particular…just kind of how he looks at us. I think he's lonely."

"Yeah, well he is the one. I've seen bruises on him sometimes, and he won't talk about them. But I really don't know for sure because River won't talk about a lot of things. I somehow don't think he'd appreciate us interfering."

"Perhaps…well, anyway, he's welcome here whenever. Besides, I think he comes over for more than just a meal. I think he likes you."

"Of course he likes me. We're friends." Sierra didn't understand why her mother would state the obvious.

24 NOVICE LEVEL

When competing, it is always the horse who is the star, not the competitor. – Max Gahwyler, *The Competitive Edge.*

The weeks of summer were passing way too fast.

Sierra spent every morning with João. First they did the chores, then he rode Fiel and Sierra watched, paying close attention as he explained the aids he used. Then it was her turn to ride. After the first few lessons, João took her off the lunge line and Sierra re-learned how to use the reins lightly, relying more on her core muscles, weight, and legs. Fiel finished his lessons snorting in contentment and nudging at both João and Sierra for the treats he knew they carried and that he deserved for doing so well. The way he walked, carried his head, and looked around seemed to Sierra to state as clearly as in words, *I am relaxed and happy and I enjoy my work.*

João trusted Sierra with Fiel. After riding, they walked Fiel back to the crossties and untacked. Then João left Sierra to rinse off, groom, and turn Fiel out in the pasture while he went back to the house and prepared the morning tea.

Sierra was falling in love with Fiel. Good-natured and patient, he willingly put up with her efforts to ride; all his mannerisms indicating he wanted to figure out what she asked him to do. She loved the dappled color of his coat and his luxuriously thick mane that hung below his neck and his forelock long enough to fall over his eyes.

"You are beautiful inside and out," she told him and the look in his eye seemed to agree with her. His posture, his attitude, his entire bearing was regal and proud.

After riding and taking care of Fiel, Sierra sat with João on his porch and they talked for an hour or two over tea; mostly about horses. João answered her questions about riding and to her delight, had read most of the same books she had read and praised her for taking the trouble to learn all that she could. It was great to have a knowledgeable adult confirm that the books were not just idealistic principles, but were the basis of his own style of riding.

He loved to talk and tell stories and willingly told Sierra his own history. His father had been a horse breeder in Portugal, but some bad luck and bad investments had resulted in the loss of his farm. At age eighteen, the boy João moved to the United States where a relative worked at a thoroughbred breeding farm. João had grown up riding dressage horses, but found better opportunities to make a living as a jockey in America. With his small size and experience, he had no trouble finding work as an exercise boy at local tracks. He proved himself adept with the thoroughbred colts and fillies and after getting his jockey license, established a reputation that kept him in work. He had been riding in races for ten years when he met River's mother, an ambitious and talented woman in her early twenties. They formed a friendship when they discovered they both had a background in dressage and both loved the heart and soul of horses.

After years of racing and two serious injuries, João knew he should plan for a future when he could no longer work as a jockey. He began taking accounting and business courses through an on-line university, one or two classes at a time. When he retired as a jockey five years ago, he had earned a business degree and had already started a business as a financial and investment consultant. His mornings he devoted to Fiel and his chores around the farm. In the afternoons he worked from a room in the house he had set up as an office.

He had been married once but had divorced before there were children. His ex-wife grew tired of all the time he spent away from home during the racing season and had no desire to follow him around from track to track. He had no other family except a sister still living in Portugal.

With just a few questions from Sierra, she also learned more of River's background. Both Renee and João had ridden horses for Cray Blackthorn, River's father. João described him as a handsome man with a lot of charm and an eye for all the ladies. One of the first horses Renee rode for him, Raging River, was a long shot winner. João suspected that Renee, in the excitement of winning and the attentions from the handsome trainer, had had a brief affair with Cray. It didn't take long however, for both Renee and João to discover that Cray was unscrupulous in his business dealings, and resorted to unethical as well as illegal methods in training his horses. When Renee caught him drugging a horse she was to ride, and then he blatantly lied to her about it, she refused to ever ride for him again. She hated Cray after that. She told João and he backed her up; also refusing mounts from Cray.

"Nevertheless, Renee chose to have her baby. She was perhaps not a conventional mother," João reminisced. "But she loved that little boy with all her heart. I am afraid it would break her heart to know that Cray has custody of him." He sighed deeply. "Ah, poor River. That man is using him as he uses the horses. All is about profit."

"Didn't she have any other family that could have taken him?" Sierra asked.

"Renee was born in Haiti and an orphan since the age of three. She was adopted by an American family and given many wonderful opportunities; riding and dance lessons and a college education. But they disowned her when she chose a career as a jockey. So sad and unfortunate."

After the morning tea, Sierra insisted on washing up the few dishes, and from there, she began doing light housework for João. At first he was reluctant to allow it, but Sierra pleaded for the opportunity to repay his generosity; and he finally agreed. She dusted, vacuumed, and swept once a week, and kept the kitchen and bathroom scrubbed and polished. She wandered around outside and weeded and watered his flower beds and flower boxes when needed. It was easy work and she didn't think anywhere near compensated for her lessons on Fiel.

One morning, River showed up in time for Sierra's lesson, and he stood with João, watching.

"Sit deep; now more weight on your inside seat...that's right, down through the heel. It is just a micro-shifting of the pelvis; see how he bends easier on the circle?" João instructed. "Now give with your hands...ahhh, that's right. See? See how he moves into the bit? Can you feel his back muscles underneath your seat?"

Sierra nodded and grinned, a look of bliss on her face.

"Beautiful! All right, very good. Give him all the reins now and let him stretch."

Sierra complied and then walked Fiel over to where João and River stood at the low rail.

"River!" Sierra greeted him happily as she dismounted. "How did you get away from Pegasus?"

"The horses are all turned out and Manuel wants to work with the new girl cleaning stalls." He gave a short laugh. "She's not working out all that well. Anyway, he told me to take a few hours off and come watch you ride. He misses you."

"I miss him too. Can you tell him that?"

"Sure."

"And Rosa too."

"Uh huh."

They walked Fiel back to the crossties. River helped Sierra with his care while João left to make the tea. Then they all sat down on the porch.

"What do you think of this young lady riding now?" João asked.

"She looks great on Fiel," River complimented Sierra through a mouthful of cinnamon roll.

"Yes, I think so. She has an ability and more important, a great desire to ride correctly." João fumbled on the stand behind him for his cigarettes.

Sierra blushed under the praise.

River finished his roll and reached for a scone. "I think you should let her jump Fiel."

Sierra set down her teacup, surprised at the suggestion and interested in how João would respond.

"Pah," João snorted out on a puff of smoke. "Jumping, hopping; forcing these poor animals to do something so unnatural."

"But they like it," River insisted.

"Who says, the horse? I have seen at these shows; terror in their eyes, all hot and agitated. Hmmph, does not look like they are happy to me."

River laughed. "Okay, I can't argue with that. But, Sierra, you remember the day I rode Magic in that clinic? Did he look unhappy to you?"

Sierra would never forget the beautiful image of River and Magic sailing around the field that day. "No, he really looked like he enjoyed jumping as much as you," she agreed.

"I swear, it started out with me asking and he was saying, 'you want me to go over that?' And before we finished the course, he was asking me, 'can we go over this one?'" River had a look in his eye of deep pleasure at the memory of that ride.

And nothing like talking about a horse to bring out the best of his verbal skills. It pleased Sierra to hear him speak of Magic.

"Not natural, not at all. I grant you, with a good relationship like you had with that one horse, sure, he will do anything for you," João continued to defend his belief.

"Okay, what about the horse you told me about back on your father's farm in Portugal; the one you couldn't turn out into a field because he always jumped the fences?"

"He was a stallion. There were mares in the other fields. Very natural."

Both River and Sierra laughed at his stubbornness.

"Now dressage, that is natural. You watch a happy horse, turned out fresh from his stall. Watch how he bucks and kicks up his heels. Then he goes into natural passage; brings his back end underneath him and so elegantly and natural, reaches out with his front legs." João pawed in the air with his arms, demonstrating. "And pirouette, no problem, as he changes direction. Just watch how he races around in an open space, pirouettes, and changes his leads as he reverses. Natural, all natural."

"Fiel can jump." River turned to Sierra. "João bought him from a girl who evented him."

"Really…he can jump?" Sierra asked. "I didn't think Lusitanos could jump."

"Any horse can learn to jump up to certain heights. Sure, Fiel has jumped before," João admitted.

"I think you should let Sierra start jumping him, and then enter him in the horse trial next month." River made the statement looking into the distance, toward Fiel in the pasture.

Sierra noted the squaring of his jaw and the stiffening of his shoulders. *What is this really about?* She wondered.

"River, what is on your mind?" João asked.

"Tess and Crystal are driving me crazy. Ever since Tess rapped Galaxy in Sierra's lesson, well he jumps high and wide now so he's not taking rails down. She won her last two events. Someone needs to get out there and beat her; prove there are better ways to train and ride a horse."

"You want revenge?" João asked in a gentle voice.

"I don't know what I want…maybe," River mumbled, looking down at his plate.

"River, isn't Crystal riding training level? I've only ridden beginner novice. I couldn't ride against her." Sierra stated, amazed at his suggestion.

"She's going to stay at novice level this year. You could easily ride novice level."

Sierra was surprised to hear Crystal wasn't taking Galaxy up to training level. And she knew her own abilities were probably at a level for the novice jumps; an increase from heights of two-feet-seven at the beginner novice level, to two-feet-eleven. She had been jumping three feet in her lessons with Tess. Part of her instantly wanted to jump at a chance to compete again. But she didn't need revenge against Crystal, and certainly didn't need to increase Crystal's animosity towards her.

"You miss jumping, don't you?" River persisted.

"Yes, of course, but…" Sierra looked over at João.

"It's only novice level. Any horse can do novice level." River also looked at João.

"River," João said in a tone of reprimand.

"Well, Fiel can."

João scratched the back of his head, took a last deep drag on his cigarette and then stubbed it out. He smiled at Sierra, eyes crinkling. "I will think about it."

João did think about jumping and two days later he set up cavalletti for Sierra's lesson. Fiel perked up and took the line of low jumps with energetic enthusiasm.

"Perhaps he is getting a little stale with just flat work," João commented thoughtfully as he noted Fiel's attitude.

And so it was settled. He downloaded the entry form from the website for the event and he and Sierra filled it out during morning tea.

"João, I can't afford the entry fee," Sierra exclaimed when she saw how much it cost.

"Miss Sierra, I will tell you this. I chose to live here in this area for my friend Renee. I wanted to see if I could perhaps do something for her son. But as I came to know River, I grew to love him and care for him for his own sake. When I agreed to teach you riding on my little Fiel, I did this as a favor to River. But now that I know you, I do it for the joy of your friendship and for who you are. You will let me take care of entering you in this competition for the pleasure it will give me."

Sierra nodded and with her heart filled with gratitude, she solemnly stood, stepped over to his side and gave him a hug. He hugged her in return, patting her back, and murmured, "My little equestrienne."

Over the next few weeks before the horse trial, João added jumping into two to three of Sierra's lessons each week. On the other days after working on the flat, Sierra galloped Fiel up and down the hills in the surrounding fields. Sierra spent the afternoons painting brick and stone images onto plywood panels, and then in the evenings, she and River used the panels to build cross country obstacles. River borrowed João's tractor to drag a perfect-sized log that he had spotted in the surrounding woods, to add to the course. There was a low area in the field that naturally held water after hard rains, and was conveniently within reach of several lengths of garden hose. They lined the bottom with sand and gravel to create firm footing, filled it with water from the hose, and then had a water jump.

"He could have benefited from some trail work but I think he is fit enough; the dressage gymnastics have kept him in pretty good shape and you are conditioning him on your gallops," João commented one morning as he checked Fiel's heart and breathing rate after Sierra had completed a practice course over the field jumps. As far as she could tell, Fiel seemed to recover as quickly as any horse she had ridden at Pegasus. "Yes, I think he is ready." João gave Fiel an affectionate pat on the rump as Sierra dismounted to cool him out.

Show day arrived. Sierra awoke with rampaging butterflies in her stomach, but at the show grounds, once up on Fiel's back in the warm-up arena and with João's gentle coaching, she turned all her attention to Fiel. As she concentrated on his mood and energy, trying to keep him calm and focused on her aids, she also managed to calm herself.

"Good, good," João whispered from the rail of the warm-up arena as Sierra passed him in an energetic working trot. "He is relaxed and listening to you," he encouraged the next time she rode by. "You two are ready."

Sierra rode the dressage test with her attention tuned into Fiel and consciously blocking out the distractions around the dressage ring. *We are in our own ring*, she told herself, *ride just like at home.* Fiel responded to all her aids, and after the final salute, applause greeted them as they exited the ring. João met her at the exit gate, grinning from ear to ear.

"Nice test," the next rider complimented Sierra as she passed her, entering the gate.

"Thanks, you have a good ride," Sierra replied.

"Very well ridden," João commented as Sierra dismounted.

"I am so proud of him," Sierra beamed as she loosened Fiel's girth.

"I am proud of both of you."

As Sierra led Fiel back to his stall she heard laughter and then a comment spoken in a loud voice, "What a jug-headed animal!"

"I didn't think they allowed mules in combined training," a familiar voice added.

Sierra looked toward the voices to find Crystal smirking down at her from the back of Galaxy with Gloria at his head.

The war was still on.

"Ignore such poor sportsmanship," João advised with a very disgusted look on his face.

"Don't worry," Sierra laughed, hoping it sounded light-hearted, and not wanting to admit even to herself that such comments hurt her feelings.

Fiel remained energetic throughout the competition as if the cross country and stadium jumping events were no more strenuous than his work-outs at home. He completed both courses clean and without time penalties. As Sierra led him back to his stall after each event, he danced at the end of the bridle reins, arched his neck and passaged a few strides as he passed other horses.

"You are showing off," Sierra laughed at him, but also very proud.

At the end of the event, Sierra finished in second place. Crystal came in first place, for Galaxy had also jumped clean, but they had a higher dressage score.

"I hope River won't be too disappointed that I lost to Crystal," Sierra said as she and João walked back from the booth where results had been posted, carrying her dressage test sheet and red ribbon.

João stopped in his tracks and took her shoulders to face him. "Showing your horse is not about beating the others. When you have done your best and your horse has given you his best as Fiel did today, then you have won. Do you understand?"

Sierra nodded.

"If everyone competed with a true spirit of horsemanship, then we would all celebrate every horse's performance that has done well."

"You're right," Sierra agreed out loud. Even so, she admitted to herself a begrudging disappointment that Fiel's best had not been good enough to beat Crystal.

"I do not like to criticize a judge," João said in a thoughtful tone, "but of course there is always an element of subjectivity in judging a dressage test which includes one's personal biases and prejudices. I think this particular judge was perhaps a bit over impressed with that horse's big movements. He is a very nice horse."

"You mean Galaxy?"

"Yes, your friend's horse. But I believe you rode more correctly. At this level, that perhaps should count more than natural big movements. Her horse was often behind the bit, and not always engaged from the hind end. But his conformation is such that he still appears to look as if he is on the bit and balanced. Hmm..," João made a noise to himself, thoughtful.

Although Sierra and Fiel didn't win first place, they did qualify to compete in the Pacific Regional Combined Training Championship three-day event.

25 HIGH SCHOOL

Our job as a rider is not to interfere with our horses. Our job is to allow a horse to express itself in whatever it is doing but not to interfere with that horse's expression. – Carrie Schopf

"You've grown at least three inches this summer," Pam commented as she looked over Sierra's wardrobe for the upcoming school year. Sierra wore either riding breeches or shorts all summer long and hadn't noticed her increase in height. But as she tried on her jeans from last year, there was a considerable gap between the hem of the jeans and the top of her socks. "Well, Kitten, I guess we go shopping for new clothes."

"Sorry, Mom, I didn't mean to grow so much." Sierra's tone was bitter and sarcastic, reflecting her foul mood. Not only had she awakened with a stomach ache, but she didn't even get to ride today because João had a doctor's appointment this morning. Sierra had called Allison, thinking a long talk with her friend would help improve her day, but only got her voice mail and then remembered Allison was away for two weeks at some kind of fine arts camp. So Sierra had moped around with nothing to do and not interested in finding something to do, until her mother came home from the hospital where she was doing clinical training. The last thing she wanted when her mother arrived was to try on clothes, or worse, go shopping for clothes.

As Sierra pulled off the too short jeans, a sudden sharp cramp grabbed at her abdomen from deep inside, and then she felt warm wetness gush out. She looked down and emitted a small scream when she saw the insides of her thighs red with blood. "What is…?" Then realization hit her.

Pam looked up at Sierra's distressed cry, and her own eyes followed to where Sierra stared at herself in shock.

"I think I've started a period." Sierra looked up at her mother and then burst into tears.

"Honey, Baby!" Pam gathered her daughter into her arms. Sierra sobbed with her face buried and with her emotions jumbled between feelings of distress and relief that she finally had proof of her developing womanhood.

Pam soothed and comforted her; telling her, "You're a woman now." She drew a hot bath and helped Sierra into the tub. "It helps relieve the cramps," she explained. Afterwards, she showed Sierra where she kept her own supply of feminine products. "You can share mine until you figure out what works best for you."

Later, with the promise of dinner at a restaurant of her choice to celebrate her new status as a woman, Sierra agreed to shop for her school wardrobe. She picked out three new pairs of jeans, five new tee-shirts, and two winter sweaters. Just because she was a woman now didn't mean she had to totally change her style.

The following morning, River had a few hours away from Pegasus to spend with Sierra and João.

"Tess fired the last girl and Manuel is working with the new one today," River explained over tea. This was the third person hired to fill Sierra's position. "Anybody worth anything isn't going to work for what Tess is willing to pay; except you, of course. I think Tess is realizing what a mistake she made in firing you."

Sierra couldn't help taking satisfaction that no one was working out, although she knew it increased the workload for River and Manuel. "I may be a fool, but I don't regret working there," Sierra defended herself. "At least I learned from you about handling horses, and you gave me a good start riding. I will always be thankful for that."

"Would you come back if Tess changed her mind?" River asked with a look that Sierra thought was actually hopeful.

She thought for a few minutes. "I guess I would but on different terms. I think I would ask for pay."

"Good for you," River said with sincerity.

"And I would still want my time here with you and Fiel," Sierra said, looking at João, who smiled back and pushed the plate with one last scone toward her. "But I doubt she'll change her mind." Sierra picked up the scone, her second, and João got up to refill the plate. They always needed more food when River joined them.

"She might," River stated. João returned with another full plate of pastries and handed them to River.

"I can't believe school is starting in just two weeks," Sierra changed the subject, looking toward the pasture where she could see the back end of Fiel grazing, his tail swishing rhythmically at flies. She had always looked forward to a new school year, but now for the first time in her life, she regretted the end of her summer's routine.

"Ah yes, the opportunity to enjoy free education and better yourself," João proclaimed as he refilled his teacup.

"I'm a little nervous about starting high school. River, we'll be going to the same school now," Sierra commented.

River stuffed half a scone in his mouth and said something indistinguishable.

"What subjects are you taking?" João asked.

Sierra recited her freshman schedule; all courses aimed at going on to college.

"Very good; a well-rounded curriculum." João turned his attention to River. "What are you taking this year?" Sierra detected a poignancy in his tone and noted River's posture tensing.

"I don't remember," he mumbled.

João shook his head in disgust and stated sarcastically, "How convenient."

"I don't want to talk about school," River retorted.

Sierra realized this was an old discussion for the two of them. She wondered if João was aware of River's plans to quit school.

"That's the problem with you, young man. You don't like to talk about or face anything that is unpleasant for you."

"Why should I?"

"Why shouldn't you?"

River glared at João, defensive anger rising. "I..." River started. He threw his last bit of scone down on his plate. "I just can't. I'm not good at school."

"You don't try."

"You don't know."

"You are afraid and you are a coward," João kept pressing.

"I'm too stupid," River insisted, his voice raised a decibel.

"What have I said to you about saying that?" João's own voice rose in timbre. "You tell yourself so because it gives you an excuse."

Sierra watched the two of them glower at each other, feeling very uncomfortable.

João sighed deeply, softened his expression and lowered his voice. "River, if you would only let me help you. Studying is a skill that can be learned, just like riding a horse."

"I don't need school."

"Your mother would…"

"Don't bring my mother into this." River pushed himself violently away from the table, stomped to the edge of the porch, vaulted down and took off at a jog. Storm got up from where she lay on the porch next to Charlie, shook herself, and trotted off after River, looking back once as if to apologize for her master's rude behavior.

Sierra and João watched River until he ran out of sight. "That is his answer to all his problems, run away." João sighed deeply, shaking his head. He reached for his cigarettes but tossed the pack back down and turned to Sierra apologetically. "Sierra, I am not feeling well this morning. If you don't mind I believe I will leave you to clean up. I'm going to lie down for a bit."

"Of course," Sierra agreed. She did not like the grayish hue, especially around his mouth, visible in spite of his suntanned skin. She watched as he slowly rose from the table and went inside.

The last few days of summer flew by. Sierra continued with Fiel's training program, looking forward to the upcoming championship event, the culmination of the combined training season.

On the last Sunday before school started, João coached Sierra and Fiel through a short flat lesson and then had them finish over a course of low, practice jumps. "I must admit, adding a little jumping into his work has been beneficial," he stated, noting the increased energy Fiel displayed in his daily sessions. "He is fit and ready. Our job now is to maintain that fitness without overtraining or having him injured. We have just one week before the championship."

Sierra nodded in agreement. She knew what he meant, having witnessed overtraining in so many of the horses at Pegasus.

"We will change our routine," João continued. "You come after school next week and we will have Fiel wait for you."

"Thanks," Sierra agreed, grateful that he was willing to change his routine for her.

"And if you see that River, you tell him I miss him, okay?"

"Sure, but he hasn't come over for dinner lately. I guess he's avoiding both of us."

"Yes, that is his way." João sighed in disappointment. "But maybe you will see him at school."

"I hope so."

Monday morning, Sierra stood in front of the bathroom mirror getting ready for her first day of high school. In the past, she barely looked at herself in a mirror; just quick glances to make sure her face was clean and to part her hair before braiding it. But now she scrutinized the reflection staring back at her; long wet hair hanging past her shoulders and the freckles across her nose prominent from the summer sun. *I'm almost fourteen. I'm a teenager. I have periods. I'm in high school.* These thoughts ricocheted around in her mind. Maybe it was time to give up braids and put a little more effort into her appearance.

With sudden determination, Sierra pulled out her mother's blow dryer and dried her just-shampooed hair. It fluffed out with more body than she realized her hair possessed since she always pulled it tightly into braids. The sun had bleached the color to a very pale brown with golden tones. She thought her face looked small with her hair framing it, and she wasn't sure she would be able to tolerate feeling the hair around her face all day. She parted her hair as if for braiding, and then brought the sides back and fastened them behind, letting the hair in back hang free.

Now for the freckles. She opened the drawer where her mother kept her make-up, and studied the items tossed together. Finding a tube of foundation, she dabbed a small amount over her nose and cheekbones and smoothed it in. *Yes, the freckles are almost invisible.* Next, she took up a tube of mascara and applied the brush gingerly to her top lashes. *I actually have long lashes*, she marveled, never having noticed before due to their light color.

Sierra smiled at herself, studying the effect. *Am I pretty?* It wasn't something she had ever thought much about. Her image stared back; *not ugly, but pretty..?*

She shrugged, and laughing at herself, exited the bathroom to pull on new jeans and a light blue tee-shirt. Grabbing her backpack that she had filled last night, she left the cottage to wait for the school bus.

"Wow, Sierra!" Allison exclaimed, coming up the row of lockers where they had agreed to meet as they talked on the phone last night. "You look fantastic! You should always wear your hair down."

"You're the one who looks fantastic," Sierra replied, blushing, pleased at the praise, but also feeling by comparison, rather plain. Allison looked as if she had stepped off the page of a high-fashion magazine. Her shiny, soft curly black hair framed her fine facial bone structure and emphasized her large, dark eyes. She wore three earrings in each ear that sparkled above her long, graceful neck. The colors of her patterned short ruffled skirt matched her blouse, and she wore heeled sandals that accentuated the elegant shape of her long dancer's legs. *If guys don't notice her this year, then they are total idiots,* she mused, with the teeniest bit of envy.

They walked together to home room, greeting people they recognized. Sierra saw Billy and returned his wave, but quickly urged Allison onward. She had no intention of letting him latch onto her this year.

"Sierra," someone called behind her. She turned and to her surprise, Katrina pushed through the crowd. "Hey, you look great. So, are you showing at championship this weekend?"

"Yes, are you?" Sierra was a little surprised but also pleased that Katrina seemed willing to resume a friendly attitude.

"Yeah, Calliope and I qualified."

"Uh, where are Crystal and Gloria?"

Katrina snorted a laugh. "We don't really hang out anymore; ever since I made the mistake of being honest with Crystal. I told her I thought River was a better rider than her."

"You told her that?" Sierra asked, surprised.

"I said it in a nice way; sort of hinting that maybe she should listen to him." Katrina made an 'oh well' face and shrugged her shoulders holding up her palms.

Sierra laughed appreciatively. "I guess I'll see you at the championship then."

"Yeah, are you going to ride that Andalusian?"

"Yes; actually he's Lusitano."

"Oh, whatever, he's nice. Here's my class, see ya," Katrina turned away but then called out over her shoulder. "I miss you at the stable!"

Allison and Sierra looked at each other and Allison raised her eyebrows. "Interesting," she said.

There was one other person Sierra looked forward to seeing. *How will he react to my new look?* As they entered homeroom, she spied him just sitting down at a desk. *Great, we have the same homeroom!*

"Sierra!" He greeted happily as the two girls walked in. "Sit over here. Hi, Allison."

"Hi, Luke," Sierra returned the greeting, already feeling her face flush with heightened color. She also experienced another twinge of envy, wondering if he had invited them to sit near him because he had noticed how great Allison looked. She pushed the feelings down as totally unfair.

Cheerfully, Luke asked about their summer and chatted a little about his own before the bell rang and they turned to face forward.

"Are you riding in the horse show this weekend?" he whispered as the noise in the room abated.

"Yes," Sierra whispered back.

"Great, Justin and I are going to watch the jumping. I'll see you there."

26 CHAMPIONSHIP

There is something about jumping a horse over a fence, something that makes you feel good. Perhaps it is the risk, the gamble. In any event, it's a thing I need. – William Faulkner

The Pacific Regional Combined Training Championship was held over three days on Labor Day weekend, at a large equestrian center about one hundred miles from Firwood. Friday after school, they caravanned to the center; João driving his camper and pulling his two-horse trailer with Fiel inside, and Sierra and Pam following. Pam had requested Friday and Saturday nights off from her nursing home job so she could drive her daughter to the show and stay with her.

"Mom, it is so awesome that you're finally going to see me ride," Sierra exclaimed as they followed the horse trailer.

"I think I'm as excited as you are." Pam flashed a grin. "You know, I haven't had any vacation since I started nursing school. I think this weekend is going to be a nice break for me. And I can't wait to see you ride."

"Thanks again for coming. I know we really can't afford it."

"Honey, I am so proud of how conscientious you are about money, but sometimes it's hard for me to think of my daughter having to worry about making ends meet." Pam's tone had turned serious. "You should only have to worry about keeping your grades up and relationships with your friends and your hobbies. Those are the kinds of worries a teenager should deal with; not money."

"Don't worry, Mom, I have all those worries." They both laughed.

"Besides, the extra shifts I worked during school breaks is income I didn't budget for; just to have a little extra for something special like this," Pam assured her. "So we can afford it."

They found the equestrian center easily; there were signs posted everywhere, even a freeway exit. A big sign and arrow indicating *Exhibitor's Entrance*, directed them where to pull in and find the stall assigned to Fiel.

"Well, well, here we are," João announced full of enthusiasm after they had parked. Sierra helped him unload Fiel from the trailer, remove his shipping wraps, and then settle him in his temporary home with a pile of grass hay and fresh water.

Sierra leaned on the stall door watching Fiel. He took a bite of hay, circled the stall, snorted at the walls, and finally stuck his head out next to her shoulder, as if to ask, "What's this about?" She stroked his velvety nose, whispering reassurances. He went back for another mouthful of hay and came back to look out.

"He's curious about what is going on but cannot bear to pass up something to eat," João laughed. "So, let us go settle ourselves, then you can hand walk him around the grounds so he can see everything."

The equestrian center had a large field next to the competition stabling, where competitors parked their horse trailers, campers, and motor homes, as well as others setting up tents. There was a large cement block building with public restrooms and showers. João planned to sleep in his camper and Pam had borrowed a tent, sleeping bags and pads from a friend. João and Pam moved their vehicles to a vacant spot and Sierra helped Pam set up the tent and organize their stuff inside. Then she went back to Fiel.

Horses, trainers, riders, grooms, and other support people milled around the grounds. The sights, sounds, and smells intrigued Sierra as much as it did Fiel as she led him up and down the aisles in between the rows of stalls, and then around the warm-up areas. Everyone seemed in high spirits, passing her and Fiel with friendly smiles. A few people even stopped to compliment Fiel and ask his breed.

Many stables participated with a team of riders, and they decorated their stall areas with accessories in their team colors; tack trunks, canvas chairs, racks that hooked over the edges of stalls, and banners with the name of the barn. Most stables paid for one or two extra stalls that they converted into temporary tack rooms and dressing areas.

Sierra looked for and found the scarlet and blue colors of Pegasus Equestrian Center, hoping to find River and maybe some of the horses she used to care for. There were six stalls with the horses' names on Pegasus placards, displaying the logo of a winged horse silhouette. One extra stall had been set up as a tack room with several trunks, saddle stands, bridles hanging from hooks, bales of hay, and the usual barn equipment of buckets, wheelbarrow, pitchfork, shovel, and broom. Another stall had canvas panels draped to cover the open grillwork and create a private dressing room.

"Rather posh," Sierra said out loud. In spite of herself, she experienced a brief wave of envy that she was no longer a part of such a well-turned out and prominent team. But all she had to do was recall the blood on Galaxy's leg after the rapping experience to quell any desire to be a part of Pegasus. No amount of fancy surroundings was worth that. "Seen enough?" she asked Fiel and patted him on the neck. "Let's get you back to your hay." She decided to settle Fiel back in his stall and then return to greet her old friends. She had glimpsed Calliope and Galaxy who had whinnied at her in recognition.

Someone entered the aisle leading a horse. As he came closer, Sierra recognized River and Silver Knight.

"River! I was hoping I would see you here," Sierra greeted, breaking into a grin.

"How's it going?" he replied a little sheepishly. Sierra couldn't tell if he was happy to see her or not.

"Okay; I've been leading Fiel around so he can check things out."

River led Silver into a stall and removed his halter.

"How about you?" she asked.

"Fine."

"You look busy."

"Yeah."

"Want some help?"

River turned from where he had bent over to remove the horse's leg wraps and frowned up at her.

"Are you mad at me or something?" Sierra asked, feeling hurt by his cold reception.

"No…I thought maybe you were mad at me."

"Of course not. I've missed you. So has João."

"Oh…uhm."

"I'm taking Fiel to his stall. If you want, I'll come back and help you. I don't have anything more to do for awhile."

"If you want."

"I do if you want me to," Sierra responded in a sharp tone and determined she would not return if River was going to remain in his sullen mood.

He stood up and finally, smiled. "Yes, I'm glad to see you. Please come back."

Sierra led Fiel to his stall and gave him another flake of hay, his evening grain, and made sure he had fresh water. Then she went back to help River.

"I have two more horses to walk around. You want to lead one?" River asked when she returned.

"Sure."

"Galaxy or Moose?"

"I'll take Galaxy." They haltered the two horses and led them out. "Who all is competing?" Sierra asked out of curiosity.

"Your three friends on their horses," he answered with wry humor, "and Ann on her mare. Tess is riding Moose."

"She qualified on Moose?"

"Yeah, she's riding open training level."

"Wow, she's brave," Sierra commented as she remembered her harrowing rides on the flighty thoroughbred.

"He's easier to ride now. I've been trail riding him and jumping him outside all summer long and he's finally listening to me."

"That doesn't mean he'll listen to her."

River looked at her with a conspiratorial grin. "She uses a pelham bit and running martingale to get his attention."

Sierra knew a pelham bit combined a snaffle and curb into one bit, and consequently more severe. The running martingale, since it prevented the horse from flinging his head up, also increased control.

"I see Gunsmoke is here." Sierra had noted Tess's retired grand prix horse in one of the Pegasus stalls. "She's not competing him again, is she?"

"No, she's riding him in a demo musical freestyle for the evening show Sunday night."

"That should be something to see."

"Umhm," River replied, sounding distracted. They walked along in silence awhile until River asked, "Is João here?"

"Yes, my mom's here too. This is the first time she'll see me ride."

"Where are you staying?"

"We're camping over there," Sierra indicated the field with the campers and tents. "Where are you staying?"

"I have a cot in the dressing room stall so I can be near the horses."

"What about all the others?"

"They're staying in some motel nearby. Tess took them all out to dinner."

"And she didn't take you?"

"Of course not; I'm just the hired help."

"How are you supposed to eat?"

"It's not a problem. I have a cooler full of food and there are the vendors here on the grounds. Besides, can you imagine sitting down to eat with Tess and Crystal at the same table? Talk about a stomach ache!"

Sierra laughed at the image her mind conjured up. "You should come to our campsite and eat with us. My mom and João are cooking some kind of special dish. He has his camper and he's got a stove inside and all that."

"No thanks."

"Why not? You know you'd be welcome."

"I haven't been back to see João since the day I…well, you know."

"He's not mad at you and he misses you."

River thought for a few minutes, then shook his head. "No, I better not; not here."

"River," she said, exasperated. "You should come."

He shook his head again.

"Why not?" she persisted in spite of noting how he tensed his shoulders. She was not willing to let it drop. "Every day he asks if I've seen you. He really loves you, River."

River glanced at her with a strange look on his face.

"He does; don't you know that?"

River stared straight ahead, not willing to meet her eyes. Moose suddenly jerked up his head and shied away from a paper wrapper that had been rustled by a sudden breeze.

Sierra laughed and teased, "You are so uptight you are upsetting your horse." As she had hoped, he smiled back. "So, will you come?"

"Come where?"

"To dinner," she said again, annoyed. She wanted to grab his shoulders and shake him hard enough to rattle his brains.

"No; I said not now." With that he turned Moose back towards the stalls. Sierra sighed and followed him.

Still hoping she might persuade him, Sierra hung around to help River feed and water all the horses. But he remained withdrawn and she didn't bother to invite him again. "I guess I'll see you later," she said when all the chores were finished.

River stared into Moose's stall, watching him eating in contentment. Then he said, "Sierra, people shouldn't care about me. I'll just let them down."

She could not believe what she had just heard. She walked over to him and put a hand firmly on his upper arm. "That is about the stupidest thing I have ever heard," she said, irritated. She was quite tired of his bad manners, his moodiness, and self-degradation.

"I told you I'm stupid."

"You know, a person is just about as stupid as they want to be." Sierra turned on her heel and strode away.

After dinner, Sierra went back to the stalls to check on Fiel. He had finished his hay and stood sleeping with one back leg bent, when she peeked into his stall. But a person can't sneak up on a horse. He awoke, whickered at her and strolled over for a treat. She fed him pieces of carrot.

"Good night, beautiful Fiel," she whispered to him with an affectionate pat on his nose. "Sleep well."

On her way back to the campground, River emerged from the Pegasus stalls and called softly, "Sierra?"

She stopped and waited for him to come up to her, still annoyed with him.

"I was waiting for you," he said.

"Oh yeah?"

"I wanted to apologize...so, I'm sorry."

"Okay...Stupid," she added with a grin and when he laughed, both their moods lightened. "Did you eat?"

"Yes...um, I was going to say, I'll feed Fiel for you in the morning so you can sleep in if you want."

"Thanks, that's very sweet. But I doubt I'll be able to sleep in and I'll want to check on Fiel as soon as I wake up. But I appreciate the offer."

"Sure."

"Hey, where's Storm?" Sierra suddenly remembered to ask.

"Manuel and Rosa are looking after her."

"Oh, that's good. Well..." They had reached the edge of the campground. "Actually, I could help you feed in the morning," she offered.

"Thanks, but with only six horses to feed it won't take me very long. But you can help me braid if you have the time."

"Yeah, I can do that. I don't ride until the afternoon."

"Good...thanks...well, good night."

"River..." She started to invite him once again to come and say hello to João and her mother. But he quickly turned away and back to the stall area. She watched until he disappeared from her sight.

27 DAY ONE: DRESSAGE

When it's getting really good, no matter if riding at home or in a show, dressage becomes art. When you've got a really good symbiosis with your horse, riding stops being work and becomes a celebration. – Hubertus Schmidt

Saturday, day one of the championship, was devoted to riding dressage tests.

Sierra awoke just before dawn and slipped out as quietly as she could so as not to wake Pam, and made her way to the stalls. She fed Fiel, who seemed quite at home now. Then she sought out River at the Pegasus stalls and invited him to breakfast. As she expected, he refused.

After both she and Fiel had finished their breakfasts, she led him once again around the grounds to stretch his legs and give him another chance to become familiar with the surroundings.

Then she joined River, and together they braided the manes of the five horses competing that day. Tess came by to make sure all the horses were well and preparations were on schedule. She frowned when she saw Sierra, as if trying to place where she knew the girl; but she didn't say anything.

Katrina and Ann arrived to help braid their own horses, and both girls greeted Sierra in a friendly manner.

"I didn't know you were still riding," Ann said as she worked on Lucy's mane.

"Yeah, I'm riding a friend's horse," Sierra answered.

"It's really too bad what happened at Pegasus," Ann kindly offered. "I miss you at the stable."

"Me too," Katrina chimed in.

Sierra was very touched by their friendliness.

When the Pegasus horses were all braided, River helped Sierra with Fiel's mane. Then she cleaned Fiel's stall and wandered back to help River clean the Pegasus stalls; anything to stay busy and help keep her nerves calm.

Finally, the time arrived to groom and saddle Fiel and head off to the warm-up ring. João helped her prepare Fiel while Pam looked on.

"A perfect day," João prattled on, trying to keep Sierra distracted and relaxed as he stood by while she mounted up on Fiel. "You two look terrific! You are ready for this."

In spite of trying to stay relaxed, Sierra felt nervous and overwhelmed as she noticed the beautiful, well-bred horses being warmed up. It was hard for her to believe that she and Fiel were equals, for these were all the best event horses in the region.

As if reading her thoughts, João assured her, "You are as capable as anyone here. Remember, you qualified for this event. This is no different than your last show."

She smiled weakly, and then entered the ring.

"There are about four rides ahead of you," the ring steward told her as she checked in.

Plenty of time. Sierra let Fiel, who was tossing his head and trying to prance, move off into a working trot. *He's reacting to my nervousness.* Taking deep breaths, she concentrated on images of the dressage ring at home, blocking out the other riders. Closing her eyes for a few brief moments as she moved into a spacious gap in the ring, she tuned into Fiel's muscles moving beneath her seat, and noting stiffness in his shoulders she realized how she was gripping with her thighs, restricting his movements. She pulled in her abdominal muscles, relaxed her thighs, and rolled her shoulders to relieve the tension that could travel down to her hands; and then opened her eyes. Fiel's back came up underneath her seat as he rounded his neck and head, and his stiff, choppy gait transformed into a relaxed, forward-moving working trot.

"Watch it!" A paint horse and rider almost collided with Fiel as they came around the corner on a circle. "You rode right in front of us."

"Sorry," Sierra responded reflexively and recognized Crystal warming up Galaxy. *She's the one who almost ran into us!*

"That girl almost ran into you!" the rider behind Sierra said in disbelief.

Sierra reached forward with her inside hand to give Fiel a reassuring pat, glad that someone else had noticed. She kept Galaxy in her peripheral vision from then on and stayed on the opposite side of the warm-up area.

Crystal's number was called and Sierra saw Galaxy leave the ring. Sierra was two rides behind her. At least with her out of the warm-up area she didn't have to worry about an equine collision.

"Number one-twelve, you're on deck." *My number.* Sierra completed the canter circle she had been riding and eased Fiel down to trot and then walk. He snorted and lowered his head as she rode out of the warm-up ring.

"Good warm up," João assured her as he met her coming out of the ring and walked alongside to the test arena. "He is relaxed and shows good energy." He had a soft brush that he ran quickly over Fiel's coat, and then used a rag to wipe dust off of Sierra's boots.

The rider in the ring turned her horse down the center line, halted and gave her salute. Sierra could now enter.

"In you go," João encouraged and patted her booted leg and Fiel's neck.

Sierra swallowed, took two deep breaths, and gathered the reins lightly into her fingers. Fiel immediately arched his neck at her touch and lowered his head into the bit. "Good boy," she whispered and they entered the ring at an energetic trot.

As Fiel responded to her aids, Sierra tuned out everything and everyone except her horse. He worked with impulsion from his hind end, flicking his ears at her signals and making smooth transitions right on the letter the moment Sierra asked. The test called for a serpentine figure at the trot, and their loops were symmetrical with Fiel changing the bend of his body as they moved through the figure. He jumped into a rocking canter for the twenty-meter canter circles. When Sierra released the reins for the free walk, he stretched his neck forward and down into the bit without losing energy, his walking steps like marching. His final halt was square. Sierra saluted the judge and gave Fiel the reins as they walked out of the ring, patting him on both sides of his neck; so proud of him!

Applause came from the bleachers. Pam and João stood, clapping enthusiastically, broad smiles on their faces. "Great ride," someone called out to Sierra.

She dismounted and hugged Fiel around his neck. He blinked at her as if saying, "What's the big deal? Where's my carrot?" Then Pam was hugging her and João was patting her on the back. At that moment it didn't matter what score they earned or whether they had placed. Sierra knew Fiel and she had done their best and she was elated.

When the dressage scores were posted at the end of the day, the Pegasus team had done very well. Tess was in first place on Moose in the open training division. In junior novice, Crystal was in first place, Gloria fourth, and Katrina sixth. Ann, riding junior training level, was in third place.

To Sierra's surprise, she was second in junior novice, having scored only one point less than Crystal.

28 DAY TWO: CROSS COUNTRY

A horse gallops with his lungs, perseveres with his heart, and wins with his character. – Federico Tesio

Sunday was cross country day, the most grueling as well as the most exciting phase of combined training; and also the phase where most accidents and injuries occurred. Sierra's thoughts were often on Magic's tragedy as she and João walked her course after her dressage test. This was also the phase in which she had the most nervousness and apprehension.

Sunday morning Sierra nestled a few extra minutes in her sleeping bag going over in her mind the twenty obstacles Fiel and she would face later in the day. The course included a water crossing, a ditch, and a bank. The heights of the jumps were up to two feet-eleven inches. *None of them are any more difficult than we have faced at home*, she kept telling herself to calm the increasing fluttering in her stomach.

"Time to get ready," João said, one hour before Sierra's ride. His words caused her stomach to take a sudden flip of anxiety and her face paled. He laughed, "You look just how I used to feel before a big race. Sit here." He guided her into the canvas folding chair they had set near Fiel's stall. Pam, who had come to watch the preparations, massaged Sierra's shoulders while João did the same for Fiel; massaging his back, the muscle groups of his rump and shoulders, and down his legs.

After twenty minutes of relaxing massages for the two competitors, Sierra stood up, did a few stretches, and helped João brush Fiel's coat, comb through his mane and tail, and wrap his legs with protective track bandages. Then Sierra slipped on her boots, protective vest, and helmet while João saddled and bridled Fiel.

Either Sierra's excitement was contagious, or it was in the air affecting Fiel, for he pranced at the end of his bridle reins as Sierra led him to the warm-up area. Even so, he minded his manners and never pushed himself ahead of her. Sierra flushed with pride whenever she heard passersby comment, "Look at that beautiful horse! What a magnificent animal! There's the look of a champion!"

"Begin with trotting forward; encourage him to stretch," João advised after Sierra mounted.

She nodded; her mouth dry. Horses cantered in circles in the warm-up area and some riders were going over a low cross-bar jump. She noted Crystal cantering a circle on Galaxy with Tess nearby coaching her.

Fiel snorted and pranced, unable to stand still. "Easy, boy," Sierra stroked his neck and touched the reins to get his attention. Without waiting for her signal, Fiel jumped into a canter and even kicked out in a small crow hop. "Easy, easy," Sierra repeated as she sat deep and took up an inch of rein to bring him back to a trot. He obeyed, but she could feel his pent up desire to move faster.

"Let him gallop once or twice around to get the ants out from underneath his saddle," João coached.

Sierra released the reins and Fiel jumped back into canter. She moved forward into two-point position and allowed him to lengthen into a hand-gallop as she guided him well around the other horses. When he began to snort and lower his head, releasing tension, she sat back, deep in the saddle and squeezed the reins with her fingers. Fiel came obediently to trot. "Good boy," she praised him, and touched her fingers to his neck.

"Sierra!"

She glanced toward the side of the field and saw Luke and Justin. Luke waved. Smiling, she circled Fiel back around and brought him to a walk near the boys. "Hi Luke. Hi Justin."

"Hi," Luke greeted with his usual wide grin. Justin only glanced at her. "You're riding a different horse."

"Yes, this is Fiel." Sierra brought Fiel to a halt and let Luke step up and pat his neck.

"He's nice."

"Luke, come on," Justin called. "Crystal's heading up for her ride."

"We're going to watch Crystal ride, but I'll be watching for you too," Luke called over his shoulder as he started out after Justin, already walking away.

Her anxiety had subsided as she galloped Fiel and felt his obedient responses, but a different kind of nervousness crept back in as she thought of Luke watching her. She forcefully pushed those thoughts away and moved Fiel back onto the warm-up field into working trot.

"Warm him up once or twice over the cross-bar," João called out as she trotted past him. She followed his advice, letting Fiel trot up to the rail, jump, and then canter on after landing.

"Number one-twelve," the ring steward signaled her. "You can head up to the starting box."

João walked alongside with a few last minute reminders about the best approaches to the trickier jumps on the course. He checked her girth, gave Fiel a pat on the rump, and said, "Off you go. I'll meet you at the finish gate."

"Thanks." Sierra walked Fiel in a small circle until the steward indicated she could enter the starting box.

"You start in two minutes, twenty seconds," the starter informed her, looking at his stopwatch.

Sierra nodded in acknowledgment and walked Fiel into the box and circled him around once.

Then the starter held up his arm holding a flag and started counting down, "Ten, nine, eight, seven, six, five, four, three, two…" His arm dropped down with the flag.

As soon as the flag dropped, Sierra released her holding aids, and Fiel sprang forward. Immediately she moved into two-point and let him pick up an easy canter. They were on course!

The first two jumps were easy; a rail fence and a coop, both on level ground. Then they came to the first downhill. Sierra settled back into the saddle and thrust her weight down through her heels, and Fiel galloped down without losing one stride of rhythm. At the bottom they had two strides on the level and then over the flower boxes. Sierra remembered immediately after landing, to sit back in the saddle and with a squeeze of the reins, slowed Fiel's pace to make a sharp turn, and then over a split rail fence. After that they galloped a long stretch on the level where they could pick up speed again. Fiel sailed over a brush jump and a railroad crossing jump.

"Bounce jump coming up," Sierra said, easing the pace again to help Fiel find his stride to negotiate the two fences set in a combination. Fiel jumped the first with a perfect landing and took off immediately to clear the second.

Next an uphill gallop with a log pile jump at the top, another stretch on level ground, and then a drop jump off a bank. Fiel took the bank faster than Sierra wanted, and she lost her balance and landed forward on his neck. He snorted but shortened his stride, giving her a chance to reposition herself in the saddle. "Good boy," she called out and urged him forward again into a full gallop along an even stretch of ground to the water crossing. Sierra did not detect even a flicker of hesitation as her brave horse splashed through. "Half way," she told him.

From the water they galloped to a jump of vertical stumps set upright in a row, then over a rail draped with old tires. Another easy downhill stretch brought them to a narrow ditch. Still on the level they cleared the hen house, then a combination of two green-and-white board fences.

Sierra slowed Fiel for another sharp turn and onto a stretch of road through a wooded section. They emerged from the woods into an open field and the last three obstacles. They sailed over the roll top, a stone wall, and then galloped forward on a straight line to the last jump, a thick log rail draped with a bright colored banner. Fiel flicked his ears suspiciously at the bright colors, but Sierra pressed with her legs and spoke reassuringly, "It's nothing; let's go." Fiel took the jump as if it wasn't even there.

They galloped through the flags of the finish gate; they had jumped clean and no time penalties!

Sierra brought Fiel to a walk greeted by applause and faces merged around her; Pam, João, and Luke. Strangers congratulated her. She leaned forward and hugged Fiel around his neck.

"He was fantastic!" Sierra met the eyes of João who beamed back in total agreement. She dismounted and Pam hugged her, with tears in her eyes and saying silly things like, "my baby."

Then João hugged her, no words needed to convey his pride. "Let's get this guy cooled out." He threw a cooler over Fiel's back and Sierra led him back to the stalls where she and

João pampered him with treats in abundance, a bath, another massage, and finally into his stall with a mound of hay. Pam stood by and watched, after a few attempts to help that only put her in the way.

They were about to head back to the camp site when João said, "I need a few moments to rest." He sat down on the canvas chair, his color ashen. He pulled a small brown bottle from his shirt pocket and fished out a tiny white tablet which he put in his mouth.

"João," Pam asked, concerned. "Is that nitroglycerin?"

He laughed. "Ah yes, the nursing student. Yes, I have a bit of angina. I'll be okay in a few minutes." Color was already returning to his face.

"What's going on?" Sierra asked, worried mostly by the look on her mother's face.

"It is my heart," João explained. "Nothing to worry about; I have an appointment next week for some studies." He stood up. "Much better, but I will take a little nap after all this excitement."

"Just hold him," Tess cried out as her adult student, who had come to watch the show and help out, tried to keep Moose standing by the mounting block. The thoroughbred had flung his head high and shied at every other object as he was led from his stall to the warm-up field for cross country, and his coat already gleamed with the dampness of his nerves. "Make him stand."

"I'm trying," the student answered. "He's very excited." She held tight to the bridle reins near the bit, struggling to hold his front end in place as he swung his hind end to the side.

Tess had one foot in the stirrup and leapt into the saddle. She quickly picked up the reins and shortened them into a tight hold. "You can let him go," she said needlessly for her student had already ducked away defensively as Moose half reared. "Settle down," Tess shouted at him as she dug her spurred heels into his sides to push him forward out of rearing. Moose dropped down to all four legs and bolted for the open field where other horses were warming up. Tess jerked hard left to turn him in a tight circle to regain control, and managed to bring him to a walk. Blowing loud through his nose and tossing his head, Moose fought every step.

Tess hadn't believed River when he told her that Moose was a different horse outside of a railed arena, but realized the truth when she had ridden the thoroughbred in his first horse trial early in the season. He performed well in his dressage test and in stadium jumping, so it had been a shock to find him wild with excitement when she rode the cross country course. It had been a terrifying ride but she had managed to get him around the course and they had actually placed third and qualified for the championship. His owner, a long-time client who sent Tess horses every year to train, had been thrilled that Moose had placed his first time out and qualified, and she had pushed Tess to continue to show him. Tess could not afford to disappoint her. She had River concentrate on Moose's manners out on the trail after that, and at the next two shows, he had been manageable. But Moose had thrown a shoe just a week before the championship and she had not been able to get the farrier out until the day before the show. River had not ridden him at all last week; and now she had a fight on her hands.

She wondered if she should scratch; she knew that was the sensible thing to do. She could explain to the owner that it was unfortunate he had lost a shoe so missed a week of work, and was not ready for today. It was amazing the difference in Moose when River rode him consistently. Tess truly believed it was because River was stronger than her, and therefore better able to control the thoroughbred. She didn't understand that

River got along with Moose because he rode with light and more tactful hands.

Her number was called and Tess determined to stick it out, hoping that once on course Moose would settle into his work. She headed him up the slope to the starting box, grateful it was uphill which made it easier to keep Moose under control. Inside the box, Tess kept him in a tight circle at a walk, although it was really more of a jig. The starter began the countdown. Tess waited until he reached three before turning Moose to face the exit out of the box. As the flag went down, Moose reared again and bolted madly forward at the touch of Tess's spurs.

They cleared the first three jumps too fast. Tess realized she had lost control and the best she could do was to keep him on course and stay in the saddle. She had no hope of slowing him down for he ran now as if in a race, ignoring all the pressure she exerted on the bit.

Dare I even try to finish? she considered, for the next jump was at the bottom of a downhill and at this pace…terror filled her heart.

They crested the hill and Moose careened down the descent with his ears flat and knowing only to run and run and run. The rails of the jump loomed in front of him. He was going too fast; he could not see a way over so he slid his back legs into a sudden skid and spun away.

Tess screamed as the shift in velocity and change of direction flung her from the saddle and she crashed to the ground.

"No…no." River leaned against the stall door with his arms folded tight and his mouth set in a firm line. It had taken him over an hour to cool down Moose, then bathe and groom him before finally settling the thoroughbred in his stall. Moose now munched on his hay in perfect calmness, oblivious to the havoc he had caused.

Tess sat on a bale of hay opposite the stall, her students hovering around. She had a bruise on her cheek, a wrenched shoulder and back, and she looked miserable. "River, this is extremely important. A good demonstration ride does so much for the reputation of Pegasus. You have to." Tess had been pleading with River to ride Gunsmoke in her place for the evening's performance. She had convinced the paramedics after her fall that she was not seriously injured; but the truth was her back went into a spasm if she moved suddenly or tried to stand up straight. She could barely walk, much less ride.

"I do not." River glowered back at her. He smoldered inside with anger at what he considered abuse of Moose; pushing him too early in his career. He was sorry Tess was hurt, but more than any concern for her, he was relieved that Moose was not.

"I'm willing to ride him, Tess," Crystal stepped forward to offer. "I know him well enough from the lessons you've given me on him, and I have time to learn the routine. I could do it."

Tess barely shifted her glance to Crystal. "You cannot." Her frustration was too much; she leaned forward, covering her face with her hands and burst into tears.

River's eyes opened wide in disbelief. Tess never lost control; never showed any sign of weakness. It disturbed him to see her sobbing into her hands and struggling to hold back the sounds of her misery. "Okay," he reluctantly agreed, the only thing he could think of to end the scene in front of him.

"Thank you," Tess choked out, keeping her face buried.

As River turned away from Tess, anxious to escape from the emotional group, he caught sight of Crystal staring at him icily, hatred emanating from her murderous glare.

When the scores were posted at the end of the day Crystal remained in first place. Katrina, with a clean cross country go, moved up into fourth place; the two entries previously ahead of her each had refusals on course, including Gloria. Gloria dropped into fifth place. Sierra remained in second place.

29 EVENING SHOW

There is nothing more beautiful than a horse reacting to nearly invisible aids and both horse and rider feeling as if their two bodies and souls have melted into one. – Walter Zeittl

After dinner, Pam, João, and Sierra headed over to the indoor pavilion for the evening's entertainment. They arrived early enough to procure seats in one of the front row bleachers, bringing reading material to pass the time until the show began. Sierra worked on the required reading for her history class, Pam studied her notes for an upcoming test, and João had his Wall Street Journal.

The seats gradually filled up around them, and finally a microphone squeaked. "Ladies and gentlemen," the announcer began the program. He welcomed everyone to the facility and to the regional championship. He announced the current team standings and then a few other announcements.

"Now, please sit back and enjoy the evening's entertainment." A trumpet blared over the loudspeaker. "Ladies and gentlemen, please welcome the Sunnyside Vaulting Club!"

Rousing music followed the trumpet blare as a group of ten riders on horses entered the pavilion and picked up the canter as they circled around. The riders looked to be all teenagers or younger, including one small girl riding a pony at the end of the line. They were dressed in identical red gymnastic tights with gold trim. Their horses had matching gold-trimmed red saddle pads, red track bandages on their legs, and red and gold ribbons in their manes. Instead of saddles they wore vaulting surcingles.

The riders performed a series of synchronized gymnastic moves; each rider first turning on the horse's back to face backwards, then back around and standing on the horse's back, then handstands, flips, and other feats. Then the group cantered back out of the pavilion, except for two dark bay horses. Their riders dismounted, led the horses in a small circle until eight kids on foot jogged back into the pavilion two-by-two, then split apart and formed two groups around each bay horse. The two kids who had remained with the horses now put them onto a circle at the end of a lunge line, one lunging to the right and one to the left. Then the other kids vaulted on and off the horses' backs in a series of gymnastics; forming pyramids and other formations. The two groups performed as mirror images of each other.

Their routine came to an end, and the vaulting team left the pavilion to the sound of enthusiastic applause.

"The Sunnyside Vaulting Team," the announcer called out again, and then gave a little speech about the history of the club and its members while a ground crew moved into the pavilion and within minutes, set up a dressage arena of moveable low white rails and white cones with black dressage letters.

Then the announcer introduced a series of riders performing kurs, or dressage musical freestyle routines; one riding fourth level, and one riding Prix St. George. Next, two riders on matching chestnuts performed a third level pas de

THE GIRL WHO LOVES HORSES

deux. As these were demonstration rides, horses and riders were attired informally, in costumes to match their selected music.

João made whispered comments to Sierra throughout the demonstrations, pointing out when a rider was using too much hand, or an improperly executed movement, but also complimenting when movements were done well. He opened Sierra's eyes to flaws that she would never have noticed, so intrigued by the overall pageantry and beauty of the performances.

"Ladies and gentlemen, for the final demonstration of the evening, we present a grand prix musical freestyle; Gunsmoke, owned by Pegasus Equestrian Center, a twenty-two year old Hanoverian and retired grand prix champion."

"Here comes Tess," Sierra informed Pam and João.

"Please note the change in your program. Teresa Holmes will not be riding tonight. Many of you are probably aware she had an unfortunate fall riding cross country today, but she is not seriously injured," the announcer quickly assured as sounds of commiseration wafted from the stands. "However, she is unable to ride tonight. In her place, Gunsmoke will be ridden by one of Ms. Holmes' students, River Girard."

"What?" Sierra cried out in surprise. She looked toward the entrance into the pavilion and sure enough, there sat River astride Gunsmoke. *How did Tess ever convince him to ride?* River wore a long-sleeved white shirt tucked into black breeches, black boots and his black helmet with his long hair tied back. Gunsmoke, a very dark gray, almost black in color, wore a black bridle with a white-edged browband set with sparkling clear stones, a white saddle pad, and white track bandages on his legs. They were a striking pair, all in black, gray, and white.

"Is that River?" João asked in surprise.

River nodded toward the announcer's stand, and music poured forth from the speakers, a dramatic flamenco-style guitar piece. The music fit the appearance of the black-and-white duo; they looked as if they could have ridden out of a swashbuckling tale.

Suddenly, Gunsmoke half reared with his ears back, and then he whirled, kicking out with his hind legs. *What just happened?* Sierra had never seen Gunsmoke act like that. There was a universal *ohh*, throughout the stands as the audience watched, expecting to see the rider thrown and a loose horse. A few people stood up.

With held breath, Sierra watched anxiously, her eyes on Gunsmoke. Then, among the throng of people at the entrance, she glimpsed the back of a boy ducking low and moving quickly away. She let her breath out slowly, wondering, *Justin?*

"Something spooked him," someone in the stands declared.

Somehow, River kept his seat. In fact to Sierra, it looked as if he moved as one with Gunsmoke's reaction, still in harmony with the frightened horse. Gunsmoke jumped forward in a gallop toward the dressage ring. Just before they entered at *A*, Gunsmoke flicked his ears, gathered the muscles of his back end underneath him, and gracefully arched his neck. The look in his eye changed from one of panic to one of intense concentration as his frantic gallop converted to a collected canter down the center line. Sierra knew River must be communicating with Gunsmoke although it appeared as if he did nothing at all but sit quietly on the big horse's back.

Gunsmoke came to a square halt at the center of the ring, the spot known as letter *X*. River saluted toward the announcer's stand. Then Gunsmoke moved forward into collected trot, tracked to the left and crossed to the center of the ring in a half-pass to the left. From the center, he reversed the bend in a half-pass to the right to return to the rail. Gunsmoke floated forward into passage around the short end of the arena, back to collected trot and the half-passes were repeated to the center and back. Then a serpentine through the arena at passage with steps of piaffe in the center of each loop. At the end of the serpentine he shifted back to a collected walk, then forward into collected canter with half-passes and appropriate lead changes and a canter pirouette in each direction at each end of the arena. After extended canter down the long side, he turned down the center line performing one-tempi changes (flying changes of lead at every stride); then extended canter in the other direction and one-tempi changes again down the center line. They finished the performance with extended trot across one diagonal and then into canter across the other diagonal with changes of lead every two strides, and down the center line in passage to a square halt and ending salute.

Gunsmoke moved with such lightness that he appeared to float, to dance through the test; every movement effortless and pleasurable. He snorted in rhythm with his trot and canter strides, foam collected at the corners of his mouth as he chewed his bit, his ears flicked back and forth, and his tail seemed to swish in rhythm with the music. River appeared as if a melded appendage of the mighty horse, all his signals to Gunsmoke invisible to the onlookers.

The audience stood as one and roared into applause and cheering as Gunsmoke and River walked out of the arena. "Gunsmoke of Pegasus Equestrian Center," the announcer blared over the loudspeaker. "What a performance, folks! A champion!" he gushed on. "Hard to believe the horse is twenty-two years old. Incredible! And rider, River Girard; he's fifteen years old, folks!" The applause and cheering continued even after the pair disappeared from sight.

"Sierra, I had no idea a horse could move like that," Pam sighed. "He was literally dancing!"

João had sat in silence throughout the performance. He looked at Sierra now and she saw tears in his eyes that he quickly brushed away. He hugged her with one arm across her shoulders and said, "Let's go find him." They gathered their things and pushed a way through the crowd that was filtering through the exits now that the show was over.

They found River outside the pavilion, still astride Gunsmoke and surrounded by a crowd of people praising the performance and asking questions. He looked dazed and exhausted. A rivulet of sweat trickled from his hairline down one cheek, and dampness streaked the back of his shirt.

"What kind of horse is he? Who trained him? How long have you been riding?" The typical questions barraged River, who could only stare back or answer with one word. Sierra could imagine how desperately he wanted to get away.

"River," she called out, "do you need help?"

He saw her and João and nodded yes, a look of relief on his face. The crowd moved away enough for Sierra and João to come up to Gunsmoke and take the bridle reins while River dismounted. He still seemed dazed and held onto the saddle, leaning against Gunsmoke while he stroked his damp neck.

Just then Katrina with a cooler in her arms, and Ann emerged, having pushed their way through the crowd. "We'll take him back to his stall," Ann said. João handed her the reins and then took hold of River's arm to steady him while Sierra and Katrina placed the cooler over Gunsmoke's back.

"Come, River, you need to sit down," João stated as River tried to follow Gunsmoke.

"I need to take care of Gunsmoke first," River insisted.

João laughed and Sierra smiled. She didn't think River had ever had anyone take care of his horse for him after he rode. "Let the girls see to him now," João said and began to steer River toward some tables and chairs near a snack stand.

"Is he okay?" someone in the crowd asked. Another person handed River a bottle of water which he gratefully accepted. They reached the chairs and all of them sat down.

Pam, who had been hovering at the edge of the crowd, joined them.

River tipped the bottle of water and gulped it dry, then wiped across his mouth with his sleeve. He scowled at the smear on the white cloth. "I need to get out of these borrowed clothes."

"I think you need to rest for a few minutes," João said. Then he placed his hand on River's shoulder. "I am so proud of you."

River, who had been avoiding eye contact, finally looked into the face of his friend. "All I did was ride a horse."

"You spoke to your horse and he listened, and the two of you danced together," João responded in a soft voice.

River ducked his head. "I nearly blew it. Did you see all those people? I admit they kind of scared me, all staring at us. I guess I was more nervous than I realized to have upset Gunsmoke like that."

"I saw and I also saw how you shut them out and then it was just you and Gunsmoke. Am I right?" João reassured him.

River nodded. "I had to gallop him up to the entrance to catch up with the music," he said with a short laugh.

"But you did catch up and you had him nicely collected when you entered the ring. You have a gift, boy. People spend a lifetime trying to reach a level of communication with a horse that you have had for years."

"He was so good. I should be taking care of him now." River started to get up.

João touched him back down with his hand. "You can go praise him in a few minutes, but let the girls take care of him. He will enjoy the attention just as much from them."

"River, I think…" Sierra started, but then bit back the words. She wondered if anyone else had seen Justin in the crowd. She actually didn't see him do anything to Gunsmoke, *but he must have!* She had no proof and River seemed to think it was his own nerves that had upset his horse. Instead, she asked, "What happened to Tess?"

"She had a fall from Moose on her cross country ride and hurt her back."

"Wow, that's awful for her. I'm surprised she was able to convince you to ride in her place."

River laughed. "Believe me, I didn't want to. But there really was nobody else who could. I already knew the routine because I had ridden Gunsmoke a few times at home for her so she could watch how it looked."

"He is an amazing horse," Sierra said needlessly.

"Yeah, not too bad for an old man," River smiled.

"Watch it now," João said with humor.

River ducked his head but after a few minutes he looked up at João and very humbly said, "Um, I'm sorry about...you know."

João nodded. "You should not have stayed away. I have missed you." And he hugged River.

30 DAY THREE: STADIUM JUMPING

Under a rider who has a heart for the animal, the correctly trained horse will work with joy and happiness, while a horse that carries its rider with fear and hesitation accuses him of being unfair and cruel. – Gustav Steinbrecht, *The Gymnasium of the Horse*

Monday, the final day of the show, consisted of stadium jumping.

"Compared with the cross country, not too difficult," João stated. He walked the course with Sierra coaching her on the number of strides for optimal approach and where she could cut corners if she needed to make up time. There were ten obstacles and heights were again up to two feet, eleven inches. João insisted that Sierra walk the approach several times to a double combination with two strides between the elements; to be sure she knew just where Fiel would need to take off in order to land with enough room to take his two strides. The only other jump that might be a challenge was an oxer that they would have to approach after a sharp turn. But it was a course similar to ones they had practiced over at home, and Sierra felt confident Fiel could manage this one.

Sierra fed and groomed Fiel in the morning and then hand walked him around while João studied him for any signs of lameness or stiffness after his cross country round yesterday. He seemed fine and ready to go, prancing or going into passage when passing other horses, still showing off.

Sierra also helped River with the Pegasus horses, and was pleased that he seemed very cheerful. "You're in a good mood today," she said to him.

"What do you mean? I'm always in a good mood," he quipped back, and they both laughed. "You were right," he said a little while later. "I should have gone to João and apologized a long time ago."

"I'm very glad that you did."

The only blight to the morning was when Crystal came through the stalls while Sierra was helping River clean, wanting to show off Galaxy to Justin and Luke. Sierra hadn't showered yet and felt very grimy from stall cleaning. She really didn't want Luke to see her in her unkempt condition.

In her usual snobbish manner, Crystal totally ignored Sierra and River as she brought the two boys up to Galaxy's stall. But Luke noticed.

"Hi Sierra," he called out, smiling brightly. "I saw some of your jumps yesterday. You guys were amazing!"

"Thanks," she smiled back, her face heating up with color. *Why does that always happen when he speaks to me?* She groaned inwardly.

"Hey, you're the guy who rode that horse last night to that really cool guitar music," Luke said to River, recognizing him.

River looked up briefly and returned to shoveling wet shavings without saying anything. Good mood or not, his social graces hadn't improved.

"Awesome ride, dude," Luke said, undaunted. Crystal scowled at him, very annoyed that his attention had drifted from her presentation of Galaxy. Luke turned back to peer in at Crystal's horse and made appropriate complimentary remarks.

As they turned to leave, Luke called out, "What time do you ride, Sierra?"

"At one-ten," she answered. "It should be two rides after Crystal."

"Great, I'll see you then." He waved as they left.

"Who's that guy that's been hanging around you?" River asked a while later, sounding irritated.

"Who, Luke? He's a friend from school. I've known him since eighth grade."

River turned back to his pitchfork, reticent as usual.

Thirty minutes before her scheduled stadium time, João announced, "Time to mount up. I'll finish him."

Sierra nodded and relinquished to him the body brush she had been working over Fiel's back. His announcement brought the butterflies back, flitting annoyingly around in her stomach. She stepped in front of a small mirror they had suspended on the wall next to Fiel's stall, and concentrated on tying her stock tie, using the task to distract her nervousness. Then she donned her hunt coat and smoothed down her hair before buckling on her helmet.

They led Fiel to the warm-up area as he tossed his head and pranced, aware that again, something was up.

"Working trot to loosen him up," João advised as he held the bridle while Sierra mounted. "Remember, keep him light and encourage him to stretch."

Sierra nodded, and focused all her attention on Fiel, sensing his nervous excitement through her seat and legs as they walked away from the mounting block. With a summoning of all her will, she forced all thoughts from her mind but Fiel, and whispered in self-coaching, "Easy does it. We're at home; nothing's any different except a few other horses around." She stretched and rolled her shoulders, took a few deep breaths and then allowed Fiel, already pulling at the bit, to step up to trot.

"Good, good, just like that," João assured, watching as Sierra kept her hands light and used her weight and core muscles to tell Fiel to maintain an even rhythm. Fiel stretched his neck into her giving hands and snorted. João smiled and nodded at his student, very pleased. After a few minutes of trotting, he told Sierra to walk him on a loose rein once or twice around, and then a few rounds of hand gallop.

A few low jumps were set up in the warm-up ring and a few minutes before Sierra's number was called, João coached her to take Fiel over a cross bar and then a low vertical. They were ready. Sierra left the warm-up area and walked to the stadium ring steward to check-in.

"Two rides ahead of you," he said.

Crystal just then entered the ring on Galaxy, so Sierra positioned Fiel where she could watch her go.

"Hi," Luke suddenly appeared at Fiel's side, grinning, and gave Fiel a pat on his neck.

"Hi, Crystal's just going in."

Luke stayed at Fiel's side as they watched together. Galaxy seemed tired or at least lacking enthusiasm. Crystal wore spurs and carried a jumping bat. She dug with her spurs in quick succession a few times to motivate Galaxy into a forward-moving canter as they started their beginning circle. Galaxy approached the first jump with his head high and a frightened look in his eye. He hesitated, clearly indicating he had no desire to jump. Crystal added a whack with her crop in addition to spurs to push him on. He picked up his pace and cleared the first obstacle high and wide, a style Sierra figured resulted from the rapping experience. The novice level jumps shouldn't really have posed much of a challenge to a horse of Galaxy's scope, but nevertheless, his heart didn't seem to be in the task before him and Crystal had to drive constantly. They were half way through the course with the double combination next.

"Come on, Galaxy," Sierra spoke out loud, remembering how lazy he could be. She liked the sweet-tempered horse and wanted to see him do well, and especially avoid abuse from Crystal.

As they approached the double, Crystal swatted Galaxy with the bat at the correct spot for him to take off. Galaxy laid his ears back and brought his head up, but rather than taking off, he took a short stride and then jumped, again with a foot to spare. He had taken off too late, jumping wide, and he landed too close to the next element; he would not be able to get in two strides. Crystal swatted him again and he took off after only one stride. Too far back, he crashed into the jump, knocking the top two rails down, earning four faults. Galaxy cleared the remainder of the course, but he also earned two penalties for two seconds over the time allowance. He had a total of six penalties.

Crystal left the ring scowling. As soon as she turned a corner out of sight of the arena, she jerked mercilessly on Galaxy's mouth and slashed his shoulder with her whip.

The next rider ahead of Sierra cleared the course but also with two time penalties.

"Number one-twelve," the ring steward called Sierra's number.

"Here we go," she said, glancing at Luke, and then toward the stands where João and Pam sat together, watching. João nodded, smiling; her mother stared with wide open eyes.

"Good luck," Luke encouraged and winked at her as he gave Fiel a pat on the neck.

"Hey, Luke." Just then Justin came up behind them. Sierra turned her head slightly and saw him raise a hand and pat Fiel on the rump.

Suddenly, Fiel flattened his ears with a squeal and bucked. Totally unexpected, Sierra lost her balance and found herself thrown forward over his neck and slipping off to the side. Fiel whirled to run, but a nearby spectator grabbed at his bridle and brought him to a halt. In a daze, Sierra righted herself in the saddle.

"What happened?" She heard others around her asking, echoing the question in her own mind.

"Are you okay?" João appeared at her side, her mother behind him with frightened eyes.

"Something spooked him," Sierra answered, gulping in air to still her racing heart. *Justin did something to Fiel and probably the same thing he did to Gunsmoke last night!* Suspicions barraged her brain. *Crystal's idea; an attempt to jeopardize my ride?* Sierra felt frozen, as much from fright as the realization that Crystal could do such a thing. Fiel and she as well as people nearby could have been hurt! Her mind blanked out everything but the shock of what Crystal was capable of doing in order to win.

"Do you want to scratch?" João asked?

Yes, I'm scared; I don't even remember the course. Those thoughts whirled through Sierra's mind. But then Fiel snorted, shaking his head and he took a tentative step forward. *Fiel knows his business!* Sierra looked between Fiel's ears toward the ring; where her horse had focused his attention. Fiel took another step and with his determination, Sierra's mind cleared. It was as if Fiel was telling her everything was okay now.

"We're going in," she stated and touched Fiel's sides with a whisper of her legs. The others moved aside. "Thanks, Fiel," she whispered and touched his neck as they entered the ring.

Her wonderful horse responded with eager energy. They entered at a brisk trot and right into canter for the beginning circle. Feeling Fiel's power beneath her, Sierra's mind kicked back into gear and she turned Fiel toward the first obstacle. His ears pricked forward and he jumped into a gallop with no urging from her. From then on, Sierra merely steered him around, pointing him at each obstacle of the course, and only a few times bringing his pace a little slower. But Fiel knew how to judge his distances with little help from his rider. Sierra sat back slightly as they approached the double, cautioning him, and just at the take-off point, moved forward again into two-point. Fiel took off, cleared the first element, took his two strides and cleared the second. They cleared the next vertical and then Sierra sat back and squeezed the reins to slow him for the turn; then on to the oxer. He cleared it easily; then the last two jumps of the course, and through the finish flags. A clear round!

The announcement came over the loudspeaker, "Number one hundred and twelve, no penalties." Sierra and Fiel had moved into first place.

Sierra left the arena on a loose rein, Fiel unperturbed by the applause around him with his head and neck arched proudly as if he knew it was in his honor. Sierra lavished him with pats and praise, her own face beaming.

Just before she rode up to where João waited, his own face proudly smiling, she spied Crystal and Justin standing next to Luke. Luke was watching her and waved his arms with thumbs up triumphantly when he caught her eye. But Crystal was speaking sharply to Justin, her face contorted in rage. Sierra could not help smiling spitefully to herself. *Crystal, you're not a very gracious loser.*

The Pegasus junior team retained first place for the team standings. Katrina also had a clear round and moved up into second place. Crystal dropped down to third place and Gloria finished fifth. Ann finished third in her division.

Sierra was not on a team, so she merely accepted the first place award in junior novice as an individual. It was perhaps the proudest moment of her life as she and Fiel joined the others who had placed, in a victory canter around the ring at the end of the day. She took home a fancy blue ribbon and a silver trophy of a jumping horse and rider inscribed with *Pacific Regional Combined Training Championship, Junior Novice.*

Best of all, they took home a beautiful and fit horse who seemed to have enjoyed the competition as much as she did; her wonderful Fiel!

31 JOÃO

Lived in his saddle, loved the chase, the course, and always, ere he mounted, kiss'd his horse. – William Cowper

Sierra kept up a stream of happy chatter to her mother during the drive home. "I'm so glad you got to see me ride. Isn't Fiel the most wonderful horse?"

"He sure is, Kitten."

"And he is so perfect for me. I can't believe how great it is to have met such a wonderful and kind man as João, willing to share his horse with me. You know he's given up so much of his own riding time for me? I think that's been quite a sacrifice for him, because he loves riding Fiel. And don't you think River is the best rider you've ever seen? I will never forget that amazing demonstration ride."

"Yes, Sweetie, it was certainly spectacular."

"Can you believe I won? I actually won! Me and Fiel!"

Pam reached over and patted her daughter's knee. "So, did you get your homework finished?" she asked slyly.

"Most of it. I just have to answer a few questions for history. I can easily finish those tonight. I did get all the reading done."

"You know, I'm just a little worried about João. I saw him take his nitroglycerin pills two other times."

"Mom!" That news put a damper on the perfect day.

Pam patted Sierra's leg again. "I'm just glad he is going in for tests next week. If there is anything wrong with his heart there are lots of good treatments nowadays."

"Good," Sierra said in relief. She really did not want to think about anything bad today. "Mom, River is going to sort of mention to Tess that I would be willing to work for her again. You know they haven't found anyone who's worked out yet."

"That's because you're irreplaceable," Pam grinned. "But Sierra, I really don't like the idea of you working under those conditions again. She treated you very unfairly and was unkind to you."

"I know, but I miss working with River and all the horses. I wouldn't mind working there just on weekends. Then I could still ride Fiel during the week after school. But I would only do it if she actually paid me."

"If she were to pay you what you're worth then I suppose it would be okay."

"We'll see. I still kind of doubt she'll be willing to pay me. But River says the three girls that they hired after me were getting paid."

"How that woman used you," Pam said again.

Then Sierra started in on a dissertation of all the jumps and how wonderful Fiel was at each one, with Pam politely nodding or saying, "uh huh."

"So who was the nice looking boy hanging around?"

"You mean Luke? Mom, he wasn't exactly hanging around." But that kept Sierra going for another thirty miles telling her mother all about Luke, until she finally wound down and fell asleep.

The next day at school during lunch, Allison graciously listened to Sierra's detailed retelling of the championship, and like a true friend, congratulated her heartily on her win.

"Maybe I'll come watch one of your shows," Allison said. "They actually sound pretty interesting."

"Allison, that would be so cool. But the season's over for the year. Shows won't start back up until April."

"Oh, that's fine. You know, I think I need to meet this River of yours. He sounds so interesting."

"River?"

"Oh yes. You know I heard about his ride from Katrina this morning. We have art together. It sounds like that would have been something to see."

"It was so incredibly awesome. I wish you could have seen it. I know how much you love music and dance, and it was truly an equestrian ballet."

"Doesn't River go to this school?"

"Yeah, I guess he's a sophomore or junior. But I haven't seen him around so far."

"Well, keep your eye out for him and introduce me if the chance comes up."

"Sure," Sierra agreed but somehow had trouble imagining how introducing Allison to River would go.

"From the sound of it, I think Luke is definitely interested," Allison changed the subject.

Sierra blushed. *Why do I do that?* "I don't know. It's hard to know if he's interested, or if it's just his natural friendliness."

"I can assure you it's more than just his natural friendliness. I'm still surprised he didn't ask you to the eighth grade graduation ball last year."

Sierra wondered if her avoidance of him at the end of eighth grade might have had something to do with the lack of an invitation. But that might just be her own wishful thinking. She heard he had gone to the dance with a very pretty and popular girl; much cuter than herself.

"But Homecoming's next month. You never know…" Allison said in a thoughtful tone.

"Sierra!" Calling her name in an excited squeal, Katrina pushed her way through the cafeteria tables. "I never got a chance to congratulate you on your win." Katrina sat down at their table.

Sierra smiled a welcome. "Thanks, and you and Calliope did really great too."

"Thanks. Hi, Allison."

"Hi, Katrina, have a seat," Allison said wryly, since Katrina had already sat down.

"The thing is, I've been showing for three years and this is the first time I've placed in the championship. You won your very first time. That's incredible."

"Well, I have a great horse to ride and a great teacher."

"You're lucky. Is River still teaching you?"

"No," Sierra answered. "I owe a lot to River who gave me a great start. But I'm taking lessons now from the man who owns Fiel."

"Oh, that ex-jockey; yeah," she said knowingly.

"So," Sierra had to ask. "How is Crystal dealing with not winning?"

"Oh, she is so furious," Katrina ducked her head and lowered her voice. "She can't stand that my appaloosa actually beat her expensive warmblood; not to mention you winning on a horse and with a trainer that isn't even from Pegasus."

Katrina laughed. "She had notices up to sell Galaxy even before we left the show grounds."

Sierra shook her head, but not really surprised, and hoped that maybe Galaxy would end up with a more compassionate owner.

"You would probably be wise to stay out of her way," Katrina advised, an ominous look in her eyes.

"Gladly," Sierra agreed, but with a sinking feeling in the pit of her stomach. She didn't need Katrina's warning after what she suspected Crystal had plotted with Justin to do to Fiel and Gunsmoke.

Later, Luke caught up with Sierra between classes and added his congratulations.

"Thanks," Sierra hesitated and then asked, "Luke, can I ask you something?"

"Sure," he said, breaking into his friendly grin which lit up his blue eyes.

"Do you think Justin might have done something to upset Fiel and also to River's horse?"

Luke's face fell, the bright smile replaced by a worried look.

"Please, I saw him there. Tell me what you know."

"Well," he hesitated. "I don't really know. I don't want to get him in trouble."

"I'm not going to say anything. I just want to know," Sierra promised.

"I did overhear him and Crystal whispering about something. I know he has this gadget that gives an electric shock. He likes to play tricks on kids at school with it."

Of course; that's how he tripped Billy last year! "Do you think he might have used it on the horses?"

"Sierra, I don't know. Please, forget it. No one got hurt."

"But one of us could have been hurt. I almost fell off!"

Luke nodded, looking half ashamed. "Yeah, and I'm so glad you weren't. But the truth is, I don't really know."

"Luke, how can you be friends with someone like that?"

"Justin's okay. We've been best friends since the third grade. It's Crystal…"

Sierra just shook her head, "I have to get to class."

After school, Sierra jumped off the bus and ran home to change into her grubby clothes to hurry off and see Fiel. João had said they would give him a few days off after his hard work over the weekend, but she still wanted to visit him and give him carrots and she had an apple from their tree.

She bicycled up to the barn and parked her bike in the usual space. Charlie emerged from somewhere, wagging his tail and whined a greeting.

"Hey, Charlie boy." Sierra leaned down and stroked his head and back a few times before heading off to the pasture with her treats. She entered the gate and called out, "Fiel!"

She heard his whinny and a few minutes later he emerged from under the trees and trotted up to her.

"Hey, handsome," she greeted him with hugs and pats, but he was mostly interested in what she had in her pockets. Laughing, Sierra pulled out the carrots, breaking them into pieces; and then the apple which she shared with him. She took a bite and then gave him a bite. Of course his bites were much bigger. She spent a little time with Fiel, stroking him as he turned back to grazing when the treats were gone.

"Well, I better say goodbye and get to my homework." She kissed Fiel on his muzzle when he brought his head up to nuzzle for any remaining carrot.

Sierra left the pasture and went to the house to say hi to João. She knocked to let him know she was there and then turned the door handle to go in. To her surprise, she found it locked. João never locked his door when he was at home.

"Has he gone somewhere?" Sierra asked Charlie, who sat at her feet, tail thumping. She shrugged and retrieved her bicycle. It was a bit of a mystery because both João's car and truck were parked in their usual places.

"See you later," she called to Charlie who sat in the driveway whining as she mounted her bicycle. The back of her neck tingled, sending a thread of worry into her stomach as she started pedaling down the driveway. *Something is wrong. Where is João?* But not knowing what else she could do, she tamped down her worry and headed home.

Pam would not be home until after seven, as it was one of her clinical days at the hospital where they worked twelve-hour shifts. Sierra dutifully spent the quiet afternoon finishing her homework and then started dinner preparations. She took the hamburger out of the refrigerator that she had taken from the freezer this morning. She planned to make Sloppy Joes, a recipe she had made before with great success. She grabbed an onion from the vegetable bin, and then a can of tomato sauce from the cupboard, leaving it open to study the spice assortment. *Did I add oregano last time?*

The sound of tires crunching up the driveway and then the silence of a killed motor signaled Pam's arrival. "Hi, Mom," Sierra greeted without turning; still contemplating the spices as the front door opened.

"Sierra."

The tone of Pam's voice caused Sierra to instantly turn around.

"Honey, come here." Pam stood in the kitchen doorway, her face ashen and drawn, her eyes bloodshot and her nose red. Her mother had been crying!

Speechless with dread, Sierra walked over to her and Pam pulled her daughter into her arms and held her tightly.

"Mom, just tell me," Sierra said with her face pressed into her mother's breast.

"João…" She made a choking sound.

Sierra squeezed her eyes tight, keeping her face pressed into the warmth of Pam.

"He had a massive heart attack and he died at the hospital today."

Sierra's own heart seized up in her chest. She gulped for air, sucking in the scent of her mother, her comfort and solid mass to cling to as the hot tears erupted and flowed. Pam guided her to the sofa in the living room, and the two sank onto the cushions, clinging to each other as desperately as to a life-preserver.

"It just can't be true," Sierra sobbed through her tears.

"I know, Baby, I know."

"Tell me everything," Sierra pleaded as her sobs subsided into sniffles.

"He placed a nine-one-one call this afternoon. By the time the paramedics arrived he was already down. They did everything they could. I won't go into the details but he was brought into the emergency room in full cardiac arrest. They were able to shock his heart back into a rhythm a few times, but it didn't last. All the drugs we have, nothing lasted. And finally his poor heart wouldn't even respond to defibrillation anymore."

"Mom, don't say those words to me, I don't understand," Sierra wailed.

"Honey, you've seen on TV when they use the paddles. That's what I'm talking about."

"Were you there?"

"I'm doing my clinical in emergency room this week, so I was there when they brought him in. My preceptor had told me a cardiac arrest patient was expected in and suggested it would be a good experience for me to observe. I had no idea it would be João. Oh, Baby, it was awful." Pam pulled her daughter tight again, with more tears spilling.

"I thought you said there were all kinds of treatments for bad hearts," Sierra demanded.

"If a person gets to those treatments in time…for João, it was just too late."

Suddenly, Sierra sat up straight. "What about Fiel, and Charlie? Who's going to take care of them?"

"I talked with João's lawyer before I left the hospital. Apparently he has no family in the United States and his lawyer is listed as his contact person. He was surprised to meet me at the hospital because our names are mentioned in some of his documents. The lawyer asked if you would be able to care for the animals until he can make arrangements; probably just for a day or two."

"Of course I can. I was over there today to see Fiel. In fact, I better go over there right now and bring him in from the pasture and feed him."

"I'll drive you."

Thanks," and then through more sniffles, "can we bring Charlie home with us?"

"Yes, of course."

"Can we go right now?"

They found Fiel standing at the pasture gate, tossing his head as Sierra and her mother exited the car. He trumpeted a loud and questioning whinny. Charlie bounded forward, and glued himself to Sierra's side, determined not to be left alone again.

"It's all right now," Sierra soothed horse and dog as she haltered Fiel and led him into his stall. She efficiently tossed in his hay ration and then filled the manger with his grain and supplements. She checked his automatic waterer and then around the barn to be sure all was in order. When she could find nothing more to justify lingering, she gave Fiel a hug around his neck and a pat before shutting the lights out and closing the barn doors.

"I don't like the idea of him being here with no one around," Sierra said remorsefully, as she walked away from the barn.

"I know, Kitten, but I don't know what we can do about that immediately. It sounds like the lawyer is going to work on arrangements."

A shiver ran through Sierra as she thought about Fiel being taken away; she hadn't yet thought of that. *Please, no; that can't happen!*

"Come on, Charlie." Sierra needlessly coaxed him to jump into the back seat of the car next to her. He had trailed after her, his wet nose frequently bumping against her leg for reassurance, keeping her sight and smell within his reach. "It feels so wrong driving off and leaving him alone here," Sierra repeated as Pam started the car's engine.

"It's the best we can do for now, and I'll drive you back early in the morning before school."

"Okay, thanks…that will help." Then another thought suddenly occurred to her. "Oh, Mom; who's going to tell River?"

"His name is mentioned in João's papers as well. The lawyer said he was going to try to reach him this evening."

"Poor River," Sierra sighed.

Pam glanced at her daughter sympathetically in her rear-view mirror. "Yes, this is going to be very hard for him," she agreed.

João is dead. My teacher, mentor, but most of all, my dear friend; dead. Over the next few days those thoughts constantly wafted around every other thought in Sierra's head; suddenly displacing the answer to a question on her history test, or the solution to a math problem, or the instructions in a recipe at home. And each time the thought invaded, it was like knives slicing at all the tender spots inside that could feel and care about another person. It twisted her stomach into painful knots; it coursed like a burn up and down her spine, and caused her head to throb. His was the first death of someone she was close to and had loved deeply. Her father had died before she was born so she never knew him. Her old grandfather died when she was six, and she remembered how hard that time had been for her mother. But she hardly knew that man either, and couldn't remember feeling anything at all except sympathy for her mother. But losing João was an ache that felt like a ragged hole in her chest; a hole that constantly reminded her something was missing.

The day after João died, Sierra went to Pegasus. She had to see River.

He was there working; schooling a horse in the outdoor arena over a course of low jumps. She watched him without letting him know she was there, staying back in the shade of a tree where she found Storm resting. He rode a horse she didn't recognize, a large bay that looked like a warmblood breed, probably a horse brought in for Tess to train. As usual, she marveled at the magic of watching River move in harmony with the animal he rode; quietly communicating through aids that she could never detect.

When he finished the session and dismounted, Sierra stepped out from the shade and went up to him. "Hi, River."

He looked at her with narrowed eyes. "What are you doing here?"

"You know why I'm here."

"Sierra, please go away. I can't talk about it."

She didn't say anything but kept walking next to him as he led the bay to the stable.

"Please…go," he said again.

"He was my friend too."

"Go away." River stopped abruptly and faced her.

"No, River, we can help each other."

He glared at her but Sierra refused to give in to his mood. He muttered something through clenched teeth and abruptly turned away, leading the horse into the crossties; ignoring her.

Sierra gave up, and scuffling her feet as she studied the ground, slowly walked away, her shoulders slumped in dejection.

"Sierra, eet ees so good to see you!" Manuel exclaimed as he strode up from the lane leading a horse in from the paddock.

Sierra looked up and smiled at her old friend. "Hi, Manuel, how've you been?"

"Good, good, but meessing you. Nobody, dees girls, no work like you."

"Thanks, Manuel, it's kind of you to say so." Sierra fell into step alongside him. "How's Rosa?"

"Good, she doing good. You come to the trailer to see."

"I would like to; but you know Tess told me to stay away from here," Sierra explained.

Manuel nodded, and then his face shifted into a more serious expression. "Do you know what 'appen now to Reever?" he asked.

Sierra told him about João. Manuel nodded in understanding as he listened.

"Well, I gotta go," Sierra said as they reached the stable doors. "I'm taking care of our friend's horse until arrangements are made for him, so I've got to go there now."

"You bring dees 'orse 'ere, no?" Manuel suggested.

"I don't know what will happen," Sierra sighed. "Say hi to Rosa." They said goodbye and Sierra left to take care of Fiel before she went home.

32 FIEL

Horses change lives. They give our young people confidence and self-esteem. They provide peace and tranquility to troubled souls – they give us hope! – Toni Robinson.

João had left instructions with his lawyer expressing his wishes in case of his death. He wanted his body cremated and the ashes sent back to his father's old farm in Portugal. He requested no formal funeral or any type of ceremony. If his friends wished, he hoped they might get together to celebrate the accomplishments of his life; not to mourn him.

But the dead really have no say once they are gone. João had made many friends during his racing career and then in his consulting business. A few of them arranged a memorial service held at the local Catholic church.

Sierra and Pam attended. Sierra was not surprised by the crowd of people who came to say goodbye; all strangers to her except River's father sitting a few rows away. *Where is River?* Well, no surprise; he did have a tendency to avoid situations that upset him. But after the ceremony, she caught a fleeting glimpse of him at the back of the church, leaving ahead of the crowd. *At least he came.*

A few days after the memorial service, Mr. Tanglewilde, João's lawyer, called to make an appointment with Pam. He was willing to come to the cottage.

"Mr. Mateus left a will," the lawyer informed Pam and Sierra. They sat at the kitchen table. Pam had made coffee and she and the lawyer each had a mug in front of them.

"I don't know if you are aware of his financial situation," Mr. Tanglewilde began, as he reached into to his brief case and brought out a fat folder. Pam and Sierra both shook their heads no. "He was actually quite well off; having made some very wise investments, a good life insurance policy, and also well-compensated in his consulting work. He was a very smart man." Mr. Tanglewilde coughed and adjusted his glasses as he opened the folder and studied a paper in front of him as if he had never seen it before. "Let me acquaint you with the terms of his will that apply to you or may interest you."

"He has left a considerable sum of money to his one living relative, a sister in Portugal. He has made several donations to charitable organizations including one that rescues abused domestic animals." He coughed again, and took a swig of coffee. "To River Girard, he has set up a fund that will finance one hundred percent of a college education. This fund will exist until River uses it for his education or until he reaches the age of fifty. If by that age he has not chosen to avail himself of a college education, then the money will be donated to the following charities." Mr. Tanglewilde read off the names.

Sierra gasped. *João has given River a college education!* And she hoped with all her heart that he would take advantage of the generous gift.

"To Sierra Landsing, he leaves his registered Lusitano gelding, Fiel; and all possessions that relate to his care and riding, including grooming equipment, halters, bridles, saddles, and other miscellaneous gear. In addition, he has placed in a fund, monies that are to be used for the care of Fiel, including but not limited to board, veterinary fees, farrier expenses, equipment for horse and rider, entry fees, and other miscellaneous expenses." He then passed across the table to Sierra a paper with the terms of the fund and the amount of money. She could barely believe what she read. It was enough money to care for a horse for at least ten years and perhaps longer. The lawyer waited while she looked the paper over, and then passed it to Pam.

Sierra sat as still as stone, feeling paralyzed while Mr. Tanglewilde continued reading. João bequeathed enough money for Pam to finish her nursing education as well as cover living expenses so that she would not need to work while attending school. He left a generous amount of money in a separate trust fund for River, set up in such a way that River's father could not access the account. He left his truck and horse trailer to Pam. The lawyer told them that João had requested that he continue to assist them in managing the money, to help them with any taxes related to inheritance, and that he had been provided with a fund to assure he would be compensated for his services to Pam and her daughter.

João's death dramatically changed Sierra's and her mother's lives.

The day after hearing the terms of the will, Sierra returned to Pegasus about the time she knew River would be finished with chores and leaving for the day. She waited in the lane, hoping to confront him on his way home. Her timing was perfect; within ten minutes she saw him and Storm.

"River." Sierra stepped into his path.

He glared at her, stepped around and kept walking.

She followed and grabbed his arm. "Why are you mad at me?" He jerked his arm away and increased his pace. She kept up with him. "River, stop this!"

He did stop and whirled to face her. "Sierra, can't you please just leave me alone?"

"I don't understand why you're so mad at me." She felt tears forming and gulped hard to hold them back.

"I'm not mad at you. It just hurts too much to see you." He turned away, hugging himself tightly, but at least didn't walk away.

Sierra stood frozen, staring at his back. He kicked at a stone in the lane, then bent down, picked it up and flung it into the woods as hard as he could. She could feel his violent rage from where she timidly stood, a few feet away. Storm sat looking back and forth between them, her posture tense and alert. She never even glanced in the direction of the rock.

"It hurts me to have you reject me," Sierra said to his back.

"I can't help that." He started to walk away again.

Sierra could stand it no longer. She ran after him, repeating...shouting, "Yes, you can. Yes, you can. Yes, you can." She grabbed his arm again and held on with all her strength as he tried to pull it free. "Yes...you can!" She was sobbing now, no longer able to hold back the tears. "Please, River. I've lost João. I can't stand to lose you too."

River gave up. He stopped and pulled her into his arms, holding her tight against his chest, his cheek nestled into her hair. Sierra reached around his waist, holding equally as tight, and buried her face into the smell of him. Like her mother whose particular scent was a comfort to her, the smell of River seeped in through her nostrils, a balm that soothed the painful, raw spots inside.

They stood in the lane, holding onto each other until Sierra's sobs finally subsided. The sun was setting and the nights of September chilled quickly after sundown. But she felt warm and comforted within River's arms. She felt his chest rise and fall as he sighed deeply and he whispered into her hair, "Sierra."

She shivered, but not from cold.

"You're cold," he stated. "I'll walk you home."

"I need to take care of Fiel first."

"Okay, I'll go with you." River released his hold but kept one arm around her shoulders so she kept an arm around his waist as they resumed walking. Soon, he led her off the path and onto a shortcut that led between Pegasus and João's place. It passed behind a field and in the twilight Sierra spied her cottage. She realized this was how River had known where she lived. They walked in silence except for her sniffling.

"My mom will wonder why I'm so late," Sierra said, noticing the deepening shadows. She reluctantly released her hold of River to pull her cell phone from her pocket and pressed the number for Pam's cell.

"Sierra, it's almost dark. Where are you?"

"I'm just on my way now to take care of Fiel. River is with me and he'll walk me home."

"Are you okay?" Pam asked in a worried tone.

"Yes, I'm okay. I won't be long."

"I'll come pick you up."

"I'm fine, Mom, you don't need to."

"I'm on my way," and Pam disconnected.

"My mom's going to pick me up. You should come back with us for dinner." They had just walked up behind the barn, and Sierra heard Fiel's loud whinny, demanding to know why she was so late.

"Sierra," River stopped and turned her to face him. She ducked her head to hide her tear-ravaged face. He gently lifted her chin so that she had to meet his eyes. "You are the sweetest person I know. It's more than I can bear right now and I don't know if I can face your mom too."

"What's that supposed to mean?" she asked, feeling confused.

He shook his head and let go and they resumed walking. They reached the pasture gate where Fiel stood waiting, rumbling reprimands. Sierra slipped on his halter and walked him into the barn, River walking at her side. She led Fiel into his stall and slipped off his halter.

River gathered up Fiel's hay allotment while Sierra doled out his grain ration into a bucket, and the two fed the eager horse. They stood side by side, leaning their arms on top of the stall, quietly watching Fiel eat; finding some comfort in his obvious contentment.

Sierra asked again, "I don't understand why you find it hard to be with me. Don't you know that friends help each other?"

River's face creased into a frown as he struggled to find the words he wanted. Finally he answered, "You look at me with eyes that know exactly how I feel. Why does it hurt more, to know that you know how much I hurt?"

"But River, don't you see in my eyes how much I hurt too?"

"Yeah, I see that too."

"We both loved João. We can share our memories. That helps keep him alive."

"He's dead, Sierra." River's hands balled into fists. Then he laughed without humor. "He gives you a horse and me a college education. How fair is that?"

"Do you want Fiel?" she asked, stunned. It hadn't occurred to her that River might want João's horse.

"No, I'm glad you have Fiel. It's just that I'd have more use for a horse than a college education."

Sierra, thinking deeply, watched Fiel with his muzzle buried in the manger, his eyes closed as he contentedly chewed his oats. "I know why he did it," she said after sorting through her thoughts. Silence, but she waited him out.

Finally, River asked, "Why?"

"Because he knew you would always be around horses. You didn't need him to give you a horse. He wanted you to have an education, something you would never do for yourself.

"He knew that I'll manage to get through college somehow, whether scholarships, working my way, student loans; whatever it takes. But he knew that I would give up having a horse if I had to, either to get through school or to help my mom. He gave me what I might not give myself."

She could feel River thinking about what she had said. Suddenly, he released his fists and dropped his head onto his arms. "Why does everyone I love get taken away?" he asked the question muffled through his sleeve. Then he pushed away from the stall and staggered over to the hay bales where he dropped to his knees with his back to Sierra, his shoulders hunched and shaking with silent sobs. Her heart burst with his pain.

She waited a few minutes for the most violent sobbing to subside; then went over and kneeling beside him, put her arms around his shoulders. He did not pull away, and after a few minutes, shifted so that he could pull her into his arms. For the second time that night, they held onto each other; comforting each other. Sierra thought she was cried out, but tears welled up in her eyes again.

Keeping his face buried and in a choked voice, River said, "I shouldn't care about you. I don't want anything bad to happen to you too."

"I'm glad you care about me. That's a good thing."

"It's just that bad things happen to everyone I care about."

Storm entered the barn from wherever she had been wandering outside, looking for Charlie. Whining, she ran up to the two kids, and tried to lick River's face. He moved away from Sierra and leaned back against the hay bales, wiping his eyes.

"River, nothing bad is going to happen to me. Why do you say things like that?"

River stroked Storm's head as she wriggled onto his legs that he had stretched out in front of him. "Everyone I care about gets hurt; João, Magic...my mother. You could be next."

Sierra shifted herself to lean against his shoulder with her back to the hay. "That's ridiculous. Bad things happen in life...they just happen. It's not your fault."

"It feels like my fault."

"There's nothing you could have done for João; nothing any of us could have done...or for Magic."

"But maybe him worrying about me and all the frustration I caused him doing bad in school stressed his heart."

"River, he loved you. Love is a good thing. Of course he worried about you. My mother worries about me. Without people to love, our hearts are empty and I think that's much harder on a heart. My mother says he had unfortunate genetics; he inherited his heart disease and probably his smoking harmed him much more than worrying about you."

River thought about that, unconsciously comforting himself as he stroked Storm's soft fur. "Maybe," he said, barely above a whisper.

"No maybe about it," Sierra insisted.

He sniffed and looked at her sideways with wet, puffy eyes. With a weak laugh he said, "You're so much smarter than me."

"Sometimes," she smiled back at him.

They heard a car pulling into the driveway and Sierra knew her mother had arrived.

"I don't want your mother to see me right now. Can you just go?" River ducked his head away, staring intently at Storm.

Sierra studied him, wondering if she should leave him alone.

"Please?" he looked up to meet her eyes. "I'll be okay. I just want to stay here for awhile…here at João's place with Storm and Fiel. I'll shut the lights out when I leave."

"Okay," she finally agreed. "But I'm not going to let you shut me out of your life."

"Okay, good." He smiled and ducked his head again.

Sierra leaned over and kissed him on his cheek. Then she rose, looked one last time at Fiel contentedly eating, and went out to the car.

EPILOGUE

All horses deserve, at least once in their lives, to be loved by a little girl. – Author Unknown.

In the weeks that followed, Pam dropped Sierra off at João's place early each morning on her way to the university or the hospital. Sierra fed Fiel, cleaned his stall, and then worked on homework until Fiel finished his breakfast. Then she turned him out into the pasture and rushed home to shower and change for school.

After school, she rode Fiel, groomed him, and then put him up for the night with his supper. She planned her time so that she could take the shortcut to Pegasus and meet River on his way home, and try to talk him into coming to the cottage for dinner. Sometimes he would. River was as quiet as ever, but Sierra believed there was a welcoming look in his eyes now whenever he saw her. Once, when he had finished early at the stable, she found him waiting for her; and that filled her heart with a warmth that spread throughout her body like a cherished blanket. The loss of João, and possibly even the loss of Magic, seemed to have tightened a bond of friendship between them; a knot that helped fill in the painful empty spaces.

River talked to Tess, and although Tess never spoke to Sierra directly, through River, she offered Sierra the stall cleaning job on weekends with minimum wage pay. Sierra accepted the job, but on her own terms.

The owners of João's farm had found new tenants and Sierra needed a place to keep Fiel. So she offered to clean stalls on weekends in exchange for Fiel's board at Pegasus. Even though she had the money in the fund to cover the expense, she just thought it was a good idea. She wanted to participate in as much of Fiel's care as she could manage. Tess accepted if Sierra would also agree to trail ride two or three horses each week as well. Sierra happily agreed, feeling it was a good bargain.

Katrina often sat for a few minutes with Sierra and Allison in the cafeteria, and then would go join her other friends when those two left for the library to study. Katrina was thrilled to hear Sierra was going to board Fiel at Pegasus. Sierra was surprised but also pleased to have a friend that shared her love of horses. Allison easily accepted Katrina, stating she liked her well enough, although she thought she was a bit lacking in academics.

Luke was incredibly kind and sympathetic when he heard about João. He often came by the girls' table in the cafeteria to chat for a few minutes before joining a tableful of football players. He and Justin had both made the junior varsity football team so had earned the right to sit at that table.

Two weeks after João's death, Luke caught up to Sierra as they were leaving home room. "Um, Sierra, you got a minute?"

"Sure," Sierra replied. He took her hand and pulled her in the opposite direction of the kids leaving the classroom.

"Look, I know your friend just died, and it's a really sad time for you, so you might not feel like doing this right now.

But maybe it would help cheer you up, so I was just wondering if you wanted to go to the homecoming dance with me."

Sierra nearly fainted. Luke Abrams had asked her out! She wanted to cry out, *yes, of course!* Blushing, she answered, "You know, I hadn't thought about going to the dance. But that's a good idea. It probably would cheer me up. Thanks." Funny how much she had changed from last year. Going out on a date with Luke…now that just might be fun.

"Great!" he said, breaking into his sunny smile.

Arrangements were made and Manuel drove the Pegasus two-horse trailer to João's place to pick up Fiel. Sierra had him ready to go, with shipping bandages on and his gear in a tack trunk and bags.

"Ohhh," Manuel exclaimed in appreciation when he saw Fiel. "A Spaneesh 'orse."

Sierra didn't have the heart to tell him that Fiel was a Portuguese Lusitano, not a Spanish Andalusian.

They made the short trip to Pegasus and Sierra unloaded Fiel and led him around the stable yard and up and down the lane between the paddocks to let him take in his new surroundings.

"Reever, 'ee 'as a stall ready for 'eem." Manuel found her after he had parked the truck and unhooked the trailer. Sierra followed him inside the stable and he led her to Magic's old stall; still empty.

River came up behind them. "Is this stall okay?" he asked.

Sierra smiled and nodded. She knew what it meant for him to put Fiel in Magic's old stall. "It's perfect," she answered. Then she led her own horse into his new stall and slipped off his halter. She gave him one last carrot and stroking his neck, leaned her face close to him, breathing in his warm smell. She whispered, "I miss you, João. Thank you."

The End

GLOSSARY OF EQUESTRIAN TERMS

Aids

Tools used to communicate with a horse. The natural aids are the seat (weight), legs, and hands of the rider. Artificial aids include whip and spurs.

Bend

A term used to describe how a horse's body curves in the direction of his movement, such as on a circle or around a corner.

Bit

The part of the bridle inserted in the horse's mouth as a means of communication or control. *Curb* – the most severe type of bit that uses leverage for control; *Pelham* – combination of a curb and snaffle bit and uses elements of both for control; the rider will have two sets of reins; *Snaffle* – direct pressure is applied to the lips, tongue, and bars of the horse's mouth; frequently it is jointed in the center; generally the mildest bit.

Canter

The third of the basic three gaits of the horse: a three beat gait in which the horse propels off of a hind leg while the other three are moving forward; on the second beat the horse touches down with the front leg on the same side and the opposite hind leg; on the final beat, the opposite front leg touches down. In this movement, the leg that touches down in the third beat is slightly ahead as well as the hind leg on the same side, which is called the lead.

Canter Pirouette

While in a collected canter, the horse executes a turn; half pirouette is 180 degrees and full pirouette is 360 degrees.

Collection

The horse shortens his stride, but the tempo does not change. The horse must bring its hindquarters underneath and carry more weight on the hind end which lightens the shoulders or front end.

Diagonal

In an arena, an imaginary line across from opposite corners.

At the posting trot, the rider rises out of the saddle when the horse's outside shoulder is forward, and sits in the saddle when the inside shoulder is forward.

Dressage

The training of a horse to develop, through standardized progressive training methods, a horse's natural athletic ability and willingness to perform and to maximize its potential as a riding horse. In dressage competitions, the horse is trained to perform precise controlled movements in response to minimal signals from the rider.

Extension

The horse lengthens its stride to the maximum length through great forward thrust and reach; the tempo or rhythm of the gait does not change.

Fédération Equestre Internationale (FEI)

International governing body for all Olympic equestrian disciplines.

Flying Lead Change

The horse changes the lead at the canter without breaking the gait.

Half-Pass

A lateral movement in which the horse moves on a diagonal; moving sideways and forward at the same time while bent slightly in the direction of movement. It differs from the leg yield in that the horse is bent in the direction of movement which requires more balance and engagement. In the leg yield, the horse is bent slightly away from the direction of movement.

Halt

The horse stops all forward movement; when performed correctly, the horse brings his hindquarters underneath and distributes his weight evenly on all four legs.

Hand

A unit of measure to determine a horse's height from the top of his withers to the ground. A hand equals 4 inches. Example: a horse that is said to be 15 -1, (fifteen hands, 1 inch) is 61 inches.

Inside

When riding in an arena, the side toward the center of the arena.

Lead

In the canter gait, the leading front and hind leg. In general, on a circle the correct lead is the inside lead, therefore if the horse is cantering on a circle to the right, it should canter on the right lead. Counter canter is a canter on a circle on the outside lead and is an exercise often used to help the horse learn balance at the canter.

Leg Yield

A lateral movement in which the horse moves sideways away from the rider's leg and forward at the same time, crossing his legs. The horse is fairly straight with a slight bend away from the direction of movement.

Lengthening

The horse lengthens its stride without an increase in tempo; performed at the lower levels of dressage before learning true extension of gait.

Long Rein

The reins are allowed to lengthen between the rider's hands and the bit, the rider often holding the reins at the buckle. There is often no contact with the mouth when riding with a long rein. The long rein is used to allow a horse to stretch his head down and forward and encourages relaxation.

Near

The left side of the horse.

Off

The right side of the horse.

Outside

When riding in an arena, the side toward the wall of the arena.

Passage

An advanced, collected movement at the trot in which the horse seems to pause with a moment of suspension between placing each foot on the ground; the horse almost appears to float in slow motion.

Piaffe

An elevated trot in place, an advanced movement of dressage and the ultimate in collection.

Rein Back

Walking steps backward; backing up.

Sound

A term used to describe a horse in good health without any lameness or other injuries.

Tempi Changes

The horse changes his lead at the canter every third stride (three tempi), every second stride (two tempi), or every stride (one tempi).

Training Pyramid

A guide for training the dressage horse; it begins at the base with rhythm and regularity, then moves up through relaxation, contact, impulsion, straightness, and collection at the peak of the pyramid.

Trot

The second of the basic three gaits of the horse; a two beat gait in which the horse moves diagonal legs in pairs such as left hind, right front together, then right hind, left front together; there is minimal head movement. The trot is the working gait of the horse.

United States Dressage Federation (USDF)

Governing body in the United States for dressage with the purpose of promoting and encouraging a high standard of accomplishment in dressage.

United States Equestrian Federation (USEF)

Regulatory organization for United States equestrian sports, formerly the American Horse Show Association.

United States Eventing Association (USEA)

Governing body in the United States for the equestrian sport of combined training or eventing.

Walk

The first of the basic three gaits of the horse; a four beat gait in which the horse moves one foot at a time in sequence such as left hind, left front, right hind, right front; his head moves in rhythm with the walk.

Dressage Levels
Introductory
Training
First Level
Second Level
Third Level
Fourth Level
FEI levels:
    Prix St. Georges
    Intermediate I
    Intermediate II
    Grand Prix

Combined Training (Eventing) Levels
Beginner Novice
Novice
Training
Preliminary
Intermediate
Advanced

ACKNOWLEDGMENTS

Thank you, my dear husband Dom, brother John, daughters Adrienne and Monique, and all my stable friends - Bonnie, Katie, Jessica, and Roxanne, and Jessica at the hospital; all who read the manuscript. Without your wonderful advice, criticisms, and encouragement, *The Girl Who Loves Horses* would not have been possible.

Thank you for reading *The Girl who Loves Horses*. If you enjoyed this story, please help other readers find this book:

Lend *The Girl Who Loves Horses* to a friend who might like it.

Leave a review on Amazon, Goodreads, or any other site of your choice. Even a line or two makes a difference and is greatly appreciated!

Look for *The Boy who Loves Horses*, book 2 of the Pegasus Equestrian Center series.

ABOUT THE AUTHOR

Diana Vincent's passion for horses began at the age of three when she caught her first glimpse of a horse. Ever since, she dreamed of owning her own horse, read every book about horses she could get her hands on, and finally, at age thirteen, acquired her first horse, Romeo. Since then she has owned several horses and has competed in hunter/jumper shows, eventing, and dressage. Today, Diana resides in the Pacific Northwest with her husband, and her Morgan horse, Midnight.

Diana loves to hear from readers. You may contact her at dnvncnt@hotmail.com

CPSIA information can be obtained
at www.ICGtesting.com
Printed in the USA
LVOW08s0351211217
560232LV00049B/130/P

9 781478 389514